Clover Dreams

A RETURN TO COAL HAVEN NOVEL

MARIE JOHNSTON

LE PUBLISHING

 Formatted with Vellum

I went to Vegas to get married and ended up saying "I do" to my fiancé's brother.

My dream wedding in Las Vegas turns into a scandalous nightmare when my fiancé gets married—to another woman. Pregnant, unemployed, and dangerously close to losing a house that was supposed to kickstart my next phase of life, I'm out of options.

Until Sullivan, my ex-groom's black-sheep brother, makes an offer that changes everything: marry him instead. I get to keep the house, he gets to work on his start-up in peace, and we just have to cohabitate for a year.

I don't expect playing house to feel so natural. Or to see Sullivan for who he truly is without baseless comparisons to his brother. I definitely don't expect to wish I could see what he's like as a dad beyond our year together.

Then there was that one time in the laundry room with him...and in the bathroom...and on the kitchen table. I could go for much more of that.

As the calendar pages turn, I've been wishing this was the beginning and not the end. But I was let down in the most humiliating way possible. I can't waste my clover dreams on a man who could devastate my heart worse than before.

Chapter One

Clover

For a girl who had dreamed of her wedding since she was a kid, a casino wedding chapel wasn't in my plans, but that was why I was in Las Vegas now. My wedding. My family had gathered in town with me, and my future in-laws had just arrived at the hotel. Tomorrow, the ceremony would be on the third floor. The only thing I was missing was Elijah Wagner. The groom.

"I know you said you didn't fly together, but you have his itinerary?" my mom asked.

Magnolia Duke was a smart woman, and she was trying to help me get to the bottom of everything, but there was something in her tone that put me on edge. I'd always been able to see and hear the difference between how she interacted with him versus how she was with the brothers-in-law and the sister-in-law our family had collected over the years.

Would she be thrilled if something happened to my

fiancé? No. My mom had too big a heart to act like that. Did she secretly hope that Elijah stood me up? Probably.

I knew Elijah could be hard to understand. He lacked confidence, and he made up for it with bluster and an arrogance that was often off-putting. The first time I met him, he was insufferable. A friend of a friend had introduced us at a house party shortly after I moved to Omaha. I was lonely, and I could see some of that in Elijah. So I had kept talking to him.

I'd like to have a talk with him now. Was the plane delayed and he lost signal? Was he stuck on a tarmac in the Vegas heat? I didn't know, but the growing pit in my stomach was more than the nausea that had been hounding me for a few weeks.

The queasiness surged. I swallowed down the extra saliva pooling in my mouth and nodded. "According to the ticket I bought, he was supposed to land two hours ago. He told me his meeting in Dallas wrapped up, and he was heading straight here."

He'd been a little aloof, but I had chalked it up to nerves about his new job and the wedding.

Her lips pursed, and my dad's brow furrowed. I adored my parents, and I loved their solid relationship. I thought I was venturing into the same thing. Today was the start of my new life. Elijah and I would marry. We each had jobs lined up in Coal Haven, North Dakota, where my grandma had left me a house and a small chunk of land. There was another new beginning too, one I couldn't wait to share with everyone. Once my fiancé arrived.

There was a knock at the door. My hopes soared. I might be irritated, but I smothered it. Elijah always had a reason. One of my siblings might claim it was an excuse. "That might be him."

My oldest sister, Violet, answered before I could get up. The rest of my family and Elijah's were in their respective rooms, waiting to hear what our plans for tonight were. I had wanted a low-key evening. Elijah figured he'd be tired after a week of training in Dallas for his new job. It would be just us tonight. Tomorrow night, we'd tie the knot, spend our first night as husband and wife together, then head home the next day.

Elijah's older brother, Sullivan, stepped inside, and I exhaled. No Elijah.

Only a year older than my oldest brother, Alder, Van was a quiet guy who had lived in his parents' basement for the last few years, something Elijah held severely against him.

"Hey, Van." I hated how wan I sounded. My mom's gaze sharpened, and Violet developed a worried crease in her forehead. Elijah had to be okay. I could not be stifled by my family while worrying about him. "Have you heard anything?"

The sharp line of his jaw hardened. His features were more angular than his brother's, leaner but still muscled. Elijah joked that his own muscles were manufactured, but he still had them while his brother got scrawnier each year. Van had muscles, but I stayed out of that fight.

"Hey, Clover." There was never an issue mixing up his voice with Elijah's. Van's was much deeper. Surprising, since he seemed to otherwise hide behind a curtain of glossy brown hair. The length made his angular face that much sharper. A trait Elijah also hated. Actually, Elijah was never pleasant when it came to Van. "Can I talk to you alone for a minute?"

My heart stuttered. "Oh no. Is something wrong?"

He clenched his jaw again and glanced at Mama and my sister. Their brows furrowed.

Dread lurched in my chest, and the nausea swirled fast in my gut. Would I need the support? How bad is it? "Whatever it is, you can tell me in front of them."

Van was usually a serious guy, but the intensity rolling off him was unusual. He finally nodded and crossed the room. His polo shirt was untucked, and at first glance, he seemed like he should be a sloppy guy. It was his shoulder width that gave the impression. His top draped over him, but as he walked in front of me, I caught the outline of powerful thighs.

Yes, Van definitely had muscles. But I had more important things to dwell on than the one-sided competition between Elijah and his brother.

He dropped to a chair next to me, rested his arms on his knees, and exhaled. "He sent me a text."

Delight leaped so high I almost stood. "Really? Did his plane get rerouted?"

There was that jaw tightening again. "Uh...not exactly."

"Excuse me?"

Van scratched the back of his neck, and his hair shadowed his face. He tucked it behind his ear. He might hide from the world, but he wasn't hiding from me. "The text he sent was a photo. So I called him."

"And he answered?" Why not pick up my calls?

He dragged in a deep breath. "He arrived two nights ago."

"What?" My startled shout mixed with Mom's quick inhale.

No, that wasn't right. If he was in town already, I'd have seen him. We were staying in the same room!

Van met my gaze, and the tenderness in his emerald eyes stole my breath. No—it was sympathy. He felt sorry for me, and he didn't want to hurt my feelings. The sourness in my stomach increased.

He pressed his fingertips together, but he held my attention. "He had second thoughts, Clover. He quit his job, changed his ticket, and came to Vegas early." He sucked in another breath, and his nostrils flared. "He met a woman, married her, and now he's on his honeymoon in Cancun."

"What!" Each tidbit Van dropped got worse. Quit his job? Arrived early? Met a woman?

Honeymoon. The heat of wildfire wicked up my insides. Pressure rose, and my temples throbbed. I heard wrong. "How could he have met someone?" It was too soon. I'd been with Elijah for two years, and while he admitted he hadn't been ready to marry, he'd changed his mind. By doing so, we'd get the life we wanted.

"How is any of that possible?" Van was mistaken. Did they have another brother I didn't know about? "How could he have met someone else?"

Anger not aimed at me flashed in his brown eyes. "She was working."

"Where? This is Vegas. A hotel and casino. There are slots, and there are— *Oh*." Reality slapped me hard, and my head spun. Acid lurched into my throat, and I swallowed. I wanted to cry and scream, yet I also wanted to sit quietly and insist that Van must've heard wrong. But I couldn't reconcile what he said with the way my fiancé had ghosted me.

"That two-timing twat waffle." I rolled my eyes to the ceiling. I was a cliché. "He ran off with a stripper."

She was probably leggy, in shape, and more fun than

listening to me spout the differences between rubies and sapphires—trick question. They were the same mineral, corundum, but the iron and chromium content determined the color.

I buried my face in my hands. "Two days? He ran off with her after *two* days? We weren't even going to go on a honeymoon. Where did he get Cancun money— Oh, shit. That bastard." I grabbed my phone and fumbled it, my heart racing. The device went flying.

Van caught it deftly in his long fingers and handed it back to me. There was pity in his eyes, but also understanding. He knew just what a jerk Elijah could be. I'd heard the stories, and I'd even witnessed it, but not all brothers and sisters were as close as me and my five siblings.

I took the phone and didn't bother with a thank-you. That should bug me, but panic whipped through my blood. I pulled up my bank information. We had one joint account that we put moving money into. Thousands of dollars to help us get by until our next paycheck. Money that would pay for the hotel and the food and to furnish our new place. The account was now zero. The room tilted, and a strangled cry stuck in my throat.

Elijah used to tell me that I wouldn't survive without him, that I was too naive. It was why he insisted we pool our funds, so he could help manage them.

"That bastard." I stood up, got lightheaded, and sat down again. "He drained us dry."

Sure, some of that was his, but goddammit, he cleaned it out. I could survive without him, no matter how much he'd made me doubt, but it'd be harder to do without money.

I was flat broke and stranded in Las Vegas.

Mom rushed to my side. "Oh, Clover."

I heaved in a breath and blew it out, getting faster with each cycle, close to hyperventilating. "He took it all. I've gotta start my new job in a week, and he took it all." I had quit the geology position that I loved. I couldn't return to Omaha. My replacement started today. I trained her!

"Take a nice, big breath," Mom said, her steady strokes on my back barely breaking through the mental turmoil in my head.

"I can't move into that house without a husband." I couldn't move in unless I was married. The house, the wedding, the new jobs, they were all part of my and Elijah's plan. I rocked back and forth. "I can't afford more than a night or two at a hotel." That bastard! How quickly could I cash in some retirement? We'd maxed out my credit card with all the work parties Elijah insisted would further his career. "I have no place to live. I'll have no job." My stomach flopped and heaved. I pressed a hand to my belly, and tears sprang into my eyes. "And I'm pregnant."

Silence fell around me. Mom's hand stilled. Heaving sobs racked my body.

"Clover," Violet said softly. "You know we'll all help you."

I shook my head. "I can't couch surf while I'm having morning sickness." I would've probably puked already if it was any earlier in the day. I had nothing in my gut, and the cash in my purse wouldn't buy me food for long.

Mom hugged me to her. "It'll be okay. We'll think of something."

"I detonated my old life, thinking I was starting a new one. How was it going to be okay?" And now I had a baby to think about—alone.

"There are too many of us here not to figure out a solution," Mom said. "Sullivan, how are your parents doing? Do they know?"

Tension vibrated between us, and it wasn't all from me. "They didn't come."

I whipped my head up. "But they—" I made a choking noise at the profound empathy in his gaze.

"They texted you, yes. They were buying Elijah time. I'm sorry, Clover," he said quietly. "I didn't know."

Shock muzzled my outrage. "I knew they were awful people."

Instead of arguing with me, Van dipped his head. "Yes."

His agreement was the pop my emotional balloon needed. A haze filled my vision and my body. What was I going to do?

The next few hours went by in a fog. Violet tried to feed me. My appetite was gone, but she got juice and soup into me, and that helped the queasiness. My sister Poppy offered to hunt Elijah down in Cancun and lose him in the ocean. My oldest brother, Alder, was looking at tickets for the manhunt. My younger brother, Jasper, didn't have his passport, and my youngest sister, Lily, sat with me.

My parents spoke in hushed whispers, discussing how to appeal to my aunt Linda. As the executor of the ridiculous trust my grandma left me and my siblings, she could give me the green light to stay in the house regardless. But Aunt Linda was a stickler.

Van stayed next to me. He didn't bury himself in his phone, and he handled all the questions lobbed at him about his loser brother with solemn grace. The few times I'd met Van, it was clear he was different from his family, but I hadn't determined whether it was for better or worse. How he acted today spoke volumes. And uncovered how much my fiancé—my ex—had lied.

It was well after bedtime. My siblings were yawning. They were all married with kids, except for Jasper, but his rancher's hours didn't include a lot of late nights these days. They were afraid to leave me, but I wasn't the helpless girl Elijah claimed I was. I could take care of myself. I would make sure of it.

"I need to get some rest." My soft statement was somehow heard over the cacophony of my family.

One by one, they gave me a hug. My parents were the last, and Mom eyed Van, still sitting next to me.

"Can I talk to you privately?" Van asked me, his gaze earnest.

I let out a bitter laugh. "I don't think I can handle another truth bomb."

"I hope it's something that's helpful," he replied.

I nodded at my parents. They didn't need to coddle me anymore tonight. The shock had worn off, and I was exhausted. I needed rest, and in the morning, I could come up with a game plan. As if I'd get any rest.

Once we were alone, Van cleared his throat. Nervous tension rode across his shoulders.

A sudden urge to see proof, to hurt myself more, took over. "What was the picture?" Van tipped his head, and his hair fell across his face. I leaned over. One Wagner could hide from me, but not both. "You said he sent you a picture."

"Yeah, I did," he said begrudgingly. "I mentioned it in case you didn't believe me. He sent two of them."

Odd that I hadn't thought to ask for proof. Had I been harboring suspicions that Elijah wasn't my handsome prince? Had I known deep down he was a frog, but the years were ticking by, and I'd allowed it? "I'd like to see it now."

Van held my gaze for a few moments before he produced his phone. His jaw went hard again when he pulled up the screen.

"What did he say?" I asked roughly, tipping my forehead to the text exchange.

"He said he hit the jackpot."

That knife stabbed right into my chest, and I leaned close to Van to see. His clean linen scent washed over me, settling my upset stomach.

Elijah: When you're in Vegas, find yourself a life like I did.

The first picture was of a handcuffed Elijah. He was waving with the silver cuffs on, and his rakish grin was charming. A dark police vehicle was behind him. The second picture was another of the man I thought I'd spend my life with, handcuffed again. Only in this image, his pants were around his ankles, his dick was hard, and those same handcuffs were still on. He was looking at the person holding the camera like she hung the moon. My heart twisted.

He had never looked at me like that.

I scooted all the way to the other side of the couch. No more pictures. "I thought he ran off with a young dancer or something."

"I wasn't sure if it was better for you to think that."

"Don't. Don't lie to me like that again, please."

Horror rippled through his face. "I won't. I'm sorry. I didn't know what to do."

I nodded because I did understand, and as much as I wanted to lash out at Van, none of this was his fault. He could've left anytime.

"Apparently," Van said, "he hit it off with the cop who arrested him for trespassing."

Trespassing while finding a life away from me. My heart wrung itself out.

Van tucked his phone away like he sensed I felt better the farther away it was. "I gathered from the conversation that you need to be married in order to live in the house you planned to move to?"

"Yes." I was hoarse. He pushed over a bottle of water. I chugged it, thirstier than I imagined. "Grandma was some sort of romantic and tied our inheritance into properties that we have to be married to get. To even live in." I snorted and fought off the tears collecting in my eyes yet again. "I guess it worked for all my other siblings. I thought I was going to be the oddball. I fell in love first and then got married instead of saying my vows just to get the place. Except for Violet, but she and Evander sort of— Never mind."

If I rambled more, Van might understand why his brother ditched me. Maybe he already did. Who knew what Elijah had said about me?

"And you need a place to live to secure the job you got?" Van asked.

"Yes." Hopelessness filled my chest. My new position paid well, and I could work from home. It would've been perfect if I had a home.

"And you need this place even more now that you're pregnant?"

My siblings would all help, but they had homes and were growing their families. They didn't need me underfoot, proving Elijah right one day at a time. It was getting hard to swallow. Hearing it echo in my head was somehow better than having him say it. "Yes."

"What if I marry you?"

I blinked. "Hmm?"

"What if we get married?" His expression was a mix of nervousness and determination. "We get the house, you start your job, and I can build my business without my parents' interference."

"I'm... What? Are you serious?"

I came to Vegas to marry one brother. I couldn't just marry the other one.

Chapter Two

Clover

Last night, after Van dropped his bombshell offer of marrying me in his brother's absence—like we'd walked into a Jane Austen novel or a George R. R. Martin one—I called my parents. Dad said he'd talk to Aunt Linda. This was an extenuating circumstance. She was a stickler for the rules, but I needed help. I didn't have an answer yet.

Van retreated to his room, claiming he had some things to take care of if he was going to move to Coal Haven, and I had a restless night. Was Van going to run off with a show-girl or a hot cop, too, after being faced with the prospect of marrying me?

I had also sent Elijah a message that I was pregnant. No response. That was that.

As soon as I was out of the shower, there was a knock at the door. I was in the complimentary robe with my teeth freshly brushed after a morning heave session. I peeked outside. My parents and Linda. All my siblings. I would be filled with dread, but I was too tired.

"Mind if we come in and talk about this?" Mom asked from the other side of the door.

I opened it and stood aside. "I need to get dressed."

Elijah had planned to wear a nice suit like what he usually wore to work. I had found a long ivory dress decorated with green clovers swirling up the hem to the rest of the garment. It was soft, feminine, and just the right amount of casual for a—planned—Vegas wedding.

Did I still wear it?

Why the hell not? That asshole wasn't going to rob all my joy.

"Can you call Sullivan down here?" Mom asked.

"Van," I mumbled. "He likes being called Van."

She smiled. "I thought so, but he never invited me to refer to him as that."

He was used to everyone ignoring him. He never said so, but I filled in the blanks. I'd been around his parents enough, and after a couple of visits, I limited my time with them.

"I'll text him real quick." The thought of dialing him up and hearing his deep voice on the other end sent my stomach sideways. He didn't sound like Elijah. It was too weird.

Clover: The whole crew is here and would like to talk to us. FYI, this is not an uncommon occurrence. The Dukes are a big group, and we're nosy.

His reply was instant.

Van: Give me twenty minutes.

A knot loosened between my shoulder blades. That was it? He wasn't going to pepper me with questions before deciding to come to my room? This whole weekend had to be inconvenient for him. Extra time off. Money spent for no reason. And he was ending up with a pregnant wife.

"He'll be here in twenty minutes." I jerked my thumb to a bathroom. "I'm going to get dressed."

I took much longer than twenty minutes. I heard when Van arrived, but I continued to listlessly vogue in front of the mirror. My pale face didn't go with the dress as much as my bronzed skin from working outside much of the summer. I kept running a hand over my nonexistent baby belly. I'd known for a week. I wasn't even a full month along, but being on a reliable twenty-eight-day cycle had its benefits, and knowing when something changed immediately was one of them.

I couldn't put this off much longer. I might be getting married today, and it was to a man I barely knew. I'd had all of five meals in my life with Elijah and his parents and brother.

Van seemed different than the rest of his family. How? Was I fooling myself? Did I have a choice? I blew out a long breath and exited the bathroom.

My family murmured to each other. My sisters and Alder chatted with my aunt Linda. None of their significant others was here. A tall man stood in the middle of the room, his head bent and his hands in his pockets. A nice black suit draped perfectly over his shoulders, and the black trousers creased down to his wing tips. His trimmed brown hair was combed to the side, leaving a hard jaw fully visible.

Did a model get lost on his way to catch a limo? I was on the tenth floor. What's this guy doing here?

He looked up, pinning me with emerald eyes. Van.

My heart pounded. Did I think his long hair softened his sharp features? How apt. The shortcut made him look ruthless. The color of his eyes intensified yet darkened.

Butterflies exploded in my stomach, and I pressed a hand to my belly.

"Are you feeling sick, hon?" Mom asked.

No, I was— Yes. I was in the middle of morning sickness. I was ill. That was it. "Just the normal first-trimester stuff." I slid my gaze to Van, but it was like looking at the sun. "You cut your hair."

And he got a suit. With fancy loafers.

A ghost of a smile passed over his lips. "Figured if I was getting married, it was time."

Despite the change, he didn't intimidate me. The man in front of me wasn't the Van Wagner I knew. But then, I didn't really know Van.

"Now that we're all here," my dad said, "we can get started. I've talked with Linda about your request."

My nausea swelled. I really was going to be sick. Linda didn't go for our plan. She wasn't going to let us in the house.

"Linda," Dad said, gesturing to my quiet aunt. Where Dad's hair was pitch black with scattered gray, Linda's was plain brown, also pin straight. She gave off a dour vibe but was usually pleasant, if a bit stern.

Her mouth tightened, and I bit back a laugh. Dad was throwing her under the bus. Linda could outstubborn the best, and my dad wouldn't do her dirty work.

That wasn't fair. She was doing what my grandma Annie trusted her to do.

If she said no, then I wouldn't be getting married, and buying this dress and wearing it was a waste. Could I move back in with Mom and Dad? Van and I would have something in common—living with our parents.

Linda sucked in a deep breath. "I want to help, but I

can't let you stay in the place for the whole year. It wouldn't be fair to your siblings."

The flat look on each of their faces told me that they didn't care. It was a Linda thing.

"I understand." I was proud of how strong I sounded.

"Three months," she said.

I gave my head a shake. "For what?"

"You two can stay there for three months." She folded her hands on her lap, but tension radiated across her shoulders.

The urge to be relieved passed. The trust said I got a year if I was married before Linda had to decide if our union was real enough to keep the property. "But we'd be married."

Linda's back went rigid. "Not for real."

Her logic stoked the fury in my chest. "You don't decide that until the end. We're supposed to be married for a year before you sign off on us. Can we live there for three months without getting married?" Would Van go for that?

"No, you have to be married to be in there." She nodded, and I heard her unspoken *those are the rules.*

"I don't get it. Then why three months?" Why couldn't she bend just once?

"This is a hard time for you." She was too damn calm. "But I can't let you be in a sham of a marriage for an entire year. The baby will be born, and then what? I have to sign off on kicking out a couple and a kid?"

I saw her point, but couldn't she see what a hard spot I was in? "I can promise—"

"Three months or nothing." Linda shot a glare at my dad. He returned her glower. That was where Alder got it from when my siblings or I pissed him off.

I caught Van's intense gaze. The same punch of awareness hit me in the chest. He was different from his brother. That was all.

"We can make that work," he said.

"Yes," I said, more relieved than I should've been. I just need a little boost to be independent. If Elijah hadn't stolen my funds, I wouldn't be in this position. "I guess we'll have to."

An hour later, I was standing across from Van, and the officiant said we could kiss each other.

I froze. Kiss? Van?

He ducked his head to catch my eye. What was the saying? In for a penny. Might as well take the whole pound. Or something. I gave him the faintest of nods.

The way he towered over me when he bent sent shivers through my system. He paused for the briefest of moments, his mouth hovering above mine. His clean linen scent with a hint of cedar didn't wreak havoc with my heightened sense of smell. Then he closed the distance. Firm lips pressed against mine, and my eyelids fell shut. This kiss was soft yet commanding. One second later, he pulled away and took his heat with him.

A chill gusted over my skin, and I opened my eyes.

Well, it was done. I was married, but not to the man I came to Vegas to wed.

Chapter Three

Van

I stopped at the end of the driveway, unsure of whether to be thrilled or not. I had packed up my stuff at my parents' house when I knew they'd be gone for work. The dark basement hadn't seemed that much emptier once my pickup was loaded. A dismal chapter in my life had closed, and the relief I felt mingled with remorse for Clover. I'd only known her as pleasant. The most tolerable of Elijah's relationships.

A good thing since I had married her.

What had I been thinking? I'd seen a way out of my own hole while watching her fall into one. I'd helped us both. Right?

I'd make sure of it. I was better than Elijah.

My new home for the next three months stared back at me. It was a small house, ten miles out of town on a few acres, sandwiched between fields of sunflowers and corn and sweeping pastures dotted with cattle. A red SUV was out front.

After the wedding ceremony, I had told Clover that I needed a few days to clear my stuff out of my parents' house, and I needed the extra time to do it when they weren't home. I was half afraid she'd think I ran off with someone like my brother had.

One, I'd never take someone else's money. I wouldn't have been living in the basement of the home I'd grown up in if I was that kind of person. And two...well, I could no longer say I wouldn't marry a woman I'd just met. I hadn't known Clover much more than Elijah knew his new wife. Maybe I was more like him than I thought.

I continued toward the house. A wooden fence that surrounded the main five acres was missing a few posts, but the property was otherwise in good shape. According to her dad, Weston Duke, the house had been rented for twenty years by a couple who recently moved to Florida. They cared for the place but weren't able to do as much in recent years. The cold was hard for them.

The three months I was living with Clover—my wife—should go just fine.

Steeling myself, I took my foot off the brake and coasted the rest of the way. I parked outside the garage by her vehicle and frowned. The kindling of warmth in my belly was only nerves. Clover was a nice person, but she was my brother's ex. His pregnant ex. I wasn't attracted to her.

I pulled out my suitcase and checked my phone one more time.

Clover: I'll leave the door open. I'm doing some cleaning.

By the front door was an oblong brown rock with

indents that made it look like it could've come from the moon, and a mat that said Gneiss Of You To Stop By.

What the... Right. Clover was a geologist. My mom's comment to Elijah ran through my head. *"Why'd you get someone who plays in the dirt?"*

Now he'd gotten someone who was probably going to play him.

I stepped inside. Cool air swarmed around me, and the smell of freshly baked cookies filled the air. My stomach growled. How long had it been since I've had a freshly baked cookie?

Leaving my suitcase in the entry, I walked through the bare living room with one wall painted a light lavender and the others a pleasant cream. The holes from whatever the previous occupants had hanging on the walls were visible. Hardwood floors, stained a dark maple, carried through the entire house.

A dining room separated the living area from the kitchen, which was empty. No furniture. None. The magnitude of my decision was only starting to sink in. Married. New life, new town, new home. Nothing in it.

I'd remedy that. I had the freedom to now, thanks to this marriage.

A plate of chocolate chip cookies sat on the edge of the island. Were these open season? Shoving one in my mouth, I grabbed another two.

A twangy country beat drifted in from somewhere deeper in the place. I followed the sound. There were only two bedrooms and one bathroom. No office? The reason I needed the next three months was to finish launching my company.

That was a problem for later, and for when I had a desk or a table.

The place was older but well-kept. In Vegas, Weston had said the basement never got finished.

I passed the bathroom, and the smell of Pine-Sol filled the air, but the light was off.

The door to what I assumed must be the largest bedroom gaped open, and I poked my head in. A small speaker was by the door, pumping out the beat. Clover danced in the middle of the room, her stockinged feet stomping and her hips swinging. Her back was to me, and she stayed that way as she danced to the left and then to the right.

Was she line dancing?

She swiveled her hips, and a tightness coiled inside me, down lower than was comfortable. When she gyrated, I averted my gaze, since otherwise I might sport an erection. Wrong woman to do that with.

I knocked on the door.

She screeched and jumped. Her feet slipped on the floor, and I dove. The cookies hit the floor, and I clamped my arms around her, but I lost my balance from the flailing Clover. I twisted to keep from landing on her and hit my ass hard on the floor.

"Oh my God!" she cried.

I braced myself for a berating, but I didn't let her go. She was pregnant, and I had almost caused a big accident.

She scrambled off me, and I reluctantly let go. She stayed on her knees next to me, looking me over. "Are you okay? Oh God, I landed right on you! I'm sorry I didn't hear you! Is it early? Late? I should've been paying atten—"

I pressed my finger to her mouth. I needed a moment to assess for damage, and she'd keep blaming herself. Now I was caught between wanting to stroke the outline of her bow lips or yanking my hand away like I touched a hot plate. I lingered for a moment too long. Her hazel eyes were wide when I removed my finger. Why *the hell* had I put it there in the first place?

"I'm fine. It's not your fault. But I need a minute." My tailbone had taken a hell of a slam, but the worst pain was already receding. Mostly, I was content to sit my ass on the floor for a while since she was right here with me.

I'd been alone too long.

"I'm sorry," she whispered.

I cocked a brow. "Why? I scared you."

"I should've expected you and turned the music down."

"I should've walked slower so I entered when the song was done," I said wryly.

She narrowed her eyes. "I should've done the hip-dip spin to the right on beat, and I would've seen you."

"It's clear who's at fault. The singer should've sung the song slower."

She laughed, and a terrible yearning formed in my chest. No. This was not for me. But I could be friends with Clover, and friends laughed together. That thought eased the throbbing in my butt even more.

When Elijah first brought her home, I couldn't believe he'd picked someone with a brain. Usually, his girlfriends had to lack some intelligence to put up with his pompous nature. But Clover was kind while having stars in her eyes around him. He was always good at fooling people. And I was always good at being fooled by him.

I got off the floor, wincing at the cracking in the knee I hurt in high school. Damn thing didn't like getting bent at extreme angles without some warning.

"You did get hurt!" She stood and wrung her hands.

"No, it's just an old snowboarding injury."

Her bow mouth formed an *O*. "Is that where you collided with Elijah?"

"Is that what he said?" I muttered, hobbling down the hall to the kitchen. I needed more cookies at the mention of my brother.

A wave of lemon-fresh scent followed me. "What happened? Didn't Elijah tell me the truth? Oh God, he lied again, didn't he? Is this what it's going to be like from now on? I'm going to find out about all the things he was dishonest about?"

She must chatter when she was nervous. My finger that had been on her lips tingled. Her mouth was way too inviting.

My brain must've gotten rattled in the fall.

"I have no doubt he thinks it's the truth." I reached the cookies and took two. I held the plate out to her.

She put her hand to her stomach. "I was craving them, but when they were done, I got nauseous. It usually passes by late afternoon."

"Morning sickness?"

She nodded, and I kept my gaze planted firmly on her face. Better than those curvy legs or the way her shirt pooled around her hips, showing off an hourglass figure. It was bad enough that I was closing my eyes and seeing her in that ethereal dress during the wedding. It had clovers on it, and it was perfect for her.

She wasn't mine.

All we had in common was this house and that we'd both been let down by Elijah. She'd asked for the real story behind my knee. I was okay blasting any rose-colored glasses she was still wearing when it came to him. "Elijah wanted to use my snowboard, and I said no. On the next run, he rammed right into me. Didn't even know he had enough skill to do that." I shoved a cookie into my mouth.

Her pretty lips turned down. "He said you got too close to him and clipped him because you were new at it."

I barked out a laugh, and a few crumbs escaped. Damn. I'd been in that basement too long, and I'd known it.

Wiping my mouth, I swallowed. "He was the noob. It's why I wouldn't lend him my snowboard and made him rent one. He refused to go on what he considered a lesser slope than me. But I think he crashed into me on purpose."

"Why?"

Surprised she didn't just brush me off, I stuffed another cookie into my mouth. My parents always took Elijah's side. I was the "oops" kid and a hard baby on top of it. He was planned and had slept a lot. I was supposed to hand everything over for his taking as the cost of being the oldest and fussiest.

Brushing my fingers off, I thought about what to say. "He's the prized child. What was mine was his." And now his fiancée was my wife. My stomach clenched around the cookie. Was that the motivation behind my bright idea? "He doesn't like being told no."

Her brows popped up. "Oh. Wow. I mean, I knew he was arrogant—and he seemed harsh when it came to you. But I thought..." She lifted her shoulders. "I thought we were kindred spirits." Her eyes misted over, and she hastily swiped at her cheeks. "Ugh. These hormones. I am *not* missing a guy who tossed me and the baby away so easily."

Did I blame my hormones for not liking how she was crying over Elijah? I wasn't surprised he could ditch her and a kid. I'd known him my whole life, and it was on trend. Clover was the one person in the world who'd believe me now, and for that alone, I'd help her.

"Maybe it's time for that cookie." She grabbed three. "Since I can't crack a cold one for a while."

"I can get root beer."

"I've got a six-pack of it. I usually drink kombucha, but I can't handle that right now either." She wandered farther into the kitchen. "What do you want for dinner? I was going to pick up more groceries, but I didn't know what you liked."

A vise crimped around my ribs. Buying groceries for each other? Too cozy. I was here to get to the next level in my career. "I can cook for myself. I can buy my own stuff too."

"Yeah. Of course." She smothered the hurt in her eyes, and guilt wrenched in my chest. She let out a nervous laugh. "I'm still used to having to cook for two." She skated her gaze away.

Ah, hell. "He made you cook every night?"

"Well, my hours weren't as long as his."

"He worked nine to five."

She recoiled. "He worked twelve-hour days."

Double hell. I wasn't going to continue to be the one breaking bad news to her. "Okay."

She pressed both hands to her gut like she was going to hurl any second. Color leached from her face. "Was he lying about that too?"

I inhaled slowly. More bad news to pass on. "He bragged about having banker's hours, and I joked it was because he was a banker."

"He was an investment banker."

"He was a loan officer, Clover," I said softly.

Tears sprang into her eyes, and her face crumbled. "I'm such an idiot." Her shoulders shook with heavy sobs, and she pivoted on a stockinged foot only to stop at the entrance to the empty dining room. "And there's nowhere to have a good cry!"

She stomped outside.

Ah, hell. I made her cry, and I didn't care it was by proxy.

Did I follow her? Did she want my comfort? I was tired of cleaning up after Elijah, but when it came to Clover, it seemed I had more in the tank.

I trailed her to the porch. She was sitting on the first step, her arms crossed on top of her knees and her head buried in them.

Dropping to sit next to her, I didn't say anything, just scanned the property that was much nicer than my parents' place.

Her sobs quieted after a few minutes. She lifted her head and sniffled. "I guess I'll ask for the full STD panel at the first prenatal checkup."

"When is that?"

"I made it for next week to establish care." She pressed her palms against her eyes.

If we were talking doctor's appointments, we should talk about other logistics. "About the furniture…"

She giggled in bursts. "That money in our account was going to buy us brand-new stuff." More punchy laughter. "I've been trying to stay positive, Van. Things are better this way. I found out early that he was a lying liar. But it's hard to be positive when I'm going to be sleeping in my car tonight." The next laugh was a choked sob. "I guess I can call Poppy. Want me to ask one of my siblings for a bed for the night for you?"

Tingles ran up and down my arms, urging me to wrap them around her and tuck her in close. She was so defeated, and I wanted to reassure her. I had to keep my distance and concentrate on recruiting investors for my company. But the furniture issue was mine as well, and when she was distraught about where to sleep, she'd thought about me too. I could do something about that without crossing any personal boundaries.

"Come on." I had researched the town I was moving to, and that had included the businesses in Coal Haven. "There's a place in town where we can order some furniture."

She hiccupped. "I can afford inflatables. That's it."

I made some quick calculations. I had prepared for a place of my own eventually. That time was now. "I've got it. Want to ride with me?"

Chapter Four

Clover

Van's pickup wasn't what I expected—more that it was a pickup and not an electric car or something. What did computer guys drive?

He opened the door for me, and his clean, linen scent filled the cab. The hint of cedar was there too. I inhaled much longer than a regular breath, and my stomach calmed.

The nerves didn't leave completely. "I'll pay you back when I start work. It's not until next week, and then I'll have a couple of weeks before I get paid. I actually start my online training later next week, and I'll get paid for that. I was surprised I could do that. Technically, I'm two hours from where I work, but they said I can work remotely most of the time. After the online module, I'll have to go in and meet everyone, learn the equipment, and get trained in— and tell them I'm pregnant." My laugh came out thready. "I'm rambling. Sorry."

"Why?" He angled the vehicle down the driveway, his big hand clamped at the top of the wheel.

My cheeks heated. "It's annoying."

"For you?"

"Elijah said—"

"That's your first clue that it's bullshit."

Another laugh burst out of me. I needed that reminder. "Do I need to be deprogrammed?"

"Yes."

He said it with a metric ton of granite in his tone. I really did need to rethink my whole time with my ex. "Oh."

"My family isn't, how do I say this? Nice? They aren't normal." The corners of his jaw bunched. "Maybe they're more normal than I think, since they keep getting away with how they behave."

"You aren't close?" I had seen it for myself, but I wanted to hear what he said.

He let out a bitter laugh. "No. When I realized we never were, I made some changes."

"Can I ask…" It was none of my business, but Van hadn't said a kind word about his brother or his parents, and he'd been living with them. He wasn't giving many specifics, but his tone filled in the blanks.

"Why I was living with my mom and dad?" When I nodded, anger flashed through his eyes. The air crackled in the pickup. "Because I know exactly how you feel."

What did he mean— Oh. He didn't have to share that part of his life with me, but he did, and I didn't like the tension that created in him. "You just found out you're pregnant too?"

His laugh was so sudden I flinched, but immediately grinned with him. The corners of his eyes crinkled when he smiled, and I was almost glad he wasn't looking at me, or I'd get lost in those eyes of his.

"Close. I, uh, was engaged, and we started a business together. She wanted to be done with me, and I was forced to dissolve the company." He rolled his eyes toward me. "We had investors to pay, overhead, and somehow, she got all her student loans and debt paid out of the deal."

"That's awful." I'd only heard from Elijah that Van had failed and came crawling home.

"Yeah," he said flatly. "It was."

Businesses sprang up on either side of the road. A physical therapy office. The gas station and grocery store. A small movie theater. He passed the soccer fields where I'd watched Poppy and her husband, Jensen, coach.

It only took a minute once he turned off the highway until we were parked in front of Haven Furnishings. An insurance agency and a legal office were on the same street. He parked in front, and I was out of my seat before he could walk around and open the door for me.

I wasn't going to make the same stupid mistake and think that we were more than two strangers helping each other. When I had asked him about dinner, it wasn't like I thought we were really married. We lived together, and he was doing me a giant favor. Maybe I underestimated how badly he wanted to get out of his parents' place. But the message was clear. We weren't a thing.

Regardless, he held the door to the furniture store open for me.

A short, older woman with dark hair scattered with gray smiled at us. "Welcome. I'm Hattie. What can I help you with?"

I opened my mouth, but nothing came out. I wasn't

buying, so I had no say. I snapped my lips shut and stepped to the side so Van could take charge.

He shoved his hands in his jeans, and his shrewd gaze swept the assortment of dressers, recliners, rocking chairs, couches, and, in the far back, beds. "We need to modestly furnish a small, two-bedroom house."

She clapped her hands together. "Let me show you what I have, tell you what I can get, and then I'll ghost you two so you can chat about what you want."

Hattie did just that. I relaxed the longer we were there. Van wandered next to me, or in the narrower stretches, he let me take the lead. We didn't touch, but the moment was comfortable. He didn't interrupt as she cruised through her offerings, all quality stuff that wouldn't fall apart in a couple of years, but it came with a price tag. I kept peering at Van to see how much regret was etched across his face. There was nothing but calculation.

One time, Elijah had waxed poetic about how he wished he was closer with his brother, like I was with Poppy. But I understood Van's role now more than ever. How could he be open with someone who habitually lied and insulted him?

Unless Van was the one lying?

No. My gut didn't think he was untruthful, and he also hadn't cleaned out my savings and left me at the altar.

"Okay," Hattie said after she explained the layout of the store and how they could deliver. "I'll leave you two to talk about it."

"Thanks." After she went back to her desk, Van did a three-sixty like he was cataloging everything. Then he pinned me with that stunning gaze of his. "What do you like?'

"Me? You're paying. Get what you want."

"You have to live with it for three months."

I held up my hands. "Nope. Your money; your furniture."

"Clover." When I stood firm, he shook his head. "Can you at least pick out the mattress you want?"

He had the money; I had the house. I was okay with that deal as long as I was offering something. I'd sleep on whatever he got, but if he insisted, I could pick out the cheapest one. My skin prickled as I walked toward the displays. Looking at beds with a guy was intimate. It was personal. At least we weren't sleeping together. I sucked in a breath.

Spinning around, I smacked into his hard chest. Strong hands gripped my shoulders to steady me. This was the second time we touched, and I could just rest my head on his broad chest and hear his heartbeat. Only that would be weird.

"Sorry." I took two steps back. "What are you going to do for a bed? Wait—all this is yours. What am *I* going to do for a bed?"

"What do you mean?"

"You can't buy two beds." Two frames. Two box springs. Two mattresses.

His forehead crinkled. "We need two beds."

"And what about the office?" I asked. "Don't you do stuff with computers?"

He stiffened. "Yeah, I do *stuff* with them."

Whoa. What did I do to earn that flinty tone? "Did I say something wrong?"

His shoulders fell. "No. It's not you. Yes, I work from home." He ran his thumb and index finger along his bottom lip. "I can work at the dinner table."

"But *I'm* working from home too."

Clarity dawned in his eyes. "Oh. We can't both work at the table?"

"I have two screens. You?" When he nodded, I shook my head. The decision was clear. "You need the smaller room for an office. I can sleep on the couch."

He gave me a droll look. "I'm not letting you sleep on the couch while I get the bed. I'll take the couch." He tried to hide a wince, but I caught it.

"Your snowboarding injury?"

"A lawn mower incident. I've been doing lawns the last few years and wrenched my back. It can get finicky. We can buy two twin beds. That'll be all the bigger room will fit."

Okay. So we'd share a bedroom. No problem. No problem at all. Like a sleepover with someone I barely knew for three months. "What about a bunk bed with a full-sized lower bed?"

His lips twitched. "Do I get top or bottom?"

I chuckled at the vision of either one of us scrambling to the top. "You're taller." We both eyed the bunk bed I described a row over. The supports would block any legroom for him. Would he be comfortable? Would I?

I'd offer to take the couch again, but he probably wouldn't go for it. As touchy as he could be, he was chivalrous. So that left one other option. "We're both adults. We can sleep together and not be weird about it."

His brows notched up. "Sleep together?"

Did he have to sound so hollow? We'd be living together. This would just be living together closer. "Yeah. In the same bed. We can build a pillow wall or something."

His jaw dropped, and he blinked. Then he lowered his gaze down to my athletic shoes and traveled back up in a way that left a trail of heat. I was in shorts and a T-shirt, but he made me feel like I was in a lacy negligee.

The next second, his green eyes were cold as an agate in winter. "A pillow wall. That'll work."

I'd been half serious, but the rejection stung. Yet it was his back and knee, and I'd appreciate not snoozing on a couch, so I nodded. "Okay. One bed it is."

❁

Van

The store couldn't deliver everything today, so I said I'd load it all up into the truck. Rather, I'd intended to. We stood at the back of the store, my pickup ready to be loaded, and Hattie was waiting for me to call it and schedule delivery. I was doing mental gymnastics on how to get this done. It'd take more than one trip, and I'd have to get everything into the house. I wasn't having Clover help me haul this heavy stuff.

Logically, I knew a pregnant woman could still do normal activities, but moving heavy dressers and chairs wasn't normal for Clover. It would've been had my brother been doing this.

Computer stuff. What had he told her? That I play games all day?

Again, if I used my brain, I knew she probably understood as much about my career as I did about geology and her work with an oil company. But I learned to be defensive about my interests—about anything I was interested in.

"I can call my brother," she offered.

We had no chairs and no beds. We'd have to get a room for tonight, and we did this whole marriage thing to get the house. "I don't want to bother them."

"My siblings love to help." She crossed her arms. "They love to be nosy, and they're going to be curious about us and worried about me. This gives them both."

When she explained it like that, it wasn't so bad. My family wouldn't lend a hand, or they would blame me for needing it. "Okay. If you have someone with trucks available, I could use the help. I'll pay them."

She clicked through her phone. "They won't take your money."

She sounded so certain. They would truly be happy to help? Huh.

Alder arrived moments later, along with Violet and Evander. My tension slowly leaked from my muscles. One trip for each of us and we'd be done. I kept waiting for snide comments, underhanded compliments, or hell, anything other than the way they all deferred to me about what we moved first and where it went.

We went to work, and at the house, it was the same. Alder and Evander jumped in where some strength was needed, and Violet stuck by Clover's side. No criticism, and Violet complimented my taste.

Huh.

Now they were inside with Clover, and I was parking my and Clover's vehicles in the garage.

Once I got Clover's car inside, Alder was waiting for me.

"Taking off?" I asked.

He nodded, his gaze appraising, just like it had been in Vegas. "Anything else I can help you with before I go?"

"There's not much else to do but settle in." Years ago, I gave up all my stuff when I had to move out of the home I had shared with my ex, Hillary, leaving me with just my clothing and laptop. I hadn't had much to move out of my parents' place.

From the meager boxes Clover had stacked in the living room, she must've pared down for the move too.

Alder nodded, but he didn't leave. He traced the perimeter of the garage, looking from the concrete floor to the roof. Only the walls shared with the house were finished.

A heaviness emanated off him.

"Something on your mind?" I asked. The defensiveness crept back into my shoulders.

He stopped pacing and pinned me with a direct stare. "I wish Clover would've just stayed with us."

Ah. He didn't like to see his sister marry a stranger and then live with said stranger.

I understood her need to be independent. We were both in our thirties. Elijah said she was a few years younger than him, which made her closer to Alder's age. Living with successful family members while struggling stung the ego more than one would think. "She had her reasons, and none of them are related to how much she cares for you and your family."

"Appreciate that, but it's that she doesn't know you."

Fair. I could give him all the platitudes in the world, but she was his little sister. Normal siblings worried about each other. I tried another route. "I know how to take care of myself. She seems scrappy, but I think I can outrun her if needed."

The corner of his mouth lifted, and he gave me one nod. "She is scrappy, and she has a lot of family looking out for her."

A pang hit my chest. "Lucky girl."

He inspected me as if to judge my tone. I was serious.

Not many people had what Clover did. Then he inhaled and looked around. "Daisy and I planned to live together to get the house too."

Daisy was his wife, and from what I could tell, they'd been married for a few years. "Decided you needed more time to really secure the place?"

He flashed a grin. "It took some convincing on her end. I set out to win her back after being divorced for fifteen years."

Surprised, I nodded. I didn't know much of the Dukes' history. I knew their names after last weekend, and who they were married to. I could probably even recite their kids' names, but I didn't know them personally. The Dukes were now in-laws. For three months anyway.

"I'll quit beating around the bush," Alder said. "You seem like a better guy than Elijah."

"You'd be surprised at what a compliment that is."

He cocked his head like he was taken off guard that I'd admit that much. "I'm worried for Clover. Beyond physical safety."

"All I can promise is that I'll try not to add to her stress. This arrangement is supposed to help both of us."

"I feel like I need to warn you—we're a big family, and we're in each other's business. Is that going to be an issue?"

Alder probably butted out of Clover's life most other times, but not now. Not when she was hurting and trying to start fresh. My respect for him grew. Clover had warned me, but I hadn't anticipated how much I'd respect them for it. "Don't know why it would be. Not for me. It's Clover you'll have to deal with."

"That's what I'm worried about," he muttered. He strolled out of the garage. "I'm only a phone call away. Give me a ring if you need anything."

"Thanks for the help today." I reached into my wallet. "I can pay you for your gas and your time."

His expression turned incredulous before he barked out a laugh. "We aren't taking your money. Just make sure Clover's okay, and we're square."

All right.

When he was off, I went inside. The living room was no longer empty. A plush couch and coffee table were flanked by recliners on each side. Why'd I get two? Like we were going to have company, or hang out together? It was like I slipped and planned for a real family.

It was done. I could always sell a chair after I moved out.

Music was coming from the back of the house again. I admired the simple dining table and chairs in the dining room as I passed. Clover's gaze had continued to stray toward those pieces while she steadfastly refused to tell me what to buy. She said she'd work at the dining room table, and that was another offer that was more like a demand. I'd take the second bedroom as a home office.

I like the openness of the dining room anyway, and the big window to look out.

I sensed only truth from her claim, so I had purchased a simple desk that was now in the new office. My meager box of supplies sat on the floor next to it.

Clover was making the bed, humming along to the twangy country song. Did she gravitate toward upbeat music, or was she relying on it right now?

My ribs squeezed against my lungs when I eyed the bed. I should've thought this through better. Sleeping together? Three months of slumber parties with a woman I didn't know very well?

She looked up. The rays of the sun through the window

made her skin glow and caught the lighter flecks in her amber eyes. "Hey. I think we're mostly settled. Tomorrow, I'll run to Bismarck for some smaller things, but otherwise we're all set."

"All set," I parroted.

She stifled a yawn. "I might even turn in early. I can sleep through a tornado, so don't worry about waking me when you come to bed."

...come to bed.

My mind played that phrase over and over again. I had sworn off women after I broke up with Hillary, and I wasn't interested in going against my oath, but that didn't stop how much I liked hearing the phrase.

"I'll get the office set up." All it'd be was to get my computer out, my notes, and the pens I'd packed. I thrust a thumb over my shoulder. "I'm going to see if there's any lawn equipment in the shop. We'll need at least one cutting before the snow flies."

She frowned. "They hayed the rest of the acreage last month. It shouldn't need to be mowed again, but I can always check with the others. With four siblings in town, someone's going to let us use their mower."

What an odd thought. She had a network of people who'd help at the drop of a hat. "I can always buy a push mower."

She waved off the suggestion. "No need. Procuring mowing equipment is the least I can do to repay you for using your furniture for the next three months." Her smile was tight. "T minus eighty-nine days."

A few seconds ticked by before I realized she was counting down to the end of us. Something sharp plucked at my chest wall. "I can make a calendar, and we'll rip off the days."

She laughed, and goddamn, I liked that sound. "No need. But I won't blame you if you need one. When Thanksgiving comes, this house will be empty again."

Did I want that day to arrive sooner or later? The answer should be immediate. She grabbed a blanket off the floor, and that only brought my attention back to the bed. I'd be crawling in with her.

As friends.

Were we even that?

No. We were just husband and wife.

Clover

I dug through my clothing. I had all my shorts-and-nightshirt sets, but they seemed skimpy in the newlywed light being shone on them. "I have to have something else."

I yanked out a lacy negligee. Crumpling it in my hands, I looked furtively around. Van was still in his office. He'd been shut in there since we talked. I had eaten a sandwich for dinner, but I had no idea what Van had eaten.

Huffing out a breath, I shoved my clothes into a drawer and picked out the least see-through night shorts and shirt. I'd be under the covers when Van came to bed anyway.

A shiver danced down my spine. Van and I were going to be in the same bed tonight. The bedroom wasn't large, but he'd gotten a king. He was a tall guy, and he likely wanted a mattress big enough to hold him. He probably also wanted maximum distance between us.

Staying in what I wore today, I crept to the bathroom and got ready for bed. I wasn't going to shower, but I changed my mind at the last minute. I'd go to bed with wet hair, but I'd be fresh for my first night with a new guy. With my *husband*.

My shorts and shirt clung to me, and my hair was wrapped in a towel, but it was a short distance to the bedroom. I swung the bathroom door open just as the office door flung wide, and Van veered out with his brow creased. He stopped when he spotted me, and his expression went blank. His intense gaze traveled down to my bare feet, then back up, lingering on my bare legs.

I had my clothing hugged to my chest. *Please let my nipples be covered.* The AC wafted over my skin, and goose bumps dotted my arms from the chill.

"Excuse me," he mumbled and continued down the hall to the kitchen.

The hallway brightened when he turned into the kitchen as if his wide shoulders had blocked out the light. I looked down at my pale-green-tipped toenails. I had wanted them to match the lighter green leaves of my wedding dress. A nod to my name. I'd admire them if no one else did.

In the bedroom, I put my clothes in the laundry basket, draped my damp towel on top, and crawled between the covers. The door was closed, and I wouldn't wonder what Van was doing. Fresh sheets, a new bed, my clean body—I should sink right into sleep.

For several long minutes, I tossed and turned. Nerves made it too hot. Then too cold. Then too...small. Van would be coming to bed soon, and then what?

Oh! The pillow fort.

I had my body pillow, and I lined my two extra pillows down the middle. There. Now I'd be able to sleep.

No luck.

Eventually, I dozed off only to be awakened when the

door cracked open. I stayed still and listened as he quietly moved around the room. He hadn't unpacked his clothing yet, but the zipper of his luggage was loud in the quiet. Then he crept to the bathroom.

I remained frozen until he returned. I sensed him moving around until he approached his side of the bed. My heart rate increased, the thuds hitting harder, and he paused.

What was he waiting for? Was he going to go to the living room?

The bedding shifted when he pulled back his corner, and the mattress dipped under his weight.

He slid in next to me. I squeezed my eyes shut and willed my breathing to stay steady. I was in bed with a guy I barely knew, but I wasn't scared. My stomach fluttered wildly, like I was walking through one of the many pastures around the house, disturbing all the butterflies and cabbage moths, watching more take flight with each step.

No noise filled the room but our breathing. Slowly, the tension leaked out of me, and my eyelids grew heavy. The weight next to me was more comforting than I expected, and I drifted off to sleep.

Van

Pink lips curved in a sexy grin, and heavy-lidded hazel eyes met mine. Her lush hips rolled and rocked. Lust pounded through my blood, circulating through my cock, bringing a fresh supply of need with each pump of my heart.

Ride me.

I was on my back, and she was leaning over me, taking all of me inside her so perfectly.

Fuck me. I was going to come. I was going to—

My eyelids flew open. *Where the hell am I?* My hips thrust up like my pelvis had its own brain. My chest was heaving, and my pulse pounded in my dick.

Shit. Was I having a wet dream?

I rolled up and swung my legs over the bed. My erection protested at the bend of my body.

A little sigh came from behind me, and the bed shifted.

My circumstances poured into my awareness. I was in bed with a woman. My wife. Clover Duke. My *platonic* wife. Yet here I was with a pounding erection, humping the sheets. Shame and panic filled me to overflowing.

I glanced over my shoulder to check if she was awake. Bad decision.

She'd tossed the covers off in her sleep, and a strip of creamy flesh was revealed on her abdomen. The round globes of her tits pressed against the fabric, and the way her legs were cocked made her shorts ride up to the crease of her curvy thighs. Brunette strands of her hair draped over her pillow, silky and shiny.

What if we were real? I'd lie back down, roll over, and move those damn pillows. She'd have a sleepy smile, and I'd push that shirt up the rest of the way. The shorts would be next and I'd—

No.

After I stood, I grabbed my clothing and put it in front of my obnoxious dick. She couldn't catch me. I would not make her uncomfortable about this arrangement. Awkward or not, the bed was better than the couch for both of us.

I shuffled out of the bedroom, hoping I didn't wake her. When I got to the bathroom, I flipped the shower on and stripped out of my shorts and T-shirt. The cold slammed into me, but it was only a suggestion for my hard-on to calm down. My skin tightened, and I waited as the seconds ticked by. Satiny skin flashed through my head. She'd be so soft.

With a groan, I fisted myself and turned the water temperature to warm.

I had to have some other images in my spank bank. Dark hair long enough to wrap around my fist.

That was Clover.

Those legs. Spread apart with me sinking between them.

Damn. Clover too.

My shaft didn't care. I came with a series of grunts I couldn't keep quiet.

Please let her be a deep sleeper. I didn't want to be the creep she married that jacked off in the shower after our first night together.

I propped a hand on the shower wall and struggled to get my breathing under control.

What was that?

I had no answer as I finished cleaning up. What I did was nothing but physical relief. Like a workout, which I'd been lax on. Nothing more. Once I was dried off and dressed, I left the bathroom. Clover was still in bed, under rumpled covers, with her mass of hair covering her face. Relieved I didn't get busted, I went to the kitchen.

My stomach squeezed and made noises similar to me in the shower. I skipped dinner last night, wrapped up in catching up on the work I'd missed. Clover grabbed groceries yesterday, but I'd been an ass and insisted we eat separately. I did not get groceries.

I let the fridge fall shut. None of the food was mine.

Clover trudged into the kitchen, blinking her big, sleepy eyes. A fluffy robe encased her down to her shins, but her cute, green-tipped toes were on display. How could one woman be so sexy and adorable at the same time?

"Find anything good?" Her voice was husky, and my erection threatened to return.

I shook my head. "I have to get some food first. I'll get out of your way."

"You can take whatever I have and get the next round of groceries." She hugged herself and looked everywhere but at me. "I mean, if that's easier. I know you want to keep everything separate."

Maybe it was my morning masturbation session while she slumbered, or that this was the first day of the next three months of living together. We didn't have to be miserable. She wasn't my enemy. I didn't agree with her taste in men, but then I didn't have the most stellar luck picking women. We had a common denominator when it came to that.

"You like eggs?" I asked.

A green tint glossed over her face. "Not in the morning. Carbs are the best. I was going to make some pancakes."

"What about sausage?"

"That I can handle."

"I'll make pancakes and sausage while you get dressed."

She didn't move. "It's no problem."

"I'm used to making myself something every morning. Really, it's fine. I didn't run this morning, so I feel like I need to do something before I sit behind my desk." I had done something, but I refused to think about it.

"Oh. Okay." Finally, she started to spin around.

"Clover?" When she turned back to me, my determination grew. I wasn't my brother. I was better than him. "We can take turns cooking and getting groceries."

She tugged at the lapels of her robe. "I can eat in the living room. Or outside while it's still nice."

I was a jackass. She was trying to make me comfortable. No wonder Elijah latched on to her. She catered to him, made him feel important, and he probably took advantage of it.

"I won't take it as a sign of your undying love for me if we eat together. Promise."

Her lips twitched. "I was more worried that you bite."

"Sometimes."

An undercurrent of electricity crackled between us, but she laughed. "I'll keep that in mind. I'll be gone a few days next week for training. You gonna be okay?"

"Mm...you might have to cook ahead so you don't miss your share of the duties."

She nodded matter-of-factly.

"Jesus, Clover. I'm kidding. I'm a big boy, and you're not meal prepping while my ass is at home."

Shame flickered in her eyes, but she extinguished it. "Then I won't expect to find an emaciated skeleton at your desk when I return."

I patted my stomach. "Healthy as a well-fed horse."

"Okay." Her smile was almost shy, and it burrowed into my chest wall before she left the kitchen.

T minus eighty-eight days.

Chapter Five

Clover

Two weeks of married life had passed, but I'd been gone for the last few days. Before I had left, Van and I had settled into a routine of pretending we slept alone on either side of the pillow wall, working at our respective workstations all day, and repeating it in the evening. We'd been roommates, nothing more, and it had been pleasant.

So why had I slept like crap in the hotel room? Was it the stress? The training? It couldn't have been the separation. Yet, why did making a pillow wall help me drift off as if I could pretend Van was on the other side and relax?

I never had an issue sleeping when my ex was gone.

I was back in Coal Haven now and shamelessly looking forward to a better night of sleep. I turned into the driveway. The garage doors were open. Van was outside of it, behind his pickup, putting together some sort of machinery. He had a baseball hat on that shaded his face when he looked up. His gaze softened when he saw me, and my belly came alive, and not in a morning sickness way.

I gave him the most awkward wave as I pulled in to park. My boobs had been tender all week, and now it was like they had their own heartbeat when his dark gaze met mine as I drove past.

When I got out, he was waiting at the back of my car. He pulled my suitcase out of the back seat. The denim at his ass clung tight, and wow, I'd never guess he sat at a desk all day.

Only he didn't. The days we'd worked sort of side by side, he was in and out of his office. He'd pace the hallway or go outside for a short run. Any excuse to move, he seemed to use it. Meanwhile, I had to set an alarm to get my butt out of the chair for a break time.

"How was your stay?" he asked.

"Oh, you know. I'll miss the Belgian waffles with the continental breakfast."

"Do I have to add those to my rotation?"

"I won't grumble if you do."

Likewise, before we'd left, he'd also be in the kitchen, taking turns cooking like we had agreed. The way we'd settled into the arrangement should be a red flag, a warning that this guy was different in a way that could make a girl fantasize if that girl had not been dumped in an embarrassing way in front of that guy.

I collected my water bottle and empty bag of chips from the front seat and followed him inside. The ache in my boobs continued to make me hyperaware of them around him. This was something I hadn't dealt with before, but that was how every day was now. He took my suitcase all the way to the bedroom. I could stand at the end of the hallway and admire his long-legged swagger, but that would be too much.

He was my husband, and I... Gosh, had I missed him.

The days before I left had been nice. Calm. He hadn't nitpicked everything I did or questioned my choices. Why hadn't I realized that Elijah was a narcissist? Anything related to me had been critiqued by him, and I hadn't noticed. My clothing and my cooking. My job, my big family, and what I drove. Nothing was off-limits, but he had done it in a charming way that flew under the radar but chipped away at me.

Two weeks with Van, not all of the days under the same roof, and my eyes were opened.

In the kitchen, I dumped my water bottle out.

"How was your training?" he asked from behind me.

There. It was that. A simple question, and he sounded sincere, dammit. I set my water bottle down too hard. I was a smart woman, and I had let some guy demean me.

He came closer. "That bad?"

Frustrated, I pushed my hair back. I'd had it down for my training. Straightened and professional. I faced him and leaned against the island. "No. It was great. My position works on the geologic storage of carbon dioxide. We inject it into underground rock formations for permanent storage. It's fascinating, and my background in remediation is actually appreciated because the company is looking at saline aquifer storage. I get to learn new stuff and use my experience."

A divot formed between his brows as my volume increased. "That's good, right?"

"It's amazing—and I get paid twenty thousand more a year." I flung my hands out. "And the whole time I was gone, learning my new duties and new programs, I'd think about how relaxed I was. Because I'm not going to go home to Elijah and field little comments like, 'Wow, must be nice to play with rocks' or 'I managed more money than that entire company is worth before noon.'"

His expression turned aghast. "He would say that?"

"Every. Time." I dropped my arms, and my hands slapped my thighs. "How did I not see it? And here!" He jumped when my volume pitched up. "You don't make tiny complaints about my dry muffins or how wet I make the floor in the bathroom when I shower, or how dowdy my clothes are." I couldn't believe I said that. I was standing in my black slacks, pink top, and ballet flats. Something that had been deemed suitable by my ex—except for the lack of heels. "Everyone was there in jeans, and I went to work in this. It's all I packed. Because my time with Elijah made me paranoid about how I looked."

I hugged myself. My pulse had notched up while I was ranting.

Van studied me. "Can I ask you a question?"

"Are you sure I won't just blurt out all my personal information?"

The corner of his mouth kicked up. "It's okay if you do. I won't even flinch if you talk about your period."

I barked out a laugh. "Don't worry about that for eight more months."

He chuckled. "Fair." He rubbed his lower lip between his thumb and index finger. Was that his nervous move? No. It was his thinking pose. I'd seen him at his computer doing the same. "What was it about my brother? I know he's decent-looking, but he's toxic."

I pondered my answer. Hadn't I been asking myself the same thing? Time to put it into words, and while Van wasn't neutral, he was more objective than if I'd tried to discuss this with my siblings. "He's like radon." Instead of scoffing at my personal way to describe it, he cocked his head. "It comes from the breakdown of uranium, and the radiation works its way up through the soil and the foundation to our homes. But you won't know it until it makes you sick, and even then, you won't know what's causing the problem. I hadn't gotten sick yet. It hit all at once when he left me for someone he just met. Thankfully, I was saved from a possibly terminal diagnosis."

"That makes sense," he said quietly. "He always was charming. Like a fancy house."

"He was so charming. But I saw deeper. He's arrogant, but he has a way of building people up when he's not using them to feel better. And then there was the loneliness."

Surprise lit his eyes. "The what?"

I nodded. He'd heard me; he just didn't believe it. "Elijah was always looking to fit in. I thought that was behind his cockiness, but I think he was just afraid of not being included. Was he teased in school?"

His headshake was almost imperceptible. "I don't know. He never talked about it. We weren't close."

I shrugged. He never discussed it with me either. "Well, whatever. The end result was the same, and it wouldn't excuse how he treated me or what he did."

"You're right." His gaze trailed down to my ballet flats and back up again. "Hungry?"

Did he like what he saw? It wasn't how I normally dressed. Give me loose linen or sweats. "Yes. And I got paid, so I'm taking you out."

He cocked a brown brow. "Me?"

"Yes. Have you been to Rattler's yet?"

"The bar and grill?"

"It's amazing. I go there each time I'm in town." I raised my arms. "And now I live here."

"Sounds like I need to try this Rattler's place."

Grinning, I pushed off the counter. "Let me change first."

"I'll get cleaned up." He tugged on the hem of his grease-stained Huskers shirt. "I found an old mower in the shed."

"Didn't Jensen come by?"

"Yes, and I appreciate it. He seems cool. But it's nice to get out of the office and be productive. I miss tinkering in my own home." A shadow crossed his expression. "Meet you outside in ten?"

There was something about the tinkering and the home, but he wasn't telling me. Disappointment filled me. Elijah must've done all the talking growing up. "It's a date." Horror washed cold through me. "I mean—not a date."

His expression stayed neutral. "I'll go clean up. You can have the bedroom first."

When he left the kitchen, I sagged against the counter. *Way to go, Clover.*

❊

Van

The restaurant was full. I liked it as soon as I walked in. The crowd was at ease, and the decor wasn't ostentatious. Exposed wood beams lined the ceiling, and timber supports added to the rustic ambiance. Servers dressed in black polos and jeans rushed around.

Clover and I were put in a booth by the windows. She'd

changed from her cute professional look to jean shorts and a shirt that said *I Rock* with a picture of a geode. Her toenails were still a light green, and I was glad to know I hadn't missed a color.

A young server appeared at our table. "What can I get you?"

Clover smiled at her. "I'll have the surf and turf with a sweet potato and cinnamon butter on the side."

When it was my turn, I ordered the sirloin with a baked potato.

The server was about to walk away when Clover stuck her finger in the air. "Can you bring an order of mozzarella sticks? And extra buns?" she rushed to tack on, refusing to look in my direction.

When we were alone, Clover smiled sheepishly. She tore small lines into the edges of her napkin. "We can bring leftovers home."

Home. Our home. Together. I liked hearing that as much as *come to bed*, and as much as I liked knowing that I wouldn't be in that bed alone tonight. I'd kept the pillow wall in place, but the bed was somehow so...empty. "If there are leftovers. It's okay if everything's eaten before we leave."

"I can't eat much in the morning, but by dinner, I'm ravenous."

"You don't have to explain it. I don't care if you shove every morsel in your mouth tonight."

Vulnerability shone in her big eyes. "It's a lot of food."

"I will order my own buns and mozzarella sticks and have an eating contest with you, but I'm warning you—you'll lose."

She chuckled, and the tension drained out of her. The radiance returned to her face. My brother tried to dull her. She had been his shiny object, and he had taken the shine out of her. I'd make sure it was back before this marriage of ours was done.

She continued to fiddle with her napkin, but she was no longer ripping it. "So? The mower?"

"I found a push mower, an old snowblower, a weed whacker, and a lot of engine parts. I think I can get all the equipment running."

"You like fixing small engines?"

I nodded. "The yard work was usually left up to me. I used it to make extra money while working on building my business." I smiled tightly. "It got me out of the house." Which had been critical for my mindset.

A big man in jeans, boots, and a plain shirt walked by. It was the most common style of the area. Not enough that I felt out of place without cowboy boots, but Coal Haven was heavy on the farming and ranching. The vibe was laid back, and I'd been enjoying my time here.

He did a double-take at Clover, and the shorter woman with him, who had a shorter, sassy hairstyle, noticed.

She grinned. "Clover! So nice to see you."

Clover looked up like she was surprised to be recognized. "Lyric, Stetson, hi." She sat straighter. "This is my, um, Van Wagner. Evander is Stetson's cousin, and another cousin of his is Eliot's brother-in-law."

"We get to be a tangled web around here," Stetson joked.

The couple ran their curious gazes over me. The woman flashed a kind smile as we shook hands.

"Nice to meet you." Her Van? How else was she supposed to introduce me? *Meet my husband for the next three months, Sullivan. Please don't call him Sully. He likes to be referred to as a family vehicle with maximum capacity.*

Lyric tucked her arm through her husband's. "I heard you moved here, and you're working in the oil fields?"

Clover nodded. "I work out of Williston, but I'm remote."

"It'll be good to see you around," Stetson said. "Next time we have a gathering, you're invited."

Clover grinned. "I'm always invited."

"But this time you can make it." Lyric glanced at the back of the restaurant, where the host was awkwardly standing by an empty table. "We'll see you around. Enjoy your meal."

When they were gone, I couldn't help my curiosity. "They invited you knowing you were in Omaha?"

"The Barrons are a close and welcoming family." She thought for a moment. "And big like ours, but most of them are cousins and not siblings." She silently counted her fingers. "There're eight of them, I think? And now five of us Dukes between Coal Haven and Crocus Valley."

What was it like to have that many people in the family? Growing up, I thought every nuclear family was like mine —small and cold. I knew better now, but my fiancée's family had also been small with a chilly vibe. That might've been only toward me. I didn't care anymore.

Yet Clover's family was warm and inviting. Was it the number of them? The more the merrier? They were supportive without prying and protective without being controlling.

Her phone buzzed. She glanced at her purse but didn't answer it. Was she worried about being rude? Was she really that thoughtful?

"Go ahead," I said.

She smiled. "It's not work. It's probably that big family I was talking about." She gave in and looked at her phone.

Her grin froze. "Speaking of gatherings. My family's having one."

"When?"

Her laugh was nervous. "Poppy and Jensen invited us out next weekend. They'll grill."

Hunger cramped my belly. I was waiting for my food, but it'd been forever since I'd had a beer on the back deck while a steak or burger sizzled next to me.

Her brows drew together. "Is that okay with you?"

"Of course you can go. I'm not your keeper."

Her rigid smile fell. "You don't want to go?"

"I'm invited?"

"We're a package for the next two and a half months. I'll warn you—it might be every Duke in town—or former Duke."

The kindling of excitement in my belly was new. A big family gathering. That would be like going to the zoo and seeing how other mammals' family units worked. "Okay."

"Okay." Her grin brightened like the sun. "There'll be another get-together in mid-September. That one will be *everyone.*" Her gaze lifted over my shoulder, where Lyric and Stetson had gone. "And I do mean everyone."

"By everyone, you mean..."

She set her phone down. "Pumpkin harvesting."

"Like a pumpkin patch?" I'd never been to a pumpkin patch. Why'd that sound like the perfect weekend activity?

"Nope." There was that sheepish smile again. "Violet's husband raises pumpkins, and he supplies local breweries, pumpkin patches, and pantries. And it's become like a yearly thing for him to invite his side of the family, and now Violet's. And then the Knights."

The Dukes and the Barrons. "Who are the Knights?"

"Lily's sister-in-law."

"The one who's married to a Barron." When she nodded, I ran through the families like I was doing calculus. "How big is their family?"

"There's, um…" She rolled her eyes to the ceiling and figured out the equation in her head. "Five? Eight Barrons, five Knights, and, if Jasper makes it, six Dukes. Couples in total? Like, sixteen? Don't ask me to tally the kids."

"Holy shit." I didn't even think about the kids. "And they all get together in one place?"

"It's a big property that Grandma Annie left Violet."

Her family and her extended family and their in-laws were fascinating. Instead of getting a headache, I was invigorated. Her crew was…interesting. My life had been quiet for so long. "Did Violet have to be married to get her place?"

"Yes, but Evander rented it before that."

"That's how they met?"

"No, it was a one-night stand at the local motel."

I coughed out a laugh. "Okay." I liked my work, but this was all the social interaction I'd missed out on over the last couple of years. "Alder and Daisy? He kind of told me."

"Really? Makes sense. He's so happy he won her back. They were high school sweethearts who got married and divorced before Daisy was done with college. Then, fifteen years later, she needed a place to live, and he wanted the house." She leaned over the table. "He wanted her back so bad."

"He used Grandma's trust to win his wife back?"

Her smile was triumphant. "And before you ask, yes, Poppy and Jensen were going to get married to get the house that she turned into her office. But they fell in love before they married."

"And Jasper?"

Her grin faltered. "I don't know. There's a time limit from when Grandma passed. I think it's two years from now, but Jasper would have to be married in a year. His property is a cabin by the river with some acreage."

"Nice."

"I think it would be, but he's been managing the Knight family ranch, and he likes it."

The threads running through the three families were plentiful. Then there was me and Clover. I brought nothing to the table, but I could help her get the house.

"It's okay if you don't want to go. I know we're a lot."

I hadn't had a lot. "Is it like the wedding?" I had been in front of her parents and siblings, marrying their loved one, whom I barely knew, with all their wary, slightly disapproving eyes on me. It wasn't an experience I wanted to repeat. Would every sibling want to tell me that they're watching me, and one word from Clover, and I'd disappear?

"Oh no. It's much more fun and laid back. Nothing formal. We just like to hang out. We were all scattered for most of our twenties."

"I can't imagine."

"Elijah never talked about anyone. Didn't you have cousins or big gatherings?"

"I was close to my grandparents, but they weren't close to Elijah or my parents." I paused as our food was delivered. Drawing a breath grew difficult when Clover's face lit up.

She squeezed her hands like she was going to pump her fists in the air. She gave the server a big smile. "Thank you so much."

This was the Clover I'd seen glimpses of when she'd been over for dinners. The radiant girl who wanted to celebrate everything. She'd hidden herself around my parents, and she'd likely tempered her personality in response to my brother's controlling ways.

How would she be around people who loved and accepted her? I'd seen her with them in Vegas, but the circumstances hadn't been ideal. I had witnessed their unconditional support, and it had gotten to me—so much so that I had stepped into the shoes my brother left behind. "Yeah, it's fine."

And that wide smile got aimed my way.

Chapter Six

Clover

I didn't realize how little Elijah had to do with my family until we arrived at Poppy and Jensen's place. My stomach flipped over and over. Would Van like them? He hadn't said much at the wedding, and well, that whole situation was different.

Van was driving, but he gestured to the back where I stashed the tote with my pudding dessert, a cookie salad. "I threw some pretzels in there if your stomach is giving you trouble."

My insides turned all gooey. I munched on pretzels when I couldn't handle a heavier breakfast in the morning. "My stomach is calming down, but thanks."

He parked by Alder's pickup off the driveway, and by the time I climbed out, he was grabbing the tote. I waited for him to hand it off to me, but he gestured for me to lead the way.

When we turned, Jensen's son, Auggie, waited for us.

He dribbled a ball between each foot and studied Van. "Do you play soccer?"

"It's been a long time, but I used to," Van said.

Auggie's face lit up. "You're on my team. Poppy!" He sprinted toward the garage. "I found another player!"

"My sister used to play soccer, and now she coaches his team," I explained.

"I played in high school until I hurt my knee."

Concern shot through me. "You don't have to play—"

"It's fine. But thanks. For thinking of me."

I nodded, but my insides were in tangles. Whenever I did something nice, he either shut down or seemed astonished. This was another manifestation of the loneliness I had seen in Elijah. My ex might've gotten the most attention from their parents, but it hadn't been enough, and he'd likely been pitted against Van from the beginning. Which must've left Van isolated.

I led him to the shop. Its doors were thrown open, and Jensen was stationed outside, manning the grill.

"Hey, Clover." Jensen waved a metal spatula. "Did you bring the cookie salad?"

"You know I did."

He grinned and nodded at Van. "Glad you could make it. The food table's inside. I'll have the first batch of burgers in a minute."

Van glanced at the gathering of my siblings on the concrete pad in front of the shop and tensed.

"I'll go with you." I started walking.

My brothers and sisters and their spouses greeted us as we approached.

Alder propped open two coolers. "This one is the pregnant-woman-friendly one." He grinned at Van. "And this is for the rest of us."

After I had my lemonade and Van took a beer from a local brewery Stetson's sister ran, we joined the crowd. Kids ran around on the grass. Daisy's daughter kicked the ball back and forth with Auggie, and Violet and Evander's oldest tried to keep up.

Alder shook Van's hand. "Hear you got a mower now."

Van glanced at me, as if a part of him was still waiting for us to give him a hard time for needing help. "Yeah, I got it started. Needs new blades, though."

I trusted my family with Van. They might be protective of me, but they weren't jackasses just because they could be. While they talked small engines and ordering parts, I let Poppy tow me into the shop. I caught Van's eye and raised a brow. A silent *will you be okay?* He gave me the slightest of nods.

"Are you telling me a secret?" I asked her. We were surrounded by cabinet samples and scraps. Jensen's desk was farther inside, but he always opened the shop for family gatherings.

Violet joined us, tugging Daisy with her.

"We want the details." Poppy crossed her arms over her gray Casper, Wyoming, sweater. Her curly hair was gathered in a bun. Mine was the same shade but with looser curls. "What's he like? What's living with him like? Do you feel safe?"

"Geez, Poppy." I laughed and sought out Van again. His guarded gaze connected with mine, and that familiar sizzle streamed between us.

The poor guy was surrounded like me. Evander was on the edge of the group, beer in hand, keeping an eye on the kids, but his presence wasn't exactly calming. Violet and her husband were perfect together, but they looked like opposites. She was a serious chemist, quiet but bossy as the oldest sister. He was a gruff man who lived in cargo pants and worn T-shirts that only showed how muscular he was.

Then there was Alder and his intimidating CEO attitude. I would trust Jensen to put Van at ease, but if Poppy said the word, Jensen would likely turn into a giant dick. Same with Lily's husband, Eliot. The easygoing cowboy would turn into a prick. They had my back, but who had Van's?

Please don't scare Van away. I needed him for two and a half months yet. After that... Well, I didn't really want to think about it.

"So, it's like that," Poppy muttered, and the rest of my sisters nodded their heads.

I scowled at each of them. "Like what?"

"You like your husband." Violet wasn't asking.

"No, it's not. Yes, I'm safe with him." I snorted. "Trust me, he's not interested."

Violet scooted to the side so her back was to Van. "You think that man gives you uninterested looks?"

Poppy kicked a hip out. "Mm-hmm."

"Yes?" I gave them a *hello?* look. "I'm having his brother's baby."

"I'm not one to talk," Lily said as if I hadn't spoken, "because I didn't know my husband either when I married him, but Eliot did not look at me that way."

"Yes, he did," Violet said.

"Not as intense," Poppy agreed. "But Eliot was very much interested; he just wasn't as brooding."

"Eliot could work a crowd." Violet peeked over her shoulder. "Van looks like he's in a zoo, and we're all the animals."

That part made sense. "His family is not close. They're pretty awful, actually," I said quietly, and it struck me. This was the first time I was admitting that to them. My sisters were my best friends, and I hadn't told them. They would've recommended I never speak to my almost in-laws again, and I hadn't been ready to hear it. "I'm sure this is... new...for him."

Deep laughter reached us from all the guys. Eliot's hands were flying. He must be the one telling the story.

"Your husband seems to be doing just fine," Daisy said. "This group has a way of making everyone feel welcome."

"Aw." Poppy pulled her in for a quick, one-armed hug. Daisy hunched her shoulders, but she smiled. The woman acted like she never knew what to do with being touched, but she never seemed to mind beyond her own awkwardness. Of course, that was absent when it was Alder grabbing her hand or pulling her in for an embrace. "You're one of us. That's why it's easy."

"I'm glad to be one of you again," Daisy said softly.

Poppy turned back to me. Damn. She hadn't forgotten about her interrogation. "Are you really telling me that you and Van haven't, you know..."

"Poppy! No. You know it's not like that."

Daisy shook her head, and I gave her a quizzical look. She blinked her owlish eyes. "Sorry. It's just that you two remind me of...me. You're, like, super aware of each other and worried about what the other thinks of you."

Did I like that insight? The answer wasn't critical right now. "He's becoming a friend. He's thoughtful and easygoing. A total opposite from his brother. And he doesn't try anything creepy in bed."

Four pairs of eyes blinked at me.

"What?" I touched my cheeks. Was something on my face?

"You two sleep together?" Lily whispered.

Oh. That. Warmth infused my cheeks. "Not like that. We share a bed. It's only a two-bedroom home, and we both need a place to work."

"So you don't share an office, but you share a mattress?" Poppy's brows were at her hairline. "You hussy."

"Stop it," I whispered with a hiss. "It's not like that."

Poppy shrugged. "Maybe it should be."

Violet coughed out a laugh.

I shot her a glare. "Unlike you, I'm not pregnant with *his* baby. Why would he want me?"

"I'm not going to pretend the why doesn't matter," Poppy said. "But he does want you. We established that."

Frustrated, I had to finish this conversation. I didn't come to get reminded that I was living with an attractive man who kept his distance while we lived in the same house and slept in the same bed. "Say he's interested? He doesn't want to be, and that's not good enough for me. Elijah was going to marry me, and I wasn't enough for him."

Violet wrinkled her nose as if saying my ex's name was enough to cause a stench to rise up. "That situation had nothing to do with you. That was all your loser ex."

"Exactly." I swallowed down the burn in my throat. "I picked that loser. What does that say about me? Van doesn't have a choice but to be related to him, but I was going to walk down the aisle with the guy."

I had been so happy, I would've sprinted to that altar.

Lily patted my back. "I know it feels that way, but it's not you. And when you meet the right guy, he'll show you that we're right."

Envy ripped through me so strong and fast, my world spun. I wanted what she had. I wanted what all my sisters had. A man who was dedicated to them, to their family. A guy who acted like they were the most valuable and desirable thing in the world. A partner who was my own.

I was thirty-four. I thought I'd be in their shoes by now. When I met Elijah, I thought my chances were slipping by, like sand in an hourglass, only there would be no flipping over to start again. I was destined to be the fun aunt. The aunt who took her nieces and nephews on walks and chattered about the shale we passed. The one who explained how the Badlands ended up with the multicolored striations.

That was fine, but it wasn't all I wanted, and I was tired of settling.

I might not be getting a real husband, and in a little over two months, it would be like I was never married at all.

❧

Van

"And then we went sailing over the side." Eliot laughed and made a crashing motion with his hands. I was standing with him and Alder as we lined up for a game of kickball, something I hadn't played in years. "We were airborne. I thought for sure that even if we weren't dead, I was going to be when Cali told her the story."

Alder laughed. "I think Laila would gut me herself if I ever took her on a sledding trip like that. Then she'd want to do it again."

I chuckled, enjoying their easy stories and the humor that had been prevalent throughout the day.

Poppy was laying out bases. When she tossed home

plate on the ground, she put her fingers to her lips and whistled. "Everyone ready?"

"You good to go?" Jensen asked.

"I haven't kicked a ball in years," I admitted. I was doing a whole lot of things I hadn't done in a long time. When had I become a hermit?

The answer rose in my head. It was when I moved out of a home where I thought I'd be married with kids. Well, I was married now. Might as well enjoy what could've been mine. And I was having a good time.

"Just don't hold back." Jensen grinned. "No one else will."

This whole day had been bewildering since I'd arrived and was welcomed into the guys' group around the grill. I had hung out with them since Poppy had abducted Clover, and there hadn't been one underhanded comment—not about the jeans and shirt I was wearing. Not about the moving and mowing they had helped me with. Would that come later? Was I getting lulled into a false sense of security?

I didn't think so. They just seemed to like hanging out. When something about helping each other was brought up, it was to check that everything was okay.

How was the furniture working? How was lawn care going? They stressed that I should give them a call if it snowed before I moved out and the snowblower didn't work.

Each one of them reminded me of my grandpa, and a tightness formed in my chest.

Before we had eaten, knots had loosened in my shoulders. Clover had sat next to me and given me an extra piece of brownie that she was too full to eat. I caught Poppy watching the exchange, but she only smiled, her eyes twinkling.

Now I was on the same kickball team as Poppy, and my worry for Clover was increasing.

She was heading to third base. When she turned, she bent and propped her hands on her knees and squinted at Auggie, who was up first.

Everyone knew not to ram into her, right? She wasn't that far along, but what if she collided with someone? What if the ball hit her right in the stomach? Would that be an issue? It wasn't like she was eight months pregnant, though she'd probably still put herself on third base if she was.

The corner of my mouth tipped up, but I jerked my gaze away from the adorable, sexy combo that was my wife. She'd put her hair up in a clip. Her loose curls spilled out of the top. She'd worn loose jogging pants and an oversized shirt. She'd warned me her family liked to play lawn games. I'd expected bocce ball or cornhole. Kickball took more than a lawn, but Poppy and Jensen had the space.

Their place reminded me of Clover's. With two stories, their house was much bigger, and he had the shop that he ran his cabinet business out of. But his home was surrounded by pastures and fields, all getting leased out to ranchers.

With five acres, Clover could hold a gathering like this. Food and lawn games. We could use the garage for space. I could clean out the shop and set up a grill like Jensen. Except Clover and I had little more than two months left together. Still, it would be nice to return some of the hospitality. Someday.

Poppy pitched the ball, and Auggie kicked it impressively far. I clapped and cheered for him with the others. He made it to first. When was the last time I'd been loud and celebratory? In this crowd, I'd stand out more if I wasn't. More tension drained out of my shoulders.

Lily was next. She had a nice kick, but her oldest daughter caught it. Everyone cheered for that play, even my team and Lily.

Next was Jensen. The ball bounced, and his kick was wonky, but it worked out. He got to first, and Auggie advanced to second.

Jensen had staggered adults and kids in the lineup. Another kid was next. Laila. Alder's stepdaughter. The strength of her kick caught me off guard. My fault for underestimating a quiet eight-year-old.

"Bases are loaded!" Poppy called, tossing the red ball up and down. The sound of that thing getting kicked brought me right back to elementary school. Coincidentally, that was the last time I'd played kickball. This was a much better experience than that.

"No pressure," Clover called, but she was grinning.

I shook out my arms and rolled my neck. The adults had all done this before. The kids were killing it without their parents helping them. The line of spectators that was the younger kids was more expectant than a regular crowd. The weight of Clover's gaze was the heaviest.

Don't look like a wimp in front of her.

Clover and I were married out of sheer convenience, but the depths of my brain didn't know that. It was natural for a husband to want to impress his wife.

I envisioned my kick, and when the ball came rolling toward me, it was like it was in slow motion. I took a few loping steps toward it, gauging when I'd swing my leg. The boing of the ball sounded and faded as the damn thing soared.

"Whoa!"

Was that Clover? I took off running. Rounding first, I had to slow down, or I'd take out Laila and her much shorter legs.

Poppy cupped her hands around her mouth. "Bring it in, Eliot!"

I hit second, and by then, Laila hopped on third and was sprinting home. I chanced a look, and Jensen and Auggie had made it home. *Yes.* Eliot fielded my ball and lobbed it toward Clover.

She was laughing and waving her hands to catch it. I put on a burst of speed. I'd round third and sprint home. There was no way Clover could beat me. My old competitive drive surged.

Clover's laughter reached me. Just as I was about to step on base, she backed up—right into my path. I tried to curve around her, but my bad knee gave out.

We collided. The ball bounced off my head.

Shit. I clamped my arms around her, and we were flying. Twisting to the side, my shoulder took the brunt of the fall. Pain exploded through my side, but I didn't let go of my wife. Triumph soared because I'd managed not only to keep from plowing over her, but that I'd cushioned her fall. We lay still for a few moments, our breathing ragged. Then she wiggled around, kneeing me in the balls.

"Oomph." A long groan left me.

"Oh my God. Are you okay?" Her hands were flat on my chest, and she was straddling me. "I'm so sorry."

My dick forgot about the assault and decided it liked her weight on top of me.

The sun was behind her, outlining her in a full-bodied halo. A sexy, adorable angel perched on top of me. My shoulder throbbed, and twinges zipped through my knee like lightning.

Her ponytail hung over her shoulder. "Van? Are you okay?"

I blinked, and my brain came back online. "Me? Are you okay?"

"Yes. Because of you," she said softly.

Shadows surrounded us. Acid churned in my gut. They were going to yell *Because of you* for totally different reasons. They had to hate me after seeing the collision.

"Oh my God," Poppy shouted. "Did we kill him?"

"That was cool." A kid's voice. Auggie?

"Did you see them fly?" No, that was Auggie. It must've been Cali before.

"He's out," Laila said. "The ball hit him. He's out."

"He saved Clover's life." That was Jensen.

"He saved Clover's bones and probably the baby," Violet added, sounding impressed.

The baby. My astonishment that I wasn't getting berated vanished. I gripped Clover's upper arms. The chorus of voices chased the blood out of my groin. "Did you land on anything? Does anything hurt?"

"I'm fine." She lightly shoved at my chest. "Where do you hurt?"

Nowhere. Not with her round ass sitting on my pelvis and her hands prodding my torso. She pushed into my shoulder, and I winced.

"Oh no." She scrambled off me. "We need ice."

"Got it," Alder said and jogged away.

"I'm fine." I rolled to the side and pushed off the ground, careful of my leg. "It's the old ski injury." I tried to roll my shoulder and grimaced. The dull throb was superficial, but damn, it was still sharp. "The shoulder will be fine after a little rest."

Clover blinked up at me. "We'll get it iced, get you some ibuprofen or something, then you rest."

"As long as you're okay." And the baby. A strong sense of protectiveness surged inside of me. She was rattling off ways to care for me, but I'd been through worse and had taken care of myself. "You sure you're good?"

"Yes." A smile curved her pretty pink lips. "The landing was a little hard. You should have some more brownies."

I laughed, my relief acute. "I'll have a couple before we leave, but I think that cookie salad will do the trick."

"You deserve all the leftovers." She tucked an arm through my uninjured side and led me off the field.

Everyone started clapping as if this was a real sporting event. I caught myself grinning. All the pain faded away.

Chapter Seven

Clover

"You can relax," Van said. "It's really okay."

I brandished two fresh bags of ice, one for his shoulder and one for his knee. "I know you're okay, but this will make you okayer."

He was half reclined in the corner of the couch, where I put him as soon as we got home. We'd been watching a movie, and I was on an ice routine with him. I bent over his leg, tucking the bag of ice cubes against his joint. Next, I snugged the second bag under his shoulder.

Studying my handiwork, I nodded. "It's time for another dose of meds."

"Clover. Relax. You've been hovering. You need to rest too."

"I'm fine."

"You didn't hit the ground, but you still fell on me. Are you sure..." His gaze brushed against my stomach.

I put a protective hand on my abdomen. Other than

tender boobs and nausea until the late afternoon, I didn't feel pregnant. I didn't look it quite yet, either. "The nugget is only the size of a lentil. One website said a baked bean."

"A baked bean can be twice the size of a lentil."

"Right? I got a little confused. Like, which legume is it, then?"

He chuckled, his eyes crinkling. I'd seen a new side of Van today. He had chatted with my family, played ball, and just seemed so much more relaxed than normal. The Van from the few Wagner family dinners I had attended wasn't nearly as easygoing. Only then I hadn't known it wasn't the real him.

Awareness skittered through me, and I backed up. "Hungry? I have the munchies, and Poppy sent us home with a ton of food." We'd left to rehab Van's knee before the crew dug into the food again. I scurried to the kitchen and said over my shoulder, "Usually, we'd play kickball for forever, end up bickering—playfully—about the score, then we'd eat again. Sometimes, Jensen even brings out another pack of burgers, and we start all over again."

I dug through the fridge and grabbed the plates that Poppy prepared. Chips sounded good, so I stuffed those under my arm.

When I returned, Van had his eyes closed, his head tipped against the edge of the sofa. He really was good-look-ing. His hair had grown out slightly since he'd trimmed it. The longer style fit him. Made him seem less severe and untouchable and more...touchable.

I stopped and took a step back. If he was resting, I wouldn't wake him.

He cracked an eye open. "Where are you going?"

"I thought you were resting."

"I've been on mandatory rest since we got home."

"Because I crashed into you." I sat and took the plastic covering off the plates. Each had a plastic fork, cookies, brownies, a hamburger, and my cookie salad. "I should've been more aware."

"We collided." He opened the chips and dug out a giant crinkle-cut chip. He held it out to me. "It was an honest accident."

I snatched the bag out of his hands and dug around inside. "I like the big ones."

"I know."

Surprised, I tipped my head. "How?"

He lifted his good shoulder and dug out another, smaller chip. "Just something I noticed."

"Oh." My chip-size preference was a tiny detail, but he'd noticed. *Don't look into it too hard, Clover.* "Want me to heat the hamburger?"

"Nope." He took a big bite. The muscles in his jaw flexed with each bite. A little furrow crossed his brow as he studied his food, like he was deciding what to eat next. He started to lift his gaze.

Damn, I was staring. I grabbed the remote. "What should we watch next? Do you like computer movies?"

"What exactly are computer movies?" The humor in his tone wasn't teasing.

"Um, *Office Space*?"

"Computer adjacent, and I love that one. What else?"

Emboldened that he wouldn't give me a hard time about the term I used, I thought of more. "*Ready Player One.*"

"You're batting a hundred."

I bit back a smile and chewed the inside of my cheek. "*iRobot*?"

"*Office Space* is more my speed."

"Satires about the uselessness of die-hard processes in the corporate environment and how it demeans the employees?"

"There's a reason I'm working for myself. For better or worse. I like explaining myself if it's valid. I didn't like explaining myself to do a job I was hired to do."

That suited him. Meanwhile, I liked clocking in and out and leaving my job behind. "Figured it was time to strike out on your own?"

"I tried before. I'm starting again because I had to dissolve the one I built with Hillary when she cheated on me."

"Oh, damn." I detested this Hillary. "Elijah never mentioned that."

"Yeah, I'm not surprised," he said flatly, then clenched his jaw until a muscle popped. "Anyway, I'd much rather be on my own. She wanted to recruit all the investors with dollar signs in her eyes, and I wanted to be more prudent. That wasn't our money."

"But she thought so?"

"She kept it like it was. I used everything I had to settle up so I wouldn't get sued or arrested."

"I'm glad you're a free man. Mind if I ask what it is that you do?" I leaned forward to dig into the chips. It was well into the evening, and my appetite had roared back.

"I'm a software development engineer, but the business I'm launching is consulting."

"Is it easy?"

When he pinched his brows together, I panicked. "I mean, not easy. Not at all. Just that launching your own company might be fairly easy, as far as starting your own business goes. You must have a large network, know people, and then there's the low overhead. Right?" I crinkled my nose. "I didn't mean to diminish what you're doing."

He exhaled, and understanding lit his eyes. "It's all right, Clover. It's not your fault I can be defensive. I can tell from your tone you weren't being insulting." He gave me a small smile that eased my concern. "It's easier than going into an office. As for getting clients, enough to earn a living, that can be a little tougher. Especially when bridges got burned in the breakup." His jaw hardened again for a second. "It's been a slow climb back into the game, and only time and reasonable rates will change anything."

"That sucks."

"It sucks less now that I can actually work all day."

"I'm glad I'm easier to live with than your mom and dad."

"Sometimes, I wondered if living on the streets would be more productive." He shoved a brownie into his mouth. Elijah would say his brother was a lazy couch surfer, but nothing about Van held up that accusation.

"You didn't pay rent, so you were their unpaid labor?"

He nodded, confirming my suspicions.

Time ticked by, and we finished our meal. The silence was comfortable, pleasant. I could go for more nights like this.

Van set his plate on the coffee table. "Somewhere between a lentil and a baked bean, huh?"

Sudden shyness took over. With the wedding, the move, and the new job, life had been hectic. I hadn't had a chance to do more than exchange quick texts with my sisters. There'd been no long dinners to talk about my situation. No meetups. Other than today, I hadn't even gone to their houses. It was like the pregnancy was my own to deal with, and I guess it was. "A small bean that resembles a tadpole."

"So it's going to look like my brother?"

I laughed. "I hope it'll grow out of it." I put my plate next to his. "I have my appointment this week."

"Yeah? What does that entail?"

I didn't care if he was asking to be nice or if he was really interested. I had someone to talk to about it, and I had some nerves to process. "I don't know for sure. According to what's online, everything. Physical, blood work, and maybe an ultrasound."

"Exciting."

"Yeah. I think it will be." My smile was hesitant. I had been talking myself down from excitement. I had my job and living situation to figure out first. "It still doesn't seem real."

"But it is."

I nodded, a lump forming in my throat. Fear threatened to rise up, but I stuffed it down. I had a good job and a lot of siblings close by. There'd be a roof over my head no matter what. "I should probably look for an apartment."

He pushed a hand through his hair like he was still used to it being longer. "Shit, yeah. Me too."

"Are you staying in the area?" Did I sound hopeful? I had a lot of family, but after today, Van was like a friend.

He shrugged. The bags of ice shifted, and he put them on his plate. "Maybe. It's cheap here."

"Daisy said rental hunting was rough. So Alder bought them all."

"He's going to hook you up?"

I grinned. "He can hook *us* up."

"Connections. Nice."

"Use 'em if you got 'em."

"You have a lot. Your family seems...really amazing."

"They are, and they're a lot of help." I held my hands

up like I was innocent. "I earn what I have fair and square, though. Don't worry about me stealing off with any ill-gotten gains."

"You mean the blood money you earned from the shale trade?"

"It's the bribes for pretending a brine spill didn't happen." I put my fingers on my lips. "I shouldn't even joke about that. Geez, I just started my job, and I don't want people thinking I would do that or cover up for it."

"Especially when you're so shady in the first place."

I giggled and collected the plates, ice bags, and chips. His dry humor was my type of humor. "Want to find *Office Space* while I put these away?"

"I can help you." He got up and took the ice from me—the heaviest items.

"You're supposed to be resting."

"I'll get stiff if I stay still too long. I need to move, and I'm not sitting on my ass while you work."

"Are you sure you're related to—" Dammit. "Sorry. I don't want to keep bringing him up."

I rushed to the kitchen, dropped the paper plates into the garbage, and tossed the chips on the counter. The thunk of the ice packs hitting the sink resounded loudly in the quiet kitchen.

When I turned, I rammed into his broad chest.

He caught me. We were still pressed close together, and I was back to when I knocked him over and landed on his hard body. It had felt way too natural to sit on top of him. Everyone was around, but I hadn't wanted to move. "It's okay. It's okay to keep bringing him up. It's okay if you don't like my family. I don't either. In fact, I'd be more worried if you thought they were great people."

"How did you turn out so well?"

His face was shadowed as he towered over me. "I was a little prick too. Sometimes worse because I was the oldest and everything went to Elijah. Then I got hurt."

I put my hands on his chest again. It was like his pecs were a magnet and my fingers were lined with iron. "You got no help?"

"Not until my grandparents took me in. Then I saw what it was like to be unconditionally loved." He let out a derisive snort. "They wished my dad left my mom. Blamed her for corrupting him, but in the end, it was his decision to act the way he did. I don't know. Maybe they were better grandparents than parents, but they treated me well."

"Good."

"Yeah." There was something noncommittal in his tone. "You deserve to be treated well too."

"I was. Other than, well, you know, I have a great family." I brushed a hunk of hair off his forehead. He kept it neatly brushed, even if he was home all day. "I wish you could've experienced that."

"What was it like?" His voice was low, almost guttural. "Being in a big, loving family?"

"Chaotic." I was still close to him, my face tipped up. Close enough to have all of his attention solely on me. Something I liked more and more. "Sometimes, I didn't feel seen. I felt like I wasn't special when compared to everyone else. But they're always there for me." The corners of my mouth tipped up. "Someone is, anyway. And Poppy's my best friend. Which is a blessing and a curse. Sisters aren't meant to stay together forever. We've lived in different states for so long, and now we're in the same town, and I don't know. We haven't talked a lot, but it hasn't been three weeks. I just..."

"You can tell me," he murmured.

"I just wonder— Am I still special to someone?" The words poured out before I could stop them.

My breath hitched. That came out more vulnerable than I intended. I had meant to give him a glimpse into what my thoughts were, and instead, I exposed myself.

"You are special, Clover. Never doubt that." He was closer to me than before, towering over me, yet our faces weren't far apart. "You're sweet too, just like the sweet clover outside."

"Sweet clover's my favorite weed."

"It's not a weed," he murmured, his gaze dipping to my lips. "It's a beautiful flower with vibrant petals."

Could I pretend he was talking about me? "You think so?"

"Yeah." The word was a whisper across my lips. "I do."

He lowered his head the rest of the way. When his warm lips landed on mine, I curled my fingers into his shirt. His chest was hard underneath my touch, his heart beating frantically under the material.

He cupped a hand around the back of my neck, and his thumb brushed up the column of my throat. A shiver danced through my veins until I was supercharged with desire. The soreness in my breasts shifted to a demanding tenderness. I had an overriding need for pleasure. All the worry, all the stress, all the change—I wanted to forget.

He opened his mouth again, and I did the same. Our tongues touched, tentatively at first, then with growing impatience until I released his shirt and hooked my arms around his neck. He did the same, embracing me around the waist and lifting me. The squish of my achy breasts eked a moan from me that almost sounded pained.

He stiffened, and his hold went slack. Jerking his head back, he stumbled away. "Shit. I'm sorry."

I touched my fingertips to my mouth. Sorry for what? That was the most excellent kiss ever.

I kissed Van.

Oh, crap.

I kissed Sullivan Wagner. The uncle of the baby I'm pregnant with. "I-I'm sorry. It must be the hormones making me do something *completely* out of character." I winced. Did that come off as insulting as it sounded? From the way his gaze shuttered and his expression shut down, yes, it had. Dammit. "I mean—"

"No, I get it. I'm not your type."

"And what is that?" I shouldn't have asked, but his tone could've buzzed down all the sweet clover outside that he compared me to.

"Uptight business douche." Ouch. "And my type isn't my brother's castaways."

My gasp filled the room, and hurt rebounded through my body, pinging off organs and bones. Pain stabbed through my chest wall, and I put my hand on my stomach. His words were a slap, but they were also true. I was tossed away. Why would he want me?

His features turned stricken for a hot second before his jaw tightened. His guard must've slammed back into place. "I'll sleep on the couch tonight."

My embarrassment turned blinding, anger taking its place. I wasn't going to be a punching bag for a Wagner. I was Clover Duke, and I could take care of myself. "You're just like him, you know, hitting me exactly where it'd hurt the most."

Horror shadowed his green eyes, but I had no more time for this. *He* was the one who kissed *me*. I skirted around him and left him behind before he could do it to me, exactly like his brother had.

Chapter Eight

Van

A few days had passed since the kiss that would make the next two months and one week feel like ten years.

Ten years of wondering if she was soft everywhere, if she tasted just as sweet everywhere.

Ten years of knowing that my brother knew the answer. He'd experienced it. A permanent sour taste stained my tongue.

Ten years of admitting I was no better than him.

The hurt in her eyes... It had been my fault. My goddamn inner asshole reared its ugly head.

It wasn't Clover's fault. She was a desirable woman. Attractive, smart, and funny. Adorable and sexy. Unless she had bodies buried all over the property, she was the whole package, and even then, I'd think long and hard about justifying those graves before I turned her in.

But she wasn't a serial killer. I was keeping my distance as if she was one, though. The atmosphere in the house was cold and quiet. We didn't talk. I slept on the couch, claiming that it was my shoulder. My joint was fine. So was my knee. I didn't deserve the bed after the hurt I'd put in her eyes.

I was in my office for the tenth hour. I'd made more progress in the last few days than I had in three months living with my demanding parents. Amazing how productive I could be when I was avoiding the woman of my dreams.

My stomach cramped for the eighth time in the last half hour. I had skipped lunch, and it was well past dinnertime. I needed food, and I'd have to walk by Clover to get it. Whether she was at the table behind her two massive monitors or if she was watching TV, this house was too small to avoid her.

I pushed a hand through my hair. Shit. *Grow up, Van.* I didn't avoid my brother this much when he was being a peak narcissist.

With a sigh, I rose. The dining room light was off, but a dull glow flickered from the room. When I turned into it, my stomach sank. She was curled in her chair with her knees to her chest. A blanket cocooned her, and she stared at her screen. Her wan smile was a punch right to the sternum, and it wasn't aimed at me.

Why wasn't she curled up on the couch? "What are you doing?"

She didn't glance at me. "Watching *Sweet Home Alabama.*"

I stopped before the kitchen and turned to look at the dark living room. "At the table?"

"You're sleeping on the couch. I don't want to—"

"Jesus, Clover. Have you been spending your entire day in that chair?" It wasn't even padded. I was supposed to be the uncomfortable one. I was the asshole, and I wasn't pregnant.

"You spend all day in the office."

"In my gamer's chair. The one specially designed for long periods of time." I raked another hand through my hair. Not only that, but I also got up a lot during the day. My knee hurt if it was bent too long. "Go sit on the couch."

"No, it's fine." She clicked her screen off. "It's almost time for bed anyway."

"I'll put the TV in the bedroom."

"Van, it's fine."

"No, it's not." If it was, she would look at me. She'd smile at me. She wouldn't sound distant when we were feet apart. I put my hands on my hips. Was that too confrontational? I crossed my arms. That wasn't better. Hands went on the hips again. "I'll sleep in the bed tonight. Go be comfortable."

She hugged the blanket tighter around her. "I know you don't want to sleep in the same bed with me. It's okay. I can make compromises too."

"No." Frustration scratched over my skin. "No, Clover. I crossed a line and made you uncomfortable, all for a stupid kiss."

Her lips formed a troubled line. "The kiss wasn't that bad."

I paused. It was fucking amazing. For me. "Wasn't it good?" I squeezed my eyelids shut and shook my head. Her sweet moans. Her soft curves. Good was an understatement. I opened my eyes. "Never mind."

"Are you afraid I'll compare you and Elijah? Rate each of you on a scale from one to ten?" Fatigue was scrawled over her face. "Do you want to know the results?"

"It's not like that."

She flung her arms out. "All of this is like that. He got a zero out of ten for loyalty. You get a ten out of ten for cleaning up his mess. He gets a six for how he treated me before he fucked another woman, but so far, you're at a ten. I'll keep you at a ten if you don't want to pick pumpkins because I don't blame you for how you reacted about the kiss, and you don't make me feel like shit about myself otherwise. When it comes to this baby, I'm sure Elijah'll be at zero, and I know you will be too, but again, I don't blame you. But he really should be in the negative. As for the kiss, his were a seven, but yours was an eleven out of ten. There? Better?"

The numbers banged through my head, and each time I came out ahead, even when I was at a zero with him when it came to the baby. My throat was closing up. I never beat Elijah at anything, but she just rattled off a list from the top of her head. No one had made me feel so seen. No one had so thoroughly stripped me down either.

"You shouldn't give me a ten for how I treat you," I said thickly. "That should be the base. It should be zero. And I should be in the negatives for how I've acted since the kiss."

She sighed and gathered her blanket. "No, I get it. I'm your brother's ex. I didn't even have the good sense to break up with him. He ran off on me. Now I'm pregnant with his kid, and you're stuck with me. I'm sure the kiss was a solid minus eight for you."

"No, Clover." She shouldn't be brushing herself off like that. Of all the people in the world, I should understand. "You were a hundred out of ten."

She scoffed and hugged the material tighter to her. "You don't have to make me feel better. I'm a big girl, and you've been honest with me from the beginning."

"I'm still being honest. Why do you think that is?

Because I want to keep finding out where else you score an infinity."

Her lower lip puffed out, but the vulnerability shining in her eyes gutted me. "You don't mean that."

"I haven't lied to you yet. Except about my shoulder. It doesn't hurt, and it's not why I was on the couch, though you're smart enough to guess that. I'll sleep in the bed tonight. And I'm going to go pick goddamn pumpkins with you."

A small smile played over her lips. "That's the name of his patch. GD Pumpkins."

I chuckled. Evander looked like a guy who'd say that.

A loud silence fell between us. I was glad we could reach this point. We were talking, but it didn't make up for how I behaved. I was better than Elijah when it mattered, and that was because of how I treated Clover. "I have a lot of baggage when it comes to my brother."

She barked out a laugh. "I don't want to turn it into a competition, but yeah. I might have more."

I didn't smile. I wasn't digging into the weeds about me and Elijah, but I wasn't going to tell her everything. A guy had his pride, and Elijah had smashed it enough.

She poked her thumb over her shoulder. "I should get to sleep anyway. I have my appointment in the morning, and then I'll work a little later than normal."

Her first prenatal appointment, and she was going alone. It was unfair. If it was my baby, I wouldn't miss a thing. "Do you, uh...need any help?"

Sadness streaked across her face. "No," she said quietly. "I know any of my siblings would show if I said something, but I need to get used to doing all this alone. Thank you, though."

"I'm not going to be a zero." That rating had bothered

me. It wasn't about the competition with my brother. It was about her and a little bean who was my family. "With the baby. I won't be a zero."

"I appreciate that." Her tone said she'd believe it when I lived up to my word. So I would make sure of it. She lifted her chin to the kitchen. "There's some spaghetti and meatballs left over."

My stomach clenched. "Sounds good."

"It was, if I do say so. A solid eight out of ten." She continued to the hallway. "Good night, Van."

It would be now that I could sleep in the bed next to her.

❈

Clover

I put my jeans on and winced. These were getting snug. I took them off and tossed them in a pile of clothing that I wouldn't be able to wear for a while, if ever again.

I stepped into my loose shorts from the summer. Well, looser. Those were getting snugger too. My stomach wasn't any more rounded than before, but my body was already changing and shifting.

Time for my first prenatal visit. Alone.

It was just another doctor's appointment. If I kept telling myself that, maybe I'd feel it too. Anxiety, trepidation, and a large dollop of excitement swirled in a small tornado in my gut. This appointment was the most major one I'd ever had, but that also meant I was fortunate. I'd get to learn about this baby and my pregnancy. I could do this. It'd be fine.

I clipped my hair up and bypassed the makeup. I wouldn't need to impress anyone, but I had more color in my cheeks than in the last few days. Talking with Van last night had eased a lot of anxiety that had settled into my bones since the kiss. I'd also gotten the deepest sleep of my life as soon as Van's weight was next to me in bed.

I left the bedroom and went to the kitchen. My stomach protested. No, I could not eat this morning.

Van was munching on a breakfast sandwich. He shoved the last bite in his mouth and dusted off his fingers. "Hungry?"

"I'll get something after I'm done." I pressed a hand to my stomach. "I don't want to risk it."

"Nervous?" He dug his keys out and twirled them on his finger.

"Yeah. Kinda excited too, I guess."

"Let's go so you're nice and early."

Was he... No. He couldn't be. Yet he was dressed in jeans and a polo when he normally wore shorts and a T-shirt in his office. He had his shoes on. Elation could've lifted me off my feet, but I had to be misunderstanding this. He wouldn't miss work for this. Would he? "Where are you going?"

"With you."

Stunned, I stared at him. "What?"

"You shouldn't have to do this by yourself."

And I'd told him that I didn't expect my family to hold my hand. Did he think I would stress myself too much? I was too inept? "You don't have to."

"Bean is my niece or nephew. Consider me checking in early for uncle duty."

Oh. He wasn't going to be a zero, and this baby was a part of his life—if he wanted it to be.

"You don't have to, but thank you." Heat poked the backs of my eyes. I didn't realize how anxious I was until a tremble ran through my body, ending in my hands. I hooked them on my purse so he didn't see them shaking.

"My pleasure. We can take my truck."

"There might, um, be a physical, and it'll involve stirrups."

He winced. "If you said that to a dude about what his appointment would be like, he'd be running."

"Wait until you see the speculum."

Color leached from his face. "I don't know what that is, but I don't like that word."

Laughing, I headed into the garage, and he followed me.

It didn't take long to drive to the clinic. Walking in with Van should've been weirder than it was, but I was grateful to have someone by my side. We'd been living together for three weeks. Perhaps that was why. He'd met my whole family. All of them. He'd played kickball with us, we'd slept next to each other, and we'd even had our first fight.

I checked in at the counter, and we sat in the waiting room. Since Coal Haven was small, the clinic was for everyone. It was big enough to have a doctor who took obstetric patients, or I'd have to drive to Bismarck.

We scrolled through our phones, sitting side by side. He bounced a leg, and that was the only sign he might be nervous. A familiar face popped out of the door to the patient rooms.

"Clover, hi," Emery Barron said. Her hair was in a clip, the strands fanning out behind her. She wore purple scrubs. "You can come on back."

Her brows lifted when she saw Van next to me, but understanding filled her eyes. I wouldn't be surprised if news got back to her through the Duke, Knight, and Barron grapevine.

Relief flowed through me, and I smiled as I rose and followed her. Van's presence was a secure wall behind me. Once we were in the exam room, Emery shut the door and sat by the desk.

"You know my situation, don't you?" I rubbed my hands together. "It's okay if you do. The less I have to explain, the better."

Her smile was just as comforting as being with Van. "I heard the story, but trust me, lots of stories have walked through these doors. Dr. Abdallah is only concerned about you and the baby. Whoever you're comfortable with having with you is fine with us."

"This is Van." I clasped Van's strong hand and let go like I touched a hot stove. "Van, this is Emery. She's married to a cousin of Evander's."

Emery grinned. "Holden's also the cousin of the guy married to Eliot's sister."

"Lily's husband." His smile was friendly. "I don't know all the cousins yet, but I'm guessing the pumpkin day will clear it all up."

"Or make it more confusing," Emery said with a laugh. She fired up the computer on the desk. "Because all the kids will be there. I'm glad you're coming. It's a legendary weekend."

Chapter Nine

Clover

An hour and a half later, I had a physical, a series of tests, and a quickie ultrasound. Van stayed with me the whole time, quiet but attentive. We got to see Lyric again when she drew my blood. Now I was in the pickup staring at the bean in my belly.

Van started the engine, but he didn't drive anywhere. "That's bigger than a lentil."

"I think it's enlarged, but it seems to be fully in lima bean territory." The weight and responsibility of being a parent—and a single parent—piled onto my shoulders.

"Are you going to find out if you're having a boy or girl?"

I stared at the black-and-white images in my hand. It really did have a baked bean shape. "I don't know. In a way, I'd like to be prepared. But then it'd be nice to have a good surprise at the end of all this. And I really don't care if

97

Bean's clothing or bedding is pink, blue, purple, brown, or chartreuse."

"I hear the chartreuse baby bedding is a hot commodity." He exchanged a smile with me. "What about names?"

"I haven't even thought about that." I ran names through my head. Names of girls I'd grown up with—Hailey, Kaitlyn, Beth. The boys—Jackson, Dillon, Cash. None that called to me. "I've always liked some rock and mineral names, and that'd really piss Elijah off."

"Are you going to contact him again?"

"That ball is in his court." I worked to keep my grip on the slippery paper to stop me from crinkling it. "I have to imagine he saw the text."

Van tapped his finger on the wheel. "Probably."

"What if he wants a role in the baby's life?" Would he be a one-man wrecking ball? Fight me for custody? Neither of us had money for a custody fight, and my ex wasn't that ambitious when it wasn't about him.

Van shook his head. "I don't know, Clover. I don't feel like any of my family will be good for Bean."

I smiled at him, grateful he was on the same page and I hadn't needed to broach the subject first. "I like Opal or Pearl for a girl, and for a boy, I don't know. I'm not a fan of Clay or Brick. I mean, they're fine names."

"Erosion is out?"

I laughed. It wouldn't have been this easy to talk to Elijah about names. He would've canned everything I brought up, and I wouldn't have realized he was manipulating me. "I think the same goes for feldspar and limestone."

"Sandstone or strata?"

"Strong names, but no. Got any super cool family

names that aren't Elijah and Dan?" I would not name this kid after Elijah or his dad.

Van went quiet and gazed out the window again. "The grandpa I was close with was named Nolan."

"I like that name." Would it be weird to name my kid after Van's grandpa? Wait...Nolan would've also been Elijah's grandparent.

I carefully folded the images and tucked them into my purse. "Do you mind if we stop at the store? I have to get the ingredients for what I'm bringing this weekend. If you've gotta work, I can run to town later."

"I don't work for myself to be tied to the office." He put the pickup in drive and pulled out of the lot. "I'm happy to take you if the ingredients you need happen to make cookie salad."

I bit back a grin. "That's so weird. They do."

At the store, Van walked next to me and picked what he wanted. He kept his items secluded to one corner of the cart, but when we paid, he threw everything on the belt and waved me off.

"No, I got it." I handed him my card. The grocery shopping experience had been pleasant enough. I would've handed over cash for that alone. Van made normal chores enjoyable.

He didn't take my card. "You're making our contribution to the party. Please let me help in some way."

The older cashier grinned at us. "It's always so cute when married couples try to buy for each other. My husband and I shared the same account, and I got an allowance." She hit the button to run Van's card. "Now I'm single, and I get to spend all my own money. Can't take it with me."

I almost told her that we weren't a couple, but we were married, and we did have separate accounts.

Van stuffed his debit card back in his pocket. "Enjoy every penny."

He lifted our groceries and didn't bother with the cart. When his arms flared out with the load, it made his profile even more rugged, with his muscles more apparent.

The cashier looked from me to him. "I also like when they can't seem to get enough of each other."

My gaze shot to Van. He waited for me by the door. I'd never find out if I couldn't get enough of him.

"Thanks," I mumbled and scurried after him.

The rest of the day went by like normal. I worked at the table, but Van left his office a lot more than he had the last few days. When he ventured out to stretch his legs and gaze out the living room window, I popped up from my workstation at the dining room table.

"It's my turn for dinner." I stopped a few feet behind him. The sun rested above the horizon. It wouldn't set for a couple more hours, but that'd change as the days went on. "What do you feel like eating?"

He glanced at me. "Whatever you're up to making."

"You'd better be careful, or you might end up with a pan of brownies and popcorn for a meal."

"Are you trying to sell me on the options?"

My stomach picked that time to growl. "I'd do it if I didn't think I'd feel sick in the morning. The popcorn sounds good. I could make that for after. I might watch a movie."

"What movie?" He spun around, stuffing his hands in his shorts pockets. He'd changed after we returned to the house, but casual Van was still potent. If he wore a suit, I might forget all about how I promised I wouldn't make more out of sharing a bed than just us two occupying the same mattress during the night.

"I'd like a good action show, and it's getting to be *Die Hard* season."

He grinned. "You're 'Team *Die Hard* is a Christmas movie'?"

"Either that, or it's an adult version of *Home Alone*." When his brow furrowed, I nodded. "A kid uses nothing but his savvy to protect a building from the bad guys. But then it'd still be a Christmas movie."

He laughed, and I glowed inside from getting this serious guy to crack more than a smile. "The parallels are impossible to ignore. Whatever you want for dinner. I'll make the popcorn for the movie."

"Deal."

He faced the window again, arms loosely folded in front of him.

Was something bothering him? Was someone out there? "Something weighing on you?"

He shook his head. "I answered emails all day, and I have to decompress. I really like this view. It's relaxing."

I scooted over to see around his shoulder. The shop and barn were both visible, surrounded by trees with leaves that were already turning color. More brown painted the grass than green, and soon it'd take over completely. A hawk hunted over the pasture, its wings spread wide. Farther out, cattle grazed. Wisps of white clouds floated high in the sky.

"It's lovely," I murmured.

"It is."

I couldn't see his gaze in the glass, but from the way heat streaked over my skin, it was on me.

❧

Van

I waited for the popcorn in the skillet to start popping. I had a pan of brownies in the oven. Clover made delicious BBQ chicken for dinner, and she likely wasn't hungry, but she'd mentioned these. After my deplorable words when we kissed, I'd do anything for her.

I just might do anything for her, regardless. She didn't hold what I said against me. She'd been nothing but kind and funny and so damn relatable, I wasn't sure if I should pretend to be sick and sleep on the couch. I woke up this morning hugging the body pillow between us. If it hadn't been there, I might've rolled right into her and dragged her into my arms.

The first pop sounded from the pan. I took off the lid and dumped in the rest of the kernels. Now it was a waiting game.

I wandered the kitchen, and as soon as I closed in on the fridge, I came to a stop. She'd hung the images from the ultrasound up with a magnet. Bean faced me, and I stared at it.

That little bean was related to me. I would be an uncle.

Warm affection spread through my chest, but there was something else with it, something I was afraid to identify. A growing desire to be more.

I put my back to the fridge and sucked in a breath. I was more. I was helping Bean's mom get her footing. For a couple of months, I was Bean's stepdad. Once this marriage ended, I'd still be an uncle. I'd still be in Clover's life. Right?

A burn ignited behind my ribs, and I went back to the popcorn. I was the guy taking care of Bean's mom right now, and I didn't take that job lightly. This was my time to prove I was better than my family. I was better than my brother.

Was I really a better kisser?

Nope. Not my business.

The oven timer went off. I took the brownies out. Once all the snacks were done, I entered the living room with a bowl of extra-buttery popcorn and a plate of gooey brownies.

Clover straightened on the couch, the blanket falling from her chest. She wore a thin shirt and leggings, hence the throw. My hold tightened on the food. Her nipples poked through the fabric like two determined pebbles, trying to drive me out of my mind.

I could control myself. As long as I didn't wake up humping the pillow in the morning.

"No way!" Her eyes grew wide, and delight lit them up. "You made brownies? I thought you were in there for a while, and it smelled good, but I was afraid to get my hopes up." She did a little shoulder wiggle.

Fuck me. I couldn't take that image with me to bed.

"I found a box of brownie mix." I dropped to the other side of the couch and set the food on the coffee table. "I made sure to put the edges all on one side if you're an edges person."

"Hell yes, I am."

She grabbed one and bit into it. Her eyes rolled into the back of her head, and she moaned.

I yanked a throw pillow over my crotch in case my dick couldn't handle that sound, and I took a handful of popcorn.

She swallowed and licked crumbs off her fingers.

I was in trouble tonight. I barely got over kissing her, and now I was lusting over every single move she made.

"You didn't have to make these, but thank you." She popped the rest of the brownie into her mouth.

"You're welcome."

She moved the popcorn bowl to sit between us on the cushions. "I haven't enjoyed a Friday night like this in so long."

I hadn't had a girl say she enjoyed a night with me in a long time. One of the scars Hillary left inside me healed right over. "What would you normally be doing?"

Her chewing slowed, and her gaze got a faraway look. Before she answered, she took a long drink of her mineral water. "I was convincing myself that I loved cocktail bars with ridiculously uncomfortable chairs and drinks that are too strong and too expensive."

"I'm familiar with those nights."

Interest lit her eyes. "You are? I don't take you for a cocktail guy."

"There was a time." I needed a brownie for these memories. "I had to wine and dine investors, earn their trust, and make them believe I could deliver on all the things I said I would. And I could've." It was important to me to tell her. I would've kept my word. "But that wasn't how I would've chosen to spend those nights."

I stuffed a brownie between my lips.

"Since you're chewing, I'll tell you what I would've rather been doing." She brandished a piece of popcorn pinched between her thumb and forefinger. "I would've loved to go rockhounding on the weekends. Do some mild camping and hike the riverbeds. I'd love to go to the Badlands and look for agates."

"Mild camping?" I asked around my mouthful.

"I can only take so many column toilets that campgrounds have." Excitement lit her eyes even more. "You know what I'd really like to do? Get a cabin at a state park." She stuck her index finger in the air. "Running water. More of a bed—though still not comfortable." She ticked another finger up, frowned, and added a third. "And I'm right there by a river. Or Lake Metigoshe. I could look for quartz there too. What about you?"

This was it. She might think what I enjoyed was useless or weird, and she'd make comments. I could lie. Or I could be honest. I could trust Clover to be decent even if she thought I was an odd duck. "I like to game. It's my zen, and I've met a lot of cool guys."

"You sure they're guys and not twelve-year-old boys?"

I chuckled, less on guard than before. There was no condemnation in her question. "I met them first, and then we started playing together."

She turned toward me more, seemingly interested. "Is that how it works? You actually know them?"

A soft warmth started in my chest. "Not always, but for what I do, it does. I'd rather play with people I know."

"What do you play?" she asked without the censure I'd get from my old social circle, and I relaxed even more.

"*Super Mario* and *League of Legends*, usually." I shouldn't continue. I'd never reveal this to anyone associated with my brother, but the words crowded on my tongue as natural as ever. "I have Pokémon cards. I play those too."

"Like the kids' card game?"

Damn. The spark around my heart extinguished.

"Oh my God." She waved her hands in a clearing motion. "No, sorry. Obviously not just a kids' card game if you're playing it. I just didn't know that guys like you still played, though it makes sense. The game would grow with the kids who played it."

There was a tendril of comforting heat again. She only wanted to learn about what I enjoyed. Could it be that easy? "It's really popular, and it's fun to gather in person."

"Where do you meet?"

"Game shops." Since she wasn't guffawing, I offered more information. "I looked up places after I first moved. Bismarck and Minot are the closest."

"When are you going to go?"

"I should stay here." I gathered another handful of popcorn.

"Why?"

"I'm here to help you."

She stared at me for a moment. "That's sweet but not necessary. Why don't I just go with you?"

My brows crept to my hairline. That was the last offer I expected a woman to make. I was prepared to put my hobby on hold until I was no longer married. First, I had wanted to hide it, but now the clock was ticking fast. We didn't have much longer. "You'd do that?"

"Sounds fun. And if I'm bored, I can find something else to do. We're not tied at the hip."

I'd like to be connected somewhere else. More than that, I had to see if she was as genuine as she seemed. Seeing the tournament in real time, the range of ages, and how serious we were about our card game might change her mind about me. I hoped not. "Okay."

"Can't wait." She rewarded me with a wide smile. Like the sun shone just for me.

"Then that means I'll go with you rockhounding."

Her smile vanished, replaced by worry. "Really? It doesn't sound excruciatingly boring to you?"

Did she have the same insecurities? We were both worried about being the outsider in the relationship because of our interests and hobbies. "Clover, as a kid, I gamed and ran around outside with no supervision. You're offering for me to act like a kid again."

Her giggle was light. "We're returning to our childhood, then?" She let out a sigh. "I don't know if I'm up for camping, but we could go to Medora for a day trip. It's less than a two-hour drive."

"It's a plan. One weekend of each after the pumpkin harvest."

Her smile turned soft, almost shy. "It's a plan."

Chapter Ten

Clover

Van took the cookie salad from me as soon as I got out of his pickup.

"Are you going to be picking pumpkins?" He hovered next to me like he thought I'd take a header on the uneven ground.

Was it bad that I liked his attention? Any of his focus was a shiny piece of quartz, just glinting in the sun for me. "I might for just a little bit. My appetite is coming back, so I might stay with Mom and graze on all the food while waiting for everyone to get in."

We rounded the big shop that had been blocking the view of everyone from where we parked. Kids of all ages were frolicking through the yard and in the field full of orange dots of pumpkins. The older kids hung out by the tractor and the wagons with Evander and some other guys. The porch on Evander and Violet's house was decorated with pumpkins and straw bales. Adults went from the house to the shop, where all the food and seating was.

He slowed. "Whoa."

"It can be overwhelming. If you want to leave, just give me a signal or something. Or heck, leave and text me. Someone can get me home."

His astonishment turned to intensity. "I'm not ditching you."

Was his possessiveness my imagination? Or was it defensiveness? "If you need to go, I'll leave too."

"Really? Why?"

I looked up at him. "Because we're in this together."

His jaw went slack, and he nodded. "Okay. It's not that I don't want to enjoy myself. I'm just not used to...this."

Jasper broke from the crowd and jogged toward us. "Hey, you made it."

"I was a little slow this morning." I had texted my family thread to let them know my stomach was upset. It hadn't been that bad, but I'd had no clothes to wear. Everything fit, mostly, but it was uncomfortable. I didn't want the band around my belly or fabric hugging my thighs. And my boobs. Ugh. Why so sensitive? So it had taken me a while to be ready.

"No worries," my brother said. "We're here all day."

"You were able to get off for the whole weekend?"

His face fell. "Yeah. Soon, I'll have every weekend off."

"You got a new job?"

He rolled a shoulder. "Not exactly. Eliot broke the news to me last week that they're selling."

"They can do that?" Our grandma wasn't the only one who liked to include strict stipulations to her trust. The Knights' dad tied them to their cattle ranch. They couldn't break it up, and they couldn't get an income from it if they weren't working there. One by one, they all found their own way around it to be with the ones they loved.

"It is what it is." Jasper fell in step with us. "It was a lot to make the trip to do their time after all the kids were involved in stuff. They want to be free of the ties, and I don't blame 'em. Just wish I could afford to buy it."

"I'm sorry. And all that's left for you is the lake cabin."

"If I'm married in less than a year, but hey, if it sells, then Aunt Linda will get something out of the ordeal of managing all the properties."

"You're a gem for thinking like that."

He put a hand to his chest like I stabbed him. "Clover, I'm named after a tree, not the rock."

Van chuckled next to me. I liked that he laughed like he was in on the joke and not a snicker that was demeaning or politely tolerating.

Jasper clapped his hands together. "Okay, Van. Want to get all the introductions out of the way and see how many people you remember after tossing pumpkins with them for a few hours?"

"Sounds fun. Let me get Clover and her pudding dessert delivered safely to the shop."

Jasper lifted a brow at me, but there was approval in his eyes. Van was a good one. He wasn't mine, but he would make someone happy someday.

In the shop, relatives, in-laws, and relatives of my in-laws roamed around. I smiled and said hi to everyone on my way to the buffet line. Van dug out my dish and placed it in the middle with the salads instead of at the end with the desserts. No one in this crowd was going to argue.

"Grab a bite to eat," he said, folding the tote and finding a spot to stuff it under the table. "I'll go with your brother and learn my way around GD Pumpkins."

"Thank you. Remember—any time you're ready."

Jasper hovered nearby. When Van joined him, Jasper slapped him on the back. "So, you said you were a computer guy."

My brother used to be in IT before he ranched. Would he return to that career? He'd been lost when he'd gotten laid off until Eliot offered him a job. I hoped the same didn't happen.

Mom appeared at my side. "How are you feeling?"

I grinned. "Let me get a bite to eat, and then I'll show you some pictures."

Her face lit up, and once I nibbled on some crackers and cheese, I was surrounded as everyone in the shop or who swung through stopped to see pictures of Bean.

Once they were all gone, Violet pulled out a chair, dropped into it, and pushed another one out with her foot. "Evander started calling Willa 'Bud' when I was pregnant. Bean is cute."

"It just happened." I sat and adjusted my bra strap. "Where can I get good maternity clothes?"

"I'll go to Bismarck with you. Tell me when."

I nodded. Right. I had all my sisters close by. "Yes, thank you."

I had been thinking of calling Poppy, but it was the middle of soccer season for her. She'd been busy in the best ways since she'd moved back to Coal Haven. I had several other sisters in town, and I could do it myself, but Poppy and I were the closest in age and best friends. I kind of missed her. But I was a big girl and starting a family of my own. Poppy was still around. It wasn't like she left me at the altar.

One of Emery's older girls came into the shop with

Willa in tow. "Do you have some Band-Aids? She fell running across the lawn."

"I-I told her"—Willa hiccupped—"where they at."

Violet jumped up. "No worries. I'll get her cleaned up. Thank you, Afton."

Dad took Violet's vacated spot. "Thanks for bringing those pictures."

"I liked showing everyone." It was nice to share my growing excitement. Any other situation, I would've been thrilled. Now I could be again.

He angled his chair to face me, propping his elbows on his knees, and tapped his fingertips together. I stiffened. He was in CEO mode. "I know we didn't talk much about the end of the three months, but have you and Van discussed whether you're going to attempt an annulment or go for a divorce?"

"Oh, uh..." We hadn't discussed it. Tension returned in my shoulders. The three-month deadline loomed over my head, and I had yet to look for apartments or think about the logistics of going our separate ways. "Divorce, maybe? Isn't an annulment harder to get?"

"Depends on how contentious a divorce would get."

"He would get half of nothing, and from what I understand, I would get half of nothing. I don't think it'll be an issue."

"You have to prepare, Clover."

I scowled, hating that I should've been prepared, unlike I was in Las Vegas. "Van isn't like that, Dad."

Dad pressed his fingertips together. "You know that for sure?"

"Yes. Besides, why would he marry me if he was going to be worth millions before our time was up?"

Dad dipped his head. He must've thought the same

thing. "I have a friend who can draw up the papers. All you two would need to do is sign them."

My mouth went dry. The three months felt like three years, but I only had two months of it left. "I should talk to Van."

His gaze sharpened. "Do you plan to stay married longer?"

"No?" Why'd it come out as a question? "Nothing's changed, it's just that he's in this too."

Dad's eyes filled with respect. "Let me know what you two want to do."

"Yeah, sure. I'll talk to him."

Evander wandered into the shop, scratching the back of his neck. He was heading for the food before he saw Violet and veered toward his wife. A shot of envy entered my veins.

Divorce papers. Easy peasy.

Violet smiled and giggled in a way I'd never heard her do in our entire lives—until she met Evander. Hearts were in her damn eyes.

I looked out the shop doors. At the same moment, Van glanced over from the crowd of guys. The corner of his mouth tipped up, and he popped a brow like he was asking if I was okay.

I gave him a small nod, but I wasn't okay. A divorce shouldn't be easier than a marriage, even a pretend one.

❁

Van

. . .

Every time there was a lull in activity, I sought out Clover no matter where I was standing. Most of the time, she was surrounded by sisters, or sisters-in-law, or some of the grandmas who were here. Sometimes she played with the kids. I could pick out her nieces and nephews, but I had to work to remember what other kids went with other couples.

Trailers were filled with pumpkins, and Clover was standing next to one, admiring all the orange fruit—vegetable?—inside. A smile lit her face when Laila ran to her. She bent down and talked with the girl; they admired a pumpkin, then Laila ran off.

Clover laughed and straightened, her expression delighted to be surrounded by metric tons of pumpkins.

"Did you get one picked out?" Jasper asked, walking toward me. His arms were full of two different-sized pumpkins.

"I don't think I have a use for them."

He gave me a *no excuses* look. "We all take a pumpkin. It kinda makes you feel like a kid again."

Hadn't I just been talking to Clover about that sensation? This was just another moment I got to experience that I hadn't gotten as a kid. Another fun activity we could do together.

"You carve them?"

"I'll carve twelve if I can."

I hadn't carved a jack-o-lantern in years, and to hell with it. It sounded fun. Would Clover think so? "Does Clover carve them?"

"She used to when we were kids. Don't know if Douche Nozzle would've ever let her. No offense."

None taken. "I've called him worse."

Jasper started walking backward toward the line of

parked cars. "If you come up with any inventive names for me, share them."

"Will do."

Clover was alone by another trailer of pumpkins. Her gaze strayed to Poppy and Jensen laughing with Auggie, then to Lily and Eliot. Eliot had one of the kids on his shoulders. Violet was under Evander's arm as they chatted with some of his cousins. Clover's smile stayed in place, but her gaze dropped. Then her light began to fade, like it was starkly obvious that she was alone.

But she wasn't. Not yet. I jogged to join her at the trailer. "I was told I have to choose one."

Her eyes sparkled as soon as she popped her head up. "Evander and Violet are trying to get us to take five." She clapped her hands. "Aren't they gorgeous? All this color when the world around us is getting brown?"

My heart swelled at her enthusiasm. Damn, she was cute. "Yeah. Want help? I haven't carved one in forever."

"I haven't either. Are you up for ten?"

I'd make sure I was. "Absolutely."

She tapped one that was by the edge. "This one has a nice, broad face. Perfect for an elaborate design."

I lifted it out and put it in the little pull-behind trailer next to her.

Her grin widened, and it was like I'd opened the floodgates. "I was eyeing this one. See this blemish? It'd make a perfect witch's wart. Oh, and this one has such a nice stem, I might not even carve it."

She went through three more and insisted I choose the next ones. Since she'd put actual thought into her selection, I did the same. "I'm going to carve a game controller."

"That'll look awesome. I'll buy some tea lights. We're going to have the craziest porch in the county."

After I made all my selections, I took the handle of the wagon. "I can load these and come back for your food container."

"Oh, it's already been packed, along with a ton of leftovers. Evander's mom is a sly one about cleaning up after."

"We're off dinner duty for a few days?"

"Lunch and dinner." She pressed a hand to her stomach. "Truth be told, that leftover pulled pork sounds good for breakfast."

"Then do it."

We reached the pickup, and I loaded our stash in the bed. I'd put them in the garage to store until it was time to carve them. When we both got inside, she was quiet. As I drove us home, she didn't make much conversation, staring out the passenger window.

I pulled into our drive and backed up to the garage. When I killed the engine, she didn't move.

"Clover?" I asked softly.

She twisted her fingers together. "My dad talked to me."

Since Weston had chatted with me too, she must mean it wasn't idle chitchat. "Okay."

She wet her lips, and seeing her tongue was just another item on the list of all things Clover I needed to forget in order to behave.

Well, I'd behave no matter what. But I'd remember how she moaned, her pert little nipples poking against her shirt, or that pink tongue. I was just asking for misery.

"He offered to have divorce papers drawn up," she said deliberately. "I guess we'll need them, but I said I'd talk to you."

Disappointment gathered in my gut. No pumpkin harvest for me next year. Who would Clover pick out pumpkins with? "Yeah, we'll need them."

"Right." She left her hands on her lap. "Do you have your own person?"

"It seems weird to say yes, but I do. The firm I used when I broke up my company has someone I could use."

"My dad would pay for it." Her offer was tentative. "Like an end-of-wedding gift."

I puffed out a weak chuckle. "Who keeps the toaster?"

"You," she said wryly. "You keep it all; you bought it."

There was nothing about her statement that sounded good. "What will you do?"

She wrinkled her nose. "I'll talk to Alder. He might have a rental by then, but yeah. I should start looking for a place. You?"

"I should too."

"Where?"

I rubbed my chin with my thumb and forefinger. "I don't know. I'm not going anywhere near Nebraska." That'd be too far from my niece or nephew. Too far from Clover. "I'm talking with a big potential investor, and two more have replied to my emails. That's heartening. If I land that first account, it'll be a springboard."

"Really? How?"

Something about the sanctity of the pickup made it easier to talk to her about something I'd kept close to my chest since I began. My trust had been shattered by a woman before.

Though it hadn't been Clover. "If I can work with them, I'll get word of mouth. Others will see, and I'll get more work. I can hire people. Buy my own house."

"Revolutionary," she said wistfully. In that, we were together. Two adults, trying to be adultier. Trying to prove to ourselves that we could do it.

"It's all online, but I'd like a headquarters. An office."

"Not a home office?"

I shook my head. "It's lonely—when I'm not married." I aimed a grin her way.

"You think so?" Her mouth formed a troubled line. "Do you think I have to plan for being lonely?"

"You'll have a baby."

A flash of fear coursed through her eyes. "Yes. Me and the baby."

"And all of your family."

She relaxed, slinking farther down in her seat. "I'll have them too. I'll be a divorced, single mom."

My stomach twisted. Divorced. Single mom. Clover was a people person. She loved her family, and she was fun to be around. I never knew staying home could be so nice, but I'd take watching a movie with her over heading out to a game night any time.

I could do both.

For the next two months.

She sighed and peered in the rearview mirror. "We have a lot of pumpkins to unload."

"I'll take care of them."

"I can help."

Not when I was around. She wasn't alone yet. "You can take in the food. I'm gonna need some of that cookie salad."

Her eyes twinkled. "I made double and kept a batch here. Just in case."

My whole world tipped over at that admission, and it might never be right.

Chapter Eleven

Clover

The hubbub of the lunch crowd at Rattler's made the booth I was in seem more private.

I had invited Van to the lunch with my brother to discuss rentals Alder might have available or know about, but Van had an important call. It must've been a critical one because he paced the hallway a few times before I left. I'd hear steady typing from his office and then his stockinged feet hitting a steady rhythm on the hardwood.

I had my oldest brother mostly to myself, which didn't happen often.

Alder juggled eight-month-old Lee like a pro with one arm while he took a drink of water. He'd taken the day off as soon as I asked him when we could meet. The weekends were busy with rec soccer for Laila, and she'd be in school during the week. Daisy was at work, but Alder had picked up Lee from day care.

"I still can't get over this." I gestured to him and my tiny nephew. Soon I'd be the Duke juggling a baby.

The dreamiest smile spread across his face. "Yeah? Why?"

"You were always bossy growing up and thought you were in charge."

"I was in charge."

"But I was a kid. And then as adults, well, you were a single guy for so long, off conquering the oil refinery world." Except for the short stint when he and Daisy were married right out of high school.

"I'm still conquering it."

"You're also conquering your personal life. Before, you didn't have one." I'd see him on the holidays, and he'd be a bossy older brother. He'd also been a little aloof, like he knew where his place was; he just couldn't get back to it. "Now you do."

"Now I have Daisy." He got the easy grin again. "And Laila and Lee."

"All right. Stop before I gag," I said jokingly when I really was getting queasy, and it wasn't due to morning sickness. "I just want to preface this to say that if you don't have a rental, please do not stress and do not search for one for me."

He dug into the diaper bag next to him. "Actually, I already did."

My stomach dropped. I appreciated his help, but this task hung over my head. Like it was task number one for me to conquer to earn the independent-woman title. "Oh. Okay."

He frowned slightly. "Does that upset you?"

"No," I said quickly, but yes, my gut was churning

before I could order my food. "It just means it's real." That was also true.

Sympathy crossed his face. "Being on your own?"

Not sharing a place with Van. Not watching any more movies with him. Not cooking for each other. "Must be."

"I know you're probably stressed about you and the baby, but I swear, Clover, we'll be there. All of us. Even Jasper."

"He's moving here?"

Alder nodded. "He was asking about a rental too, but he said you get first dibs."

Appreciation for my brothers grew. I would be taken care of. I'd have a roof over my head, but I wanted it to be my roof. I wanted it to be the one that I was sleeping under now. And I wanted Van in the same bed too.

Oh God. I was falling for him.

Was it the proximity?

No. He was a nice guy. Considerate. *Hot.* I lived for catching glimpses of him hunched over his desk, squinting at his screens.

"Clover?"

I jerked my attention back to Alder. "Sorry. What?"

My gaze had strayed to the window, like I was seeking out the guy in my thoughts.

He had a finger on an address on his printout. "I was saying that you could look at this one. The renter just notified me he'd be moving at the end of October. I could hold it for a month."

"I can't let you do that." Alder wasn't hurting for money, but I couldn't be a burden on all my successful siblings. They secured their own places and shouldn't be inconvenienced because I had shitty taste in guys. I could find another place. There were a few small towns nearby. Maybe one of them had openings.

"I don't have an issue with it." He went down the list of apartments and houses for rent, rattling off details he knew if they weren't his. "You can drive by them when you have a chance and let me know."

My head bobbed, but I wasn't thinking about driving by anything.

Alder ducked his head, a divot between his brows. "I've lost you again."

"No, I'm just numb. It's all coming at me, and..." Was Alder really the one I was going to bring this up to? It wasn't like I was confessing undying love. I was just admitting that I was afraid of being alone. "The company has been kind of nice."

Alder's eyes narrowed slightly. "You like hanging out with your husband?" There was more weight in his light tone.

"He's cool. The house isn't empty when I'm home all day, and I have someone to chat with during meals. And at night, we watch movies and stuff." I laughed when I thought of how we chowed down on leftovers and junk food. "He made popcorn and brownies the other night—I was craving brownies—and we got gut rot so bad that when we woke up the next morning, he made us oatmeal as an apology." My snickering faded when astonishment filled Alder's eyes.

"That's nice." He tilted his head like he was looking at someone unfamiliar. "He seems like a decent guy."

"He is. The polar opposite of his brother. I guess he spent some time with a set of his grandparents who were better role models than Mr. and Mrs. Wagner." I caught myself nodding too fervently. I wanted my family to like

Van. They'd met him a few times now and hadn't given me any indication otherwise. So why was it so critical? Van was another uncle. That was all.

"Makes sense." Alder's attention stayed on me, his gaze shuttered.

I blew out a breath. "What?"

He didn't flinch. "Nothing. I haven't seen you this... yourself...for a while."

"What's a while?" I pressed my lips together.

He took some time, like he was mulling over his words. "You were always adult Clover, and now you're just Clover."

"That's a good thing?" It didn't sound like it.

"Yes."

Oh. He said it so quickly and simply, I had to sit with it. Had I acted that much differently with my ex? At least he didn't say I was pretentious Clover. I had tried to soften Elijah's personality without realizing it until I didn't have to do it around Van.

"Are you afraid to be on your own?" Alder asked so gently it almost made tears spring into my eyes.

"No." I blinked rapidly. I was a big girl. I had been on my own for a long, *long* time before Elijah. "It's not that."

"You'll miss him."

Denying it was on the tip of my tongue, but it stayed there. "Yes. He's becoming a good friend."

"And that's all?"

"Yeah, what do you think? We're going to fall madly in love and stay married?"

"It could happen."

"Alder," I barked out, and Lee jumped, his little arms flailing. "Sorry, but you can't be serious."

"I mean...it's happened before."

I clamped my mouth shut. I couldn't refute it. Lily was a shining example. She hadn't met Eliot long before she'd married him. Then there was Daisy. Poppy and Violet hadn't married their guys, but the sentiment was similar. "It won't with me. I was with his brother. I'm not pregnant with Van's kid. But we're friends, and I need a friend right now more than I need to fall in love again."

Van

Clover was out with her brother discussing apartments, and I was researching rockhounding in North Dakota. It seemed my priorities were fucked around her. I had interested potential investors. They wanted me to fly out and meet them after the first of the year. If I nailed the account, I would be solid as a business and finding a place to live wouldn't be as critical. If I didn't, my ass would still be hustling out on the street, and I'd be living there too.

Yet instead of working on some big presentation that would clinch funding, I was scouting the best place to find agates on the portion of the Little Missouri River that runs through Medora. In addition to that, I had information on campsites and hotel rooms.

I was fucked.

The front door opened, and her steady footsteps padded down the hall toward me. A sound I was going to miss when I lived by myself again.

She appeared at the door, her cheeks flushed and her eyes bright, and brandished a coffee mug. "I got you a coffee. I figured if it's too late to drink it, you can heat it up in the morning."

"Thanks, I'll put it in the fridge so I don't keep you up tossing and turning."

She smiled and juggled the coffee while digging her phone out. "I took a quick pic of a flyer I saw hanging at Rattler's. You probably already know about it." She turned her screen to an image announcing days and times for a Pokémon tournament in Bismarck. "It's a local con in two weeks. Thought we could go."

I couldn't stop the grin from spreading if I tried. The laughter started next. I swiveled my monitor around to show her the threads I'd been reading about rockhounding. "Then we can do this next weekend."

Her eyes lit up, and she leaned over my desk. The V-neck of her top gaped open, and goddammit, I looked. I yanked my eyes up to the ceiling, grateful I wasn't behind her when her ass was sticking so temptingly in the air.

"You were looking all this up?" she asked.

I tabbed through all the windows I had open, careful to look her only in the eyes. "During my breaks." Mostly instead of working.

"Oh, wow. I love it," she gushed. "But you don't have to."

"Sweet Clover, I want to."

She blinked at me, and what I said finally sank in. I called her a pet name, and it flew out of my mouth like a lever had been flipped.

Heat crept up my neck. "It'll be fun and get me out of the house." I'd take the cowardly route and pretend I never said a thing. "Did you find a place?"

She dug in her purse and took out some folded sheets of

paper. "There are options. I thought you might want to see them too."

I didn't. Rip them up and throw them out. Burn them. Make paper airplanes and fly them into the slough down the road, where they could get soaked and sink to the bottom. "Thanks."

"There isn't much available for decent house rentals, but Alder found a couple. I just don't think I can do an apartment." She dumped her phone in her purse. "I'm thinking too hard, and I choose not to think at all about it right now. I should get to work anyway."

"Sounds like a plan. While you're here, let me show you this." I selected a tab that showed one of the hotels in Medora. "It might get cold at night. Want me to reserve a room instead of outdoor camping? The cabins are all taken."

"Let's do a motel. I want modern plumbing and to not pack all my own bedding."

"I like that train of thought."

Her smile made all my lost productivity worth it. "Okay. I'll make it happen." The next question I had gave me pause. "I can get a room with two beds."

Her face froze for a heartbeat before she nodded. "Right. Yes. What a novel idea."

"Downright revolutionary." My insides matched her nervous laughter. Disappointment ricocheted through my organs.

I'd still be spending the weekend with her. Why couldn't I shake the sense of loss? We'd be in the same motel. In the same damn room. But when I woke up in the morning, she wouldn't be right there, on the other side of the pillow.

The best thing for me would be two separate rooms, but I didn't even think to offer that as an option.

129

Chapter Twelve

Clover

When Saturday rolled around, we packed our stuff and drove the hour and a half to Medora. He had rolled into the shallow valley of town, passing prickly hills that thickened with stubby shrubs the closer we got. I had never been so excited to look for rocks.

We hadn't checked into the motel yet. He had gone straight to the parking spot where we could hike one of the trails close to the Little Missouri.

The river trickled next to us. The weather was on the cool side, and it was spitting rain, keeping my proximity to the river limited. I wasn't interested in the muddy spots as much as the sandier parts of the shore, but I also didn't want to drag a ton of mud into Van's pickup or into the motel room.

Van remained undaunted. He had pulled out ponchos that he'd procured from somewhere and packed without me knowing. I wore some of my old hiking boots, and he had pulled on a pair of new ones before we took off.

The two of us were living together, partially to get back on our feet, but he'd purchased new clothing. We might be getting divorced, but he was setting the bar for any future guy, and he was placing it out of their reach.

I didn't want a future guy. "How are your toes?"

"Fine."

"No blisters?" Because of his thoughtfulness, I was hyper-concerned over his well-being.

"Clover, you don't need to worry about me."

"Would you tell me if I did?"

His smile was quick. "Painted Canyon was aptly named, huh?"

I rolled my eyes so he could see, and his grin only widened.

"Is it like a geologist's dream?" he asked.

I was touched that he kept thinking of my career and asking questions. "Doesn't everyone want to distinguish between siltstone and sandstone?"

"If they don't, they should."

"Hard agree." I veered off the trail, stepping carefully closer to the water's edge. "There's a little curve here, and the water level is down from earlier this year." I crouched at the edges where it was still a little gritty. There was a gentle slope, and then a portion of the bank had been cut out by the river's flow.

Van crouched next to me. "Is this another spot?"

"Possibly." I'd found some petrified wood earlier. Van's mind was blown that they weren't rocks. Well, they were now, but they hadn't always been. Though if we were to use the Wayback Machine, most had started as something else.

A tiny knob stuck out of the ground, and something

about it called to me. I scraped the cold, wet dirt around it with my finger. More rock was exposed. I widened my attempt. "Ooh, this is just the tip of the iceberg."

Gently, I moved enough damp sand aside, and my anticipation grew. I found a nearby twig instead of digging into my tool kit. Why use a small pry bar when my finger would work? I was on the hunt for small treasures found in nature. I didn't want to disrupt nature to do it. My normal job did enough of that, and it was also my job to mitigate the damage. With my hobby, I liked the challenge of finding what was right in front of me.

"Is that it?" Van had been patiently waiting. Now he was leaning over so far he might tip into the wet dirt.

"I think so." I brushed as much sand off it as I could. It got splattered with rain, and I used the moisture to wipe off the surface. "Yes—there." I traced a faint, dark line. "There's pitting, and this here is banding. I bet if we polished this up, it would turn a rich brown."

Holding it up, I inspected the more translucent areas. Satisfaction seeped into me like the light rain soaked into the ground.

"You're killing me, Clover. Agate or not?"

Chuckling, I handed it over. "We found an agate."

"Nice." He turned it several different directions, a faint smile on his face. "That's cool."

The shrewd but astounded way he looked at what others would see was a rock sent me tumbling right over the edge. He was enthused about the petrified wood, and he'd gotten new hiking boots.

I was never going to find another guy like him, and I didn't want to. But because I'd settled for someone in the first place, I'd ruined my chances with him.

He'd make someone a good partner someday. Whoever

had broken up with him and tanked the company they were building together was likely an awful person. Now it was clear she was an idiot.

He lowered his arm, and our gazes collided. The depth of emotion staring back at me robbed words from my brain. The air sizzled between us so strongly that steam should've formed.

"I like your hobby, sweet Clover." He handed the stone back to me.

"Thank you." I carefully tucked it back into the dirt. "I'm not a lawbreaker, though."

"No taking stuff from state parks." He reiterated an instruction I had discussed with him on the way here.

"I'm not sure if we're technically in a state park, but I just like finding them." I rose and stretched my back. "I'll admire someone else's work cleaning them."

"I like that plan."

"Good. On the way back, you can teach me everything Pokémon."

"You're going to regret asking about it."

"Doubt that."

"It's going to sound like I'm speaking a different language when I really get going."

He could speak gibberish, and that deep voice of his would keep me riveted. "If I get really intimidated, I'll throw out a geological term to make myself feel better."

"And then we can each look it up when we get a signal again."

I laughed, and we started back to our parking spot on the trail. We walked side by side, his hand so close to mine I could feel the heat emanating from him. "I had fun today."

"Walking in the rain and digging in the mud. You're an easy date." His gaze flickered. Was he worried I'd think he meant a real date, and this marriage between us would get more awkward than it was?

"It often scares guys away. Either that or I just give it up."

"Never give it up. For anyone." He kept his gaze on the path in front of us. "The right guy won't ask you to miss out on it just because they don't like it."

If I looked too hard into what he said, I'd also worry I thought this was a real date. "I agree and ditto."

"The only girl who hasn't laughed at me about Pokémon is you and a buddy's twelve-year-old daughter who'd come to some tournaments."

"Then you're hanging out in the wrong crowd."

He glanced over, but I couldn't read the expression in his eyes. "Think I should surround myself with different people?"

"Yes." Unless that didn't include me.

❀

Van

After eating dinner at a rustic saloon, we were tucked into our motel room. The rain was heavier than earlier, so we didn't plan to go out again, and that was just fine with me. I packed my laptop so we could watch movies if we had nothing to do.

We'd watch them from our separate beds.

I bit back my indignation, all aimed at myself. What a time to be responsible.

She was in the shower now, her clothes from earlier folded neatly on the dresser by her luggage. Our ponchos were hanging in the bathroom in case we went out tomorrow, and it was sprinkling again.

Today was fun. Despite the clouds, Clover glowed like the sun shone just for her. She could see a plain, dirty rock and discover a gem, then carefully tuck it back where she found it.

She came out of the bathroom, scrunching her hair with a towel. She wore loose flannel pajamas with little suns all over them, and her shirt was white with a giant sun in the middle. Spots of dampness spread from her shoulders. I couldn't look farther down than that. There was less forgiveness in the motel room than in the house for errant erections.

Her gaze landed on the laptop I had open on the bed next to me. "Do you have work to catch up on?"

"Nope. I have the movie options up. I can hook this to the TV."

"Ooh, that'd be great." She plopped on the bed, and it bounced. This time, I lost the battle of wills and caught a glimpse of her tits jiggling against the fabric. I moved the laptop onto my lap and focused on getting a menu of movies pulled up. "I made a selection of geology movies."

Her laughter was becoming a favorite part of my night. "Please say you chose *Dante's Peak*."

Pride sang through my blood. "Yes. I did."

"*San Andreas*?"

"If you promise to tell me everything they got wrong." I turned my screen to her. "I've also got *Gold*, *Journey to the Center of the Earth*, and I would be remiss if I skipped *Armageddon*."

"You would be. Who knows more about drilling into asteroids than Ben Affleck?"

"Billy Bob Thornton?"

She threw her covers back and slid between the sheets. "*Armageddon* it is, but I have to warn you, my knowledge on asteroids is limited, but it likely has silicate materials, ferronickel, or a combo of both."

"See? I've learned something already."

I drank in the grin she flashed me as she was cozy and tucked in not far from me. I pulled up the movie. Once I got it linked to the TV, I dug out M&M's from my luggage.

She sat up so fast her covers slipped down. "You have candy!" Smashing her fingers against her lips, she grimaced. "I'm going to get us kicked out."

"I'll take the blame." Gladly, if I could get that reaction from her. I doled out the candy and grabbed a sparkling juice from the fridge.

She wiggled until her back was against the headboard. "This baby is going to get used to late-night junk food gorging."

"Just fill the bottles with Gatorade. It'll be fine."

"Instead of pureed carrots, I'll just sub it for some butterscotch pudding."

"Late-night snack of champions."

She wrinkled her nose but laughed.

I hit play while my mind spun. Being playful like this? Was this how it should be? Joking with her about the baby? What if it was my baby she was pregnant with?

Why couldn't it be?

I kept my gaze glued to the TV. That question was loaded with so many what-ifs, I couldn't tackle it. Clover and I were giving each other a hand, thanks to our vows, but it was never supposed to be about any of that. If we changed things, it would become complicated. We had our plan. She was looking for apartments. Divorce papers were getting written up.

Simple.

Easy peasy.

Fucking divorce papers. My fingers twitched to rip them up, and they were likely still a concept on some lawyer's computer.

We watched the movie, and Clover yawned through the whole thing, slipping farther down in the bed. I mostly paid attention to the screen and not the alluring woman only feet away.

She laid her head on the pillow as the credits rolled. "Sorry, I'm not super exciting tonight. All that fresh air tuckered me out. Must be the first-trimester fatigue."

We hiked a few miles, and while it was over fairly mild terrain, the weather had been chilly and rainy. I shut the TV off. "Get some rest, Clover. Good night."

"Night, Van."

I put my laptop away and shut off the light.

Her steady breathing lulled me, but sleep didn't come. I stayed on my back and stared at the dark ceiling. Clover huffed out a breath and flopped to her other side. I could make out her curvy outline in the dark, but the more I looked...the more I looked. Gritting my teeth, I forced my attention back to the dark ceiling. My back began to ache.

I flipped to my side, my back to Clover to keep from taunting myself. I counted backward from a hundred three times, tensed and relaxed all my muscles until it became its own workout, and inhaled, held, and exhaled my breath until I got lightheaded. Going through all the tricks, I could not shut my brain off.

Flopping to my back, I huffed out a sigh.

The other bed shifted. "Can't sleep?"

Aw, hell. I bothered her. "Sorry, did I wake you?"

"No. I thought for sure I'd pass out right away, but I closed my eyes and nothing."

"Same."

"Maybe it's being all alone in this giant bed."

I chuckled. "A double doesn't do it for you?"

"Maybe it's the pillow wall I'm missing. What about you?"

"I don't know. My mind is whirling. You should've made me hike farther."

"Too much fresh air? Woke you up?"

"Has to be it."

The fan on the wall unit kicked in, drowning out the few cars that were driving by. Neither of us said anything for a few moments.

"Should I build a pillow wall?" she asked softly.

"I've got two for you."

"What if it's you I can't sleep without and not the pillows?"

I stopped breathing. What if it was? What if what she said resonated so hard I nearly jumped out of my bed and into hers? What if that was the same issue for me? I didn't have Clover on the other side of the pillow wall. I didn't have to work hard not to think about her, so I wasn't drifting off mentally exhausted. I didn't have to worry that the person slumbering next to me had been out with my brother. I wasn't ruminating over what it all meant.

"I can move over there," I offered. Bad idea, but not a suggestion I could take back.

"You don't mind?"

In a heartbeat. "If you think it'd help."

There was a pause that nearly stopped my heart. "Okay."

I rolled out of bed, grabbed all the pillows, and padded

to the other side of her bed. After I got between the sheets, her body heat caressed my legs. She was much closer than normal, and the warmth seeped through my skin and into my veins. The two pillows between us did very little to separate us at all. One kept tipping on me, then on her, and the second fell to the floor when I tried to roll so my back was to her.

"Shit, sorry." I retrieved it from the floor.

"Do we need it?" Her question was almost tentative.

There would be nothing between us but our clothing, yet I wanted to hurl this damn pillow across the room. I tossed it onto my bed instead. "I promise I'll be good."

"That could mean a lot of things, Sullivan Wagner."

Grinning, I put my back to her to avoid any inappropriate temptation to stare at her in the dark. Her breathing quickly evened out. Within minutes, I was asleep.

<h1 style="text-align:center">Chapter Thirteen</h1>

Clover

I was going to bed for the second night in a row with Van in a small bed that fit only us and little more, and I couldn't be giddier. This was just another night. No different than at home.

Yet as I wiggled around to get comfortable, I kept straightening my clothing and pushing my hair off my face. Van was in the bathroom, and the shower had just shut off. I had washed up earlier and blown my hair dry.

We weren't watching a movie tonight. We'd hiked, and then we'd driven to Dickinson to visit the dinosaur museum and eat. He'd never been to Montana, so we headed an hour in the other direction and stopped for a drink at Wibaux. He had a beer, brewed not far from the restaurant, and then I drove us back. We had explored a trail before we'd frolicked over western North Dakota and into Montana and back, so I was tired in the nice and worn-out way. That was the part I missed about being a staff geologist. I wasn't out in the elements, scouring the earth.

Tonight was the most fun I'd had since…last night. This whole weekend had been the lowest-key, affordable enjoyment I'd experienced in a long time. Easy and casual. The motel cost wasn't even that bad since it was the offseason. I was taking one night, and he was paying for the other. He'd insisted on both, but I arranged with the front desk to split it when the shower first started.

His hair was spiky when he came out of the bathroom. The way his shirt plastered against his chest should be illegal, but the real crime was how I stared at him. Call me a stalker and lock me up. Only I didn't have to stalk him when he was so close to me in bed that I wouldn't have to reach far to touch him.

He paused at the foot of the bed. "Were you going to read or anything, or should I shut the lamp off?"

"You can shut it off."

The room went dark, and the bed dipped when he climbed in. The butterflies in my stomach rose in a cloud and veered all over. I should've been building immunity to Van after so many nights sleeping next to him and not touching him. There was a comfort between us that I hadn't been able to sleep without last night.

But now?

My breasts grew tender, only it wasn't pregnancy related. Hormones, yes. And stronger than ever. Licks of desire curled through my blood, tucking themselves in places that should be stone cold next to my ex's brother.

A steady thrum grew between my legs, and I rubbed them together as if acting like a cricket would make me less horny.

"Can't sleep again?" His deep voice so close to me didn't help. "And here I thought I was a good luck charm."

"No, it's not that. Can't get warm," I lied, embarrassed I was almost caught. I flipped so my back was to him.

"I can turn the heat up."

I would roast. "No, it's fine. Baby hormones. I'm running hot and then cold."

I curled in on myself. The way his smile lit up my entire day. His avid interest when I was studying a rock. He even inspected the claystone and shale like it was a valuable jewel. The computer nerd was athletic. He asked what to look for and scaled the steeper part of the trail. Once, he'd found two agates, and he'd traversed the trail a second time to return them.

Squeezing my legs together, I crossed my arms and grazed my sensitive nipples.

"Still cold?" he asked.

"I'm sure it'll pass." I hadn't masturbated in a long time, but I might have to now. Not in this bed. Not next to him. I had some dignity, but I needed a release. I'd never been this horny. It was relentless. Was it the dry spell?

"Here, take my blankets." The covers rustled.

Hot and turned on would be worse. "Thanks, but I'll just run some water over my hands or something." I dropped out of bed and scurried to the bathroom.

Closing the door, I left the light off. I flipped on the cold water and stuck my hands under the stream. It helped for all of three seconds until I thought of going back out there to Van in my bed.

I splashed water on my face. Again, only a temporary reprieve. The neediness roared back, along with the undeniable urge to do something about it. I could. Right here. Van wouldn't know.

It seemed wrong, like an invasion of his privacy. I shook my hands and paced the two steps between the toilet and the door. The humidity from his shower hung in the air, wrapping around me like a seductive whisper. Yep, I had to get myself off if I wanted any rest tonight.

How did I do this? Sit on the toilet? Take another shower?

Ugh. I stopped and tipped my head back. I could not fail masturbating.

Waves of lust rippled under my skin, from my full breasts down my abdomen, and kissed over my pussy.

Could it just go away?

And what? Crawl back between the sheets with Van and get worked up like a horny teen? I wasn't ever this hot and bothered during those years.

A quick orgasm and I could sleep. Van wouldn't know. How could he?

I leaned against the edge of the counter. Palming a breast, I swallowed a groan. They'd never been this sensitive. Pregnancy was wild.

I slipped my other hand between my belly and pajama pants. My top kept catching, so I whipped it off and dropped it on his shaving kit. Tunneling deeper into my pajama bottoms, I reached my drenched clit. I'd never been this wet either. A shiver rolled over me as I circled the tight nub, and a small moan slipped out.

"Everything okay?" Van called.

"Yeah! Sorry." My eyelids fluttered. The last thing I thought to pack was a vibrator. I thought what had happened in Vegas and the baby had put a damper on my libido, but it was just tired of being shut down. Van's presence had been gasoline. This trip was the match.

I was a lone bonfire in the middle of nowhere.

Shifting, I tried to open myself up more. My legs were too close together. I spread my feet apart, but they started to slide. Did I put one up on the toilet? On the counter? That might stretch my pajama bottoms too tight for my hand to maneuver.

I tried to prop a thigh on the counter. It slipped right off, and a little oomph left me when my foot hit the floor. I kept my hand between my legs, keeping pressure on my clit. Flashes of Van passed through my mind—Van standing in front of the window, Van towering over me right before he kissed me, and Van on the trail with me, smiling because I was enjoying myself. Desire hummed, and I continued stroking myself while trying to find purchase.

My foot hit the toilet lid, but it was farther away than I thought. It dropped off and caught me off-balance. I teetered to the side, and my ass slid along the edge. I got a squeak out before my shoulder hit the light switches with a thump.

"Ack!" My shoulder stung, and I flailed at the wall to push myself off without sliding down.

The door opened, and horror flooded me, but still didn't douse the desire.

"Clover?" He fumbled for the light switch, and dammit, he flipped it on. "Are you okay—shit." His eyes were saucers. He spun around and whacked his nose against the door.

"Oh my God. Are *you* okay?" I ripped my hand out of my pants to check on him, but I stilled, just staring at my digits. Had he seen? Shame burned through me. No one was supposed to know, but I got busted in the act. How humiliating.

He covered his nose with a hand. "Your, uh, your... boobs...are out."

Another gasp escaped me. I covered my breasts, but it was too late. He'd already seen them. Where did I put my shirt?

"I thought you were cold," he murmured.

Grumpy that I didn't get an orgasm and that I'd made things awkward between us, I gritted my teeth and located my top. "I wasn't."

"But you said—"

"I was horny." I flipped my shirt open and searched for the bottom hem. It was inside out, but, oh well.

"You were what?" He spun around, caught his gaze on my boobs, and pivoted back, knocking into the door again. "Fuck me." He turned again but kept his eyes closed.

Where was the damn opening? I kept flipping the flimsy material around. "You've already seen my boobs, and we're both adults." Indignation coursed through me. I couldn't handle myself, and I got Van hurt trying to help me. "I should've been able to control myself and not... Well, you *know*."

He went still and opened his eyes, pinning me with his emerald gaze. "You were masturbating?"

"Trying and failing," I muttered. "I don't know, must be these hormones."

He trailed his attention down my body to my bare breasts. "Fuck, Clover."

"I feel stupid." My pajama top hung limp in my hands.

He jumped his stare up to meet mine. His nose was red where the edge of the door caught him, and his cheeks were still flushed from the rush, but his eyes were smoldering. "Why?"

"I should've controlled myself." My conviction was weak against the intensity coming from him.

"Do you know how many times I've jacked off in the shower?"

My breath hitched, and his attention returned to my breasts, then dropped lower to where I'd had my hand shoved down my pants. "How did you do it?"

"Not well since I almost fell over." My roller coaster of emotions didn't need to take me down even more notches in front of Van's eyes.

"Show me," he said gutturally.

"What?"

"Show me how you were doing it."

This was when I should've tumbled sideways. Shock passed swiftly, leaving behind a sizzling desire to do what he told me to. I flattened my hand on my belly, and he leaned forward, anticipation tensing his large frame. His jaw was tight, and energy rippled over him, leaping between us in sharp jolts. This time, when my fingertip touched my clit, I let the moan out, long and needy.

"*Fuck.*" He caged me in with his arms, his hands on the edge of the counter. "You sound so damn sweet."

"Thank you?" I was so out of my element, but I wasn't going to stop.

"You're welcome." The corners of his mouth tipped up before he glued his fervid stare to the spot where my hand disappeared into my pants. "How wet are you?"

"Soaked."

His pupils crowded out his irises. "Your nipples are hard."

"Yes," I said on an exhale.

He caressed one with the palm of his hand.

A shiver shook my shoulders, but I arched my back. "Van."

"I like when you use that name." He closed his hand over my entire breast. "I like when you say my full name."

"Sullivan."

He groaned and lazily draped his hand over my breast. The scrape of his rough fingertips amped up my desire. My strokes grew faster, and that electricity zipping between us wound its way through me, caressing everything it touched.

"I'm close," I whispered.

"Do you need to be filled?"

I nodded. My chest rose and fell faster; my heart pounded harder.

"I was trying"—I gasped—"that's how I fell."

"Can I?"

If possible, I grew wetter. "Yes." *Please.*

He released the counter and, slowly, taking his time, pushed my pajama bottoms down. The little suns on them were earning their smiles tonight. Eventually, they were down far enough that they fell the rest of the way, pooling around my feet. Instead of being shy about being bare, it was more like it was inevitable.

"Spread your legs but keep your hand in place."

There would be no falling with him this close. Not only would he catch me, but he'd stop me from tipping in the first place.

I widened my stance, and a grunt left him.

"So fucking sexy."

I'd never been called sexy before.

Before I could dwell on whether he was telling me what he thought I wanted to hear, he covered my hand with his. The slight extra pressure was nearly enough to topple me over the edge, but he didn't move. His longer fingers were on me, touching me, stroking me.

"Keep rubbing that needy clit of yours, sweet Clover."

Spurred into action, I did as he asked. I couldn't help myself. He towered over me, and it didn't take much for him to curve his fingers and slide one through my seam. Then he pushed inside.

"Van!" My cry echoed off the walls, and I squeezed my eyes shut. Ecstasy built like a thundercloud. The moans and whimpers kept coming.

I fisted his T-shirt as I shook through the tremors. He pumped his finger in and out of me, and he held pressure on my hand, keeping my fingertip on my clit. Everything was perfect. The pressure. The stimulation. How close he was.

The lights. I blinked my eyes open. Nothing about this had been private. My shirt was still off, my nipples stiff peaks. His breathing was raspy, but he'd stilled his hand.

I tried to get a sound out that wasn't wanton, but I had no idea what to say. "I..."

That prompted him to remove his hand. He crouched down to draw my pants up. Next, he found my shirt and did what I couldn't do. He got it right side out and tugged it over my head. I was slumped against the counter, and he was dressing me.

Goose bumps rose over my skin, and he rubbed my arms. "You're cold now?"

I nodded, chilly and numb. What did I do? How did we act around each other? What happened when we got home? "Van?"

I didn't like how scared I sounded. How vulnerable.

He tipped my chin up. "Your hormones were raging, and you couldn't get comfortable. I helped you relax."

I got an orgasm. He got a weird evening and probably an uncomfortable morning. "What about you?"

He cocked a brow and tipped his head to look between

us. An impressive erection pushed out from his pajama pants. "I'll take care of it."

But I wanted to touch him, feel him, make him feel even a fraction of what he talked me through? It'd be my pleasure. But maybe he was right. We should stop here.

"I don't want this to change anything." I dug my teeth into my lower lip. "I like you."

He let out a long exhale. "I like you too, Clover." He brushed his knuckles down my cheek. "It's hormones, right? We're here to help each other, and you needed me."

Hormones. He was giving me an out. A get-out-of-this-awkwardness-free card. Would it be enough? I had to find out. Because I did not want to return to the cold Van from after our kiss. My nod was shaky.

Satisfaction gleamed in his eyes. "Let's get you tucked in."

Chapter Fourteen

Van

I scrubbed a hand down my face and stared at my computer screen. For the last week, we hadn't touched each other. We'd gone to sleep after the bathroom interlude and pretended everything was normal the next morning. Then we returned home, pillow wall in place, and acted like nothing had changed. Perhaps it hadn't for her.

To me, everything had changed. I could compartmentalize before. I could tell myself my brother's ex was a beautiful woman, but I wasn't attracted to her. I could concentrate on work despite Clover being under the same roof.

Having her come in my arms shattered all that. I was attracted to my brother's ex. Worse, I craved her. Thoughts of her consumed my time. Yesterday, I had nearly missed a call with a potential investor because I'd been listening to her on the phone with her team. I'd been hanging on her melodious laugh and recalling how tight she'd gripped my fingers when she'd climaxed.

Fuck.

I had it bad.

My screen blinked out. How long had I been doing nothing? It was Saturday, but I had taken refuge in my office.

I checked the time. We were set to leave in a few minutes for Bismarck. I had accepted that I'd lose every Pokémon match and call it quits early.

There was a light knock at the door. "Hey. Ready?"

"Yeah." My backpack with my card decks and play mat were packed. Part of me hadn't wanted her to see that the hobby my brother used to tease me about involved supplies and organization and meticulous research into card types and value. She'd been accepting, but what if there were limits?

Once we loaded up, she glanced in the back seat. "A backpack is all you need?"

"That's it."

"I thought there'd be more."

"Well, it's a card game."

She crossed one leg over the other. "There're only cards?"

Despite wanting to hide it from her, I also couldn't wait to talk about it. "Most of us keep the more valuable cards in a binder, and sometimes we trade those."

"It's like baseball cards? My dad talked about collecting those."

I nodded, relieved there was no criticism in her voice. "Exactly. My card boxes are full of my playing cards."

"You have a lot?"

"Yes." When she didn't react to that, I continued. "I've collected them since I was in middle school. I kept those and continued over the years, then the gatherings started at game shops and grew. It was a fairly cheap hobby to stick with when I was broke as hell."

"I like that."

Pleased and more than a little relieved, I hit the highway, and it went quiet again.

Her phone started buzzing. For the next several minutes, she tapped away at her screen.

Finally, she tucked it away. "I'm meeting Violet next weekend to go maternity clothes shopping."

Maternity clothes. She looked the same, but there were outfits she no longer wore. How much was her belly growing? My curiosity would skyrocket if I let it. "That'll be fun."

"I think so. Poppy's gone for a soccer tournament, and Daisy's there, too, with Laila. So it's me and Violet."

"That'll be nice." I slid a gaze toward her. My conversation skills sucked today.

"Yeah. I honestly haven't spent much time with just me and Violet. It's like I'm getting to know my bossy older sister."

"But you miss Poppy?"

She blinked rapidly, and I turned my attention back out the windshield. My fingers twitched to reach for her, but she might shut down.

"Yes, but we each have our own lives. I'm sure it's pregnancy hormones."

While that might be valid, her feelings were still legitimate. "Have you told her that you need a little me time with her?"

"No, it's a busy time for her."

I filed the Poppy topic away for later. "So. Maternity clothes?"

Clover smiled and ducked her head. "Yeah. She asked about baby furniture, but until I have a place, there isn't a point. And it's early yet." She reclined back and linked her hands over her stomach. "A lot of people don't know they're pregnant at this point, and I feel like I've known forever."

"Is that a bad thing?"

"No. I'm glad I knew at our wedding. Made it easier, I think. I would've had to move on all over again."

Not *the* wedding. *Our* wedding. "I knew I was getting a two-for-one deal."

She chuckled. "Yeah. For a little while."

Her words echoed in my head. Our time was almost up. "Have you changed your mind about finding out what you're having? My money's on a baby, but it could be a kitten."

Her laughter filled the cab. "As long as there's only one and not one that was hiding from the ultrasound. I'm not sure I'm ready for the stress of multiples. Especially if it's puppies."

"Oof, not multiple puppies."

"No." She tucked a lock of hair behind her ear. "I'm going with the surprise. Why not keep the trend up? Get dumped at the altar? Marry his brother? Only get the house for three months? Surprise, it's a pony."

"At least one good surprise."

"Maybe one of those other ones hasn't been so bad."

The adorably sexy woman was wiggling her way further into my chest wall, and at times like these, she reached out and tapped on my heart. *My brother's ex.* No matter how many times I repeated it to myself, the effect wasn't as strong as it used to be.

"Have you looked at the apartments yet?" she asked like she wanted to move on from the topic.

I gladly took the exit strategy. "Not yet. I lined up a few in-person investor meetings right away after the holidays. Next week, I can tackle a place to live."

"In person? Is that normal?"

"Sometimes, but I think with my background it's more crucial. Right away in the new year, I'll head to Denver first, then Dallas, and to keep the *D* theme, DC."

"Wow, that's a lot of traveling." Her tone was even. Was she relieved I wouldn't be hanging out? We could make a clean break, and she could be done with all things Wagner?

"Yeah, but I figured I was risking it at that time of year anyway. Never knew when it would blizzard."

"Speaking of that, do you have plans for Thanksgiving?"

I shook my head. Our time was up that Sunday. A nice set date that would leave December open for Clover's aunt to rent it out.

"Alder's having a big gathering. You should come. It's the house I was raised in until we moved to Billings."

"No kidding?" I'd see where a young Clover ran around, attached at the hip with Poppy.

"I can show you the space under the stairs that Lily always used to hide in during hide-and-seek, and I would get so upset because it scared me."

"She was playing dirty?"

"My siblings were the dirtiest."

"I guess I have to go. If any of your nieces and nephews

rope you into a game of hide-and-seek, I have to be there to go under the stairs."

Her brows lifted. "You'd do that for me?"

"Of course." There wasn't much I wouldn't do for Clover. She just had to ask, but after what happened in the hotel, she hadn't asked for a thing.

❁

Clover

Pokémon matches included a mix of mostly guys of all ages. This tournament was for adults and held in a rented room. Participants came from all walks of life, but most of the clothing they wore had some sort of fandom on it, and dark colors were a favorite.

The whole thing was sponsored by local game shops and another group. I hung out by the snacks, watched Van play, and made small talk with some players. When he laughed, all my insides lit up. When his brow furrowed in concentration, I couldn't tear my eyes off him. People responded to him, opening up and joking around. There was nothing about this hobby I found dull or repulsive if he enjoyed himself like this.

One girl, just a little younger than me, was there with her girlfriend, and she was a nurse. We chatted about school and where we'd lived before ending up at the gathering. It was a few hours of people-watching and light socializing aside from that.

I needed the reprieve after riding in an enclosed cab with him. We'd been sleeping on either side of the pillow wall. Did he want to cross it, or did he decide the hotel was the first and only time we were messing around?

I didn't want more. I *shouldn't* want more.

I did though. Badly.

Each night that went by, I was minutes away from hiding in the bathroom again. But I couldn't risk falling over and summoning him. What if he laughed the second time? What if he was disgusted that I had to get off again?

Had he done his thing in the shower since then? I could've been a massive libido killer.

Acting like everything was normal was both a blessing and a curse. Still, his growl from the night he helped get me off rang through my head at least hourly. Twice an hour. Every second.

Van rose from the table, nodding and smiling at the guy across from him who had to be in his early twenties. They laughed, and then Van's gaze went directly to me, landing on my skin like the sun's summer kiss.

I waved, and he wandered over. "Ready to get something to eat?"

People still filled the tables. Did he get out? How did that work? "Are you done?"

"Yeah, I'm getting tired of sitting."

I rose, but my gaze jumped around the room. "Feels a little unfair that I got two nights of fun, and you only got a few hours."

His smile was reassuring. "I'm not keeping score, Clover."

I believed him. Could it be that simple? He did something over the top for me and didn't expect exactly the same or more for himself? "Okay."

"Where do you want to eat?"

On him. I'd like to climb right onto his lap and get a

mouthful of him. *Mind out of the gutter, Duke!* "This is your weekend. You pick."

"Chinese."

I groaned. "I've been craving that."

His gaze intensified. "Then let's sate it."

I suppressed a shiver. I was looking too hard into his reaction.

We found a buffet after some googling. The sun had set, and tonight had a much more date-like feel than last weekend had. Over our meal, he explained more of the playing and talked about some of the tournaments he'd been to. He said he'd even gotten some guys' numbers so they could get together by themselves instead of waiting for bigger venues. And he also had a few trades lined up.

He was lighter tonight than he had been all week. Guilt threatened to turn my dinner into a lump. I should've controlled myself better.

On the drive home, I showered him with questions about his investors and his travel itinerary. The man had a plan. I hadn't even contacted a landlord. I couldn't risk my job, but dammit, I didn't want to move.

When he pulled up in front of the house, I stared at the dark shape. A night-light in the hallway was on and glowed through the blinds. Home sweet home. Just not mine. Or Van's.

After we got inside, he stretched his arms above his head. His UNO hoodie rose above his waistband, baring a strip of lean abs that I hadn't seen despite sleeping with him every night for six weeks. "I'm going to finish up some last-minute things."

My heart fluttered to the ground like the leaves this time of year. He was going back to work? After we'd spent much of the day together? "Don't have too much fun."

I trudged to the bedroom, my frustration growing about how last weekend had affected us. I stopped in front of the door. Did I keep pretending like I wasn't bothered by the distance between us? We were acting normal, but it was there. Would I make it worse by addressing the pent-up elephant in the room?

Did I want to go through another week of wondering if I had offended him? Then another week after that, and another, until we parted ways? I spun around on my stockinged feet. The office light was on. Van was inside.

At the doorway, I stalled. I wasn't brave enough to go all the way in. He was standing behind his desk, ready to take a seat. He glanced up, a question in his eyes.

Here goes. "Last weekend, did I mess this up? Like royally mess everything up?"

He propped his hands on the top of his desk, leaning forward. He might be in a sweatshirt and blue jeans, but he looked like he could command a boardroom. He'd do just that when we divorced. He'd be ready.

I twisted my fingers together. "I didn't mean to. These hormones—"

"Are they still bothering you?"

They were behind it. Living with Van was bothering me in a hot-and-bothered way. "Yes."

He pushed off his desk and came around it. Stopping on the opposite side of the threshold as me, he propped his hands on the doorframe. "Do you need help...feeling better?"

Now was my chance. "Y-yes. Wait." I held a hand up, but we were so close I put it right on his chest. "We need to talk first because I can't take another week of wondering if you regretted what happened." If he regretted me.

"No." He didn't elaborate more. A simple answer that filled me with hope.

"I didn't make you uncomfortable?"

"The erections did."

I blew out a breath. Whoa. "So you didn't mind?"

His gaze softened. "No, but I worried I crossed the line with you."

"No."

"Then..." If possible, he got closer. "We should take advantage of our time together to help relieve each other."

Yes, please. I almost said it, but another issue cropped up, an old but relevant one. "Doesn't it bother you? I'm your brother's ex."

Self-recrimination passed through his eyes. "No."

"As simple as that?" It just didn't dig under his skin anymore? He didn't act like it, but I had to know. If he rejected me again, it'd hurt more than getting left at the altar. "Because after the kiss..."

He briefly closed his eyes. "About that. I'm sure you don't have the whole story."

My libido ran and hid. There was more? About what? Me or Elijah? "Oh?"

"My ex? The one that I was starting a company with, who cheated on me and then cost me everything to fold our business without completely trashing my reputation? Do you know who she cheated with?"

I shook my head before I gave it any thought. How could I know? I'd never been around Van's social crowd. The only person we'd had in common was—"Oh." Horror and sympathy cascaded through me. Poor Van. "He didn't."

"He did. So did she. And then when he was done spending the money she kept, he dropped her."

Just like he'd taken my money and found another

woman. "What a grade A bastard. Oh God, marrying me must've been more salt in the wound. And then the kiss." The back of my throat burned. "And the bathroom. Am I making you revisit your trauma left and right?"

"Clover, I'm getting to the point where I'm going to say whatever will let me get you naked again."

Oh. His blunt tone shocked me. Heat pumped into my veins.

"The problem with that kiss," he said, "is that it showed me it didn't matter who your ex is."

Oh. A shiver whispered over my skin. I licked my dry lips, and he clocked the movement like a predator. He wanted me. The hormones I blamed last weekend on raged back. "I seem to be at a disadvantage. I haven't seen you naked yet."

He reached behind him and yanked the shirt over his head. I sucked in a breath when I was met with his bare chest. His pecs were dusted with hair just a little darker than on his head, and it merged into a trail running between his abs and down to where he was unbuttoning his jeans.

"Oh." I breathed out when he ripped the zipper down, and his underwear shifted to expose the glistening tip of his cock. "My."

My was very close to mine, and that was what I wanted to declare about that noteworthy erection.

"You're as hard as granite." Inwardly, I winced. Really? Now I was going to make a geology comparison? "Marble, really. There's a reason they carved giant slabs into statues." God, that was worse. "Those statues weren't as well endowed."

I groaned, and the corner of his mouth tipped up.

He shoved his pants down. "To be fair, sweet Clover, those statues were carved in a soft state. Not how most modern men would want to be immortalized, but I'm not sure how David felt."

He kicked off his jeans and shucked his socks off with them. Holding his arms out to his sides, he spun in a slow circle.

Now that was an ass worthy of carving. "Do you do butt clenches when you sit in the chair all day?"

"Yes."

"Oh. That actually makes me feel better." Note to self—flex some muscles while I sit all day.

"Do you want to touch?"

"Yes," I said in a whisper. When he moved closer, I wrapped my hand around his hot length. His hard-on filled my grip, and I pumped up and down. He twitched in my hand. A small reaction but a heady one. "I'd...like to do more."

He grunted and thrust his hips. "With your hand on my dick, I'm in no position to stop you."

I'd never wanted to lick something so badly in my life. The way he was reacting, and I'd hardly done anything? It was exciting. Exhilarating. Powerful. I felt sexy in a way I never had.

"What if it's my mouth?"

His jaw went slack. "You want to do that?"

To answer him, I lowered to my knees and gazed up at him. His Adam's apple bobbed when he swallowed, and his eyes were full of disbelief. He glanced around. "We can find a better spot for you."

"This works just fine." Something about sucking him off in his office appealed to me. Like maybe after we went our separate ways, whenever he was behind his screen for long stretches of time, he'd think of me.

I wouldn't forget him.

I opened my mouth and sucked him in. A long, ragged groan left him, and I would've smiled, but there was no room. He was large, and I wanted to leave an impression. My first identity to him was as his brother's girlfriend. The next was a jilted bride. Then a single mom trying to figure it all out. I wanted to be a sex goddess. Not the clumsy girl who almost took herself out masturbating in a motel bathroom.

I licked and sucked, mining my brain for any technique advice I'd heard or read over the years. It must've been working. A tremor trailed up and down his body, his raspy breathing filled the room, and he was close. His cock twitched in my mouth, and he went ramrod straight. I felt powerful.

"Christ, Clover. I'm going to— If you don't want to—"

I increased the suction and worked the base of his shaft. His hips hinged forward, and he exploded. His release filled my mouth, but I didn't let up. This had to be unforgettable. Spectacular. He gave me the control, and I would be the sweet Clover who had given him the best blow job of his life.

More groans came from him, and he swung his hips back. He popped out of my mouth, his tip glistening, and yeah, I might've been a little proud of how white his knuckles were on the doorframe.

"I'm surprised I can talk." He sounded like he just ran ten miles. He cupped my chin.

His gaze intensified, turning promising. "Your turn."

❦

Van

. . .

I had Clover's knees spread wide and pushed up as far as they'd go. She was on her back on the bed. Fuck the pillow wall. I laid her out on top of them. My arms were shoved under her ass to lift her out of the cozy cradle they made. The pillows wouldn't block me from her tonight.

I tackled her clit with my tongue, lapping and stroking until I found the rhythm that drove her wild.

She fisted her hands in my hair. "Van."

The way she groaned my name was enough to get me hard again. I'd never come like that. Her hot little mouth had robbed me of all control and brain cells. My stamina had dipped, unable to stand strong against her soft tongue.

Now it was time to redeem myself. I wasn't thinking about who I was competing with. I had to be the best. Unforgettable. Why?

Now wasn't the time to answer.

She yanked on my hair when I hit a certain spot. Mentally, I was grinning from ear to ear. I threaded a finger inside her, and she clamped on to me, riding me like she was afraid I'd stop and she'd be left unsatisfied.

She could pull every strand of hair out of my head, and I would finish her. I'd hear my name bounce off these walls.

"Van!" she shouted as if on command.

Almost there. I added another finger, and a long moan left her. Her thighs clamped around my ears, and she arched her ass off the bed. I held her to me as she shattered.

"Van!"

I fucking loved when she said my name. I loved that she was sincere.

I licked up her release. She went limp, and I kissed the inside of one thigh and then the other.

"Oh my God." She released her fingers from my hair and covered her face. "I can't believe I yelled like that."

Hell yes. "Don't hold back on my account."

I crawled up her body, laying kisses on her abdomen.

She froze. Shit. I had placed a kiss over the baby.

I traced a finger from under her ribs to the top of her pelvis. "How big is Bean now?"

"I haven't looked up how big Bean would be this week."

Scooting all the way up, I stretched out on my side next to her. All my clothes were still on the floor in my office. Hers were at the base of the bed. I'd pick up later when my obnoxious erection calmed down, if it would ever do that around Clover Duke.

"I didn't want to get obsessive," she admitted.

"It's your first baby. Obsess away." I rolled out of bed. Her phone had fallen out of her pants pocket. I retrieved it and went back.

She was wiggling to the edge of the mattress.

"Clover, if you keep trying to escape, I'm only going to turn into more of a caveman."

She grinned over her shoulder. "Promise?"

"With those tits in my face? Yes." Her creamy, round globes were emblazoned into my memory. I hadn't gotten to play with them nearly enough.

"I'll go clean up, and then we'll check on Bean's size." She found a pair of pajamas and went to the bathroom.

I set her phone on her nightstand, zoomed around the room, and ducked into the office to get our clothing. By the time she returned, I had our shirts and pants folded, and I moved the goddamn pillows. The covers on her side of the bed were pulled back, and a glass of water was next to her phone. My own body had calmed the hell down.

She stopped, blinking. "Thanks for picking up."

"I'm handy."

"Are you?" she asked playfully.

"I'd throw a pillow at you, but I piled them on the dresser." Might as well get that out of the way. "Thought we could look through first-trimester stuff together."

She crawled in and snuggled closer to the midline than she normally did, but then there wasn't a fluffy wall blocking her way. "You're interested?"

"Yes," I said honestly.

She looked at me for a moment, half a smile on her face like she was afraid I was lying.

I used my phone instead to pull up information. "What are you, nine weeks along?"

"Yes, that's what the OB figured."

The glow of the screen lit our faces. "Look at that. We're in green-olive territory."

"I can't have the martini because I have the olive."

I chuckled and read over the information. "It says you might still have first-trimester fatigue. Are you tired?"

"I've been tired for a while, but it helps to work at home."

"It's not more tempting to nap?"

"Now it's more tempting to do other things in the bed."

I coughed out a "shit." We'd been living together for six weeks, and I didn't know her hormones had been giving her ideas. I forced myself to keep scrolling, or I'd take her again, and after looking at baby stuff, this would be more than appeasing her hormones. I'd be making love, and neither of us had signed up for that. "Guess what? Its tail is going away."

"Yay?"

I grinned. "The tail's going away, but the heart is getting stronger."

"I mean, if I had to choose, I guess I'd take the heart."

"You wouldn't have a choice." I clicked the screen off and set the phone down. "You've got too good of a heart, sweet Clover. The baby is going to have a big one."

"Do you think..." Her breathing turned steady.

Did she fall asleep? "You awake?"

"Yeah," she said, almost sadly. "Do you think the baby will get more of your traits and not *his*?"

My throat got thick. She'd rather her baby get more of the Wagner traits that I have? I never questioned that I had overcome whatever poor upbringing I'd had. It was even more apparent when I moved back in with my parents and became their dude Cinderella while every little scrap of help they gave me was held against me. But nothing proved how much I'd grown away from them as much as her question. "I think with you as a mom, everything is going to be okay. But if he gets Elijah's head for numbers, that isn't terrible."

She laughed. "True. And his ability to eat anything without stomach problems."

"Are you holding popcorn and brownies over my head?"

"I'm holding the morning-after popcorn and brownies over your head. I think I weathered morning sickness better."

"Fair point. My gut was not happy." I thought about my brother. He was a dick, but there were some redeeming qualities. If it helped her to remember some of the good things, I'd do that for her. "He never got sunburned either."

"Oh my God, he didn't. Best skin ever, but I thought it was from all the products he used."

"You're fucking kidding me. He used products?"

"A cleanser-and-moisturizing combo that should've broken the bank."

"Jackass said I was just unlucky."

She chortled and let out a sigh. "Thank you, Van."

"Anytime, Clover."

The covers rusted as she rolled to her side. We weren't touching, but we were an inch away from each other. Far enough to remember that this was temporary.

Chapter Fifteen

Clover

The end of my workday was nearly done. Another weekend was approaching, and Van hadn't mentioned any plans. I didn't mind if it was mellow. Maybe he had his own ideas. The guy had a life. One I hadn't seen since we lived together. Or rather, I had been his life, and I liked that. Our nights had become orgasm fests. We hadn't had sex. It was like we couldn't figure out if what we were doing was the smart way to handle mutual pleasure, or if we were just scared to do more together. I already knew that having all of him would ruin sex with anyone else forever. Just having him get me off was doing that. So maybe limiting our contact was for the best.

I'd like to feel his weight on me, have him moving inside of me, and to really be connected. But that was where the danger waited. I was more connected with Van than any partner ever.

My phone buzzed.

Poppy: Are you going shopping with Violet tomorrow?

Me: Yes

Poppy: Then we're going out tonight.

I frowned. Was something wrong?

Poppy: Where do you want to meet?

Poppy: Rattler's or Purple Petal?

Poppy: We can go to Bismarck too.

Poppy: Wait, isn't there another place that opened in... Damn, I have to ask Jensen.

I shook my head and typed out a message before she bombarded me with eight more.

Clover: Is something wrong?

Poppy: Yes. We haven't seen enough of each other.

I narrowed my eyes on her litany of messages. Had she read my mind? I missed my best friend, but she was living her fantasy life. Yet, she texted, and I wasn't going to miss a night out.

Clover: Purple Petal. They have better fries.

Poppy: Blasphemous

Poppy: Thank God for autocorrect. I did not know how to spell that word.

Smiling, I shut down my computer. Oh, crap. "Van." I rushed to his office.

He had an elbow propped on the desk and his other hand on the keyboard. He was focused, but as soon as I appeared, he instantly switched his attention to me. I could've puffed my chest out. "Poppy wants to meet me tonight. It is my night to cook."

He shook his head. "Don't worry about it. I'll have dude food."

"What's that?"

"Lots of things, but probably some meat slapped

between bread slices and eaten while standing up and wandering around thinking of all the things I should be doing."

I'd seen Alder do that a few times before he had left the house. "I can bring you back something."

"Concentrate on your night with her."

Excitement welled up, and flutters spread through my belly. It likely wasn't the baby, but soon it would be. I could pull his hand over, and— he wouldn't be around. Those tickles went still. "Okay. I'm taking off. We're going to Crocus Valley."

"Purple Petal?"

"They have better fries. What's with the crust on all of them nowadays?" We shared a grin, and those butterflies churned into action. I backed away before I continued to stand there and smile all dopey at him.

It wouldn't take much to do it.

I rushed around getting ready. Before I ducked out the door, I nearly veered into his office to give him a goodbye kiss. The pull was almost too much to overcome. "Bye!" I shouted instead.

"Have fun!"

I was smiling when I hopped into my car.

The drive to Crocus Valley was less than ten minutes. I'd grown up loving that so many small towns were short drives away. What one town didn't have, another likely did —a movie theater, pool, or coffee shops.

Poppy was just pulling in when I got out of my car. She hopped out and stormed toward me, her curls flying behind her. She wrapped me in a giant hug and spun me around.

"Whoa." I held her, mostly to stay on my feet. "Did you miss me?"

"I always miss you, but I've been letting too much other

stuff distract me." She held me out at arm's length. "Holy shit, you're really pregnant."

I wore leggings. All my jeans were put away. The waist-bands were just too constricting. Same with any snug shirts. The top I had on was more of a long T-shirt, meant to look trendy. "I don't need much for a new wardrobe, but I want to be comfortable. Seems more important if I'm working from home."

"If you need an office, you can always lease one at the Perez house." She hooked her arm through mine and towed me toward the entrance.

Perez house was the place Poppy had inherited and made into her learning center. It was an old and beloved farmhouse in town. "But you're hiring new people."

"I am, but it's still my building to do with what I want, and if I want my sister to work with me, I get my way."

"I hate to say the kids might be an issue during my meetings."

"The oil company doesn't want giggling in the back-ground of your meetings?" she teased.

Laughing, I pulled the door open, and we were surrounded by the smell of charred meat and grease fryers. My appetite came to life.

After we were seated, I looked around. Pictures of crocuses from various nearby pastures filled the wall, and the ceiling fans looked like giant petals. "I need to come here with Van again."

She gave me a sidelong look. "Date night?"

"No," I said a little too quickly. "But I like hanging out with him."

"Is that what the kids are calling it these days?"

"Poppy, it's not like that." It sort of was, but that was between me and Van.

"You're pregnant and married to him."

I rolled my eyes and tried to play it cool. My situation with Van was private, and I hadn't figured it out yet. "You know what the deal was."

The young server appeared at our side, fighting with her notepad and biting her lip.

Poppy grinned, her eyes bright. "Peyton! Why didn't I know you worked here?"

"Hey, Coach," the girl mumbled. "I won't miss practice."

Poppy scoffed. "Don't worry about me. If you gotta balance practice with a paycheck, that's what you gotta do. We'll work around what we have to. My sister Clover will tell you how reasonable I am."

"She's really not," I said. "She'll come work your shift so you can get to practice."

The girl smiled shyly and took our order.

Poppy let out a contented sigh. A sound I loved to hear. One I longed to make, but my slightly unpredictable future put a stop to it.

She tapped her fingers on the tabletop. "How's it really going? I worried when I got that message from Van."

I frowned. "What message?"

"Oh crap. I wonder if I wasn't supposed to say anything. He said that we should get together soon."

He told her that? Did he say I was missing her? "Anything else?"

"I asked if something was wrong, but he said he didn't think so. That was it. He doesn't seem like the kind of guy to spill your business."

"No," I said softly. "He's really not. I'm trying to talk him into coming for Thanksgiving. We'll have to be moved out that weekend, but I'd like one big gathering where I can pretend everything's normal."

Understanding filled her eyes. "You want to pretend like it's going to keep going."

She didn't ask it as a question. "No. I want him to be a part of a big, supportive, healthy family."

"And fall so in love with it that he has to admit he's in love with you."

A mental *yes* popped up before I could stop it. "Poppy."

This was why I didn't want her, or anyone, to know about me and Van. My plans and his hadn't changed. Only what we were doing together in the meantime.

She didn't laugh like she was toying with me. She only tipped her head and studied my reaction. "Clover, do you like him?"

"I told you I did."

"No, do you *like him* like him?"

My cheeks heated, and there was nothing I could do to stop it.

She gasped, and several people around us turned to see why. I tried to shrink in my seat. Glancing back and forth, she leaned over the table. "Clover Jean Duke. You and your husband are canoodling."

"We are not." I might not want my private life public, but I hated lying. If I didn't, she'd be planning my next wedding, a real one, with Van. She didn't understand that Van didn't need someone like me derailing his plans. "We're not having sex," I whispered.

"What are you doing, then?" She cocked a brow, then nodded. "Thought so."

"How?" My incredulous shout caused more people to gawk at us. I ignored them.

"I know we haven't talked much, but didn't you take a trip with him?"

"Yes." Which sibling spilled that detail? Bunch of gossips.

"And that was after pumpkin day, when you two would always be sneaking peeks at each other."

"I was not." Was he?

"Why fight it? He seems like a decent guy. I wasn't sure since he's related to Elijah and lived in his parents' basement, but I didn't want to get hung up on a stereotype. And then he cut his hair for you."

"I didn't ask him to. His long hair was fine."

"His long hair needed a trim. You could tell he just couldn't be bothered with it. Until he was saying 'I do' to you."

I thought about his little self-makeover. He'd trimmed a foot of hair off and wore a suit. At home, he kept his hair combed, and he cooked and cleaned with me. We were a balanced pair, and that was significant. Elijah hadn't put those things on me to do, but he had dry cleaners and delivery services, and those were fine, but I also liked caring for my own place. The other amenities were decent, but I didn't think I was above doing them myself, and that was where the difference hid. Van didn't make himself feel important by acting like he was better than others.

"So why is Van a problem?" Poppy asked.

He was a problem because he couldn't be a solution. "He swooped in to save me. Poppy, when Elijah left, I was stranded in another state. I had no home, no money, and barely a job. I know you all would've taken me in, but without Van, I still wouldn't have a home." I had a job, but I didn't have money. "I have to be self-sufficient. I was stuck in that hotel room, with no fiancé, looking at the big ol' zero in my bank account. I'm not doing it again. I'm going to get an apartment. I'm going to pay rent. I'm going to build up everything that asshole took from me. And I'm going to raise this kid to be better than his dad."

"And Van has no role in all of that?"

My heart twisted. He did—as an uncle. "He has his own dreams, and I'm not going to be just another woman in his life who sabotages him. He needs to be free to go wherever he needs to—whenever he needs to."

"I see."

Good. Because I saw it clear as a sunny day, and repeating it all still made me want to cry, and I couldn't blame my pregnancy hormones for that.

❁

I smoothed a hand over the bodice of the shirt I was trying on. My stomach was rounded in full-baby-bump territory.

Violet smiled from her chair. She had one leg crossed over the other, and one foot was bobbing. "Is it comfortable?"

Laughing, I pivoted to see how it draped in the back. That was the first question she asked with each article of clothing I tried on. I had to drive to Williston for some in-person meetings later in the month, and I'd need a few business casual outfits.

"It's very comfy." The pants were too. They had buttons so I could let out more material until I ran out. Depending on how big I got, I could wear these until birth. "I might work in pajamas at home though." Sticker shock was real.

"I wore Evander's sweaters toward the end. I think Daisy had on Alder's basketball shorts once."

176

"He probably went out and bought ten more pairs just for her."

"You know he did."

I went into the dressing room to change back into my regular clothes. When I came out, Violet was smiling into her phone. From the way she was grinning, I didn't have to see who texted her to know. "Willa swears there's an abandoned cat at the end of the drive, and Evander's been walking the road for an hour calling 'kitty, kitty, kitty' at her insistence."

I wanted that. I wanted that dreamy smile. I wanted the husband at home with the kids, letting me know all of the sweet things he would do for them. Ugh. Someday. When I wouldn't be financially ruined if that husband ran off.

My talk with Poppy had weighed heavily on me, and I had woken up both mornings since curled against Van's side. If he woke when I pried myself away from him, I couldn't tell. Neither of us could afford to get close.

As we were walking out of the store, Violet hit her fob. "Where else do you want to go?"

"I should get back." The fatigue had hit hard today, and the chilly nip in the air only made me think of cozy blankets and warm mugs of cider. "Van was going to do some fall cleanup in the yard, and I said I'd clean the inside if he did that."

"Is he the type to have done it all before you get home?"

"Yes," I said without hesitation.

"That's sweet."

I tensed and waited for more questioning, like what happened with Poppy, but we got into her car. We chatted all the way home, and my anticipation cranked higher. Van was in the yard in a loose hoodie and jeans that framed his long legs as if they'd been tailored for him. Behind his pickup, a few garbage bags were piled in the opening of the garage. He lifted his head, and with the backward hat, I was mesmerized.

Computer-nerd Van was devastating, but yard-work Van could get me pregnant without touching me...if I already wasn't.

Violet pulled to a stop behind my spot in the driveway. The pumpkins we'd carved lined the porch. I'd tried for a geode, but only Van and I knew what it was. Both Van and I had attempted Pokémon characters, a cat, and regular jack-o'-lanterns. The rest we left and joked they were rocks.

Van jogged toward us and opened my door. "Hey, got anything to haul in?"

"Just one bag."

I was about to get out when Violet put a hand on my shoulder.

"I almost forgot," she said. "What are you two doing for Halloween?"

I met Van's gaze, and he shrugged.

"It's been years since I've done anything," he said.

"As long as it's not a cocktail in some stuffy bar, what are you thinking?" I asked her.

"Willa's old enough to trick-or-treat, and I was going to ask the others if we should just pick a neighborhood to wander. We could all get together, eat first, and then trick-or-treat. If it's nice out."

"There shouldn't be snow." Didn't mean it wouldn't be freezing. I would join them, but would Van want to? He hadn't minded yet.

He leaned down with his hands on the top of the frame. "Whatever Clover is down for, I'm in."

"You don't mind?"

This close, the darker green flecks in his eyes swirled like a hypnosis spiral. When we were this close, it was usually dark. "Yeah. It sounds like fun."

"What are you dressing as?" Violet asked.

Van's smile froze. "Dressing up?" he croaked.

Violet rested an arm across the steering wheel. "The first year we were married, Evander wore coveralls and carried a spade. Willa and I were pumpkins."

He chuckled. "Guess Clover and I will have to come up with something good."

"Really?" I asked. "You'd do that?"

"Like I said, whatever you want to do, I'm in."

Chapter Sixteen

Van

I adjusted my red hat. Next, I flipped the white collar of my blue jacket straight and tugged on the white sleeves. The last thing to put on with my Ash costume was the green, fingerless gloves.

A night that had passed with little notice over the years had turned into a big family event. And I was invited along again.

The Halloween night festivities blossomed from the initial idea of roaming Coal Haven as one large group. Poppy and Jensen were supplying pizza at the Perez house for everyone, and then we would walk the neighborhood from there. If we needed to warm up, we could dip back into the house and gorge on more pizza and cocoa.

"I love it," Clover called from the bedroom. She came waddling out in her plush yellow Pikachu costume. She'd found a full-length pajama suit with a hood that had the ears. With this, she could wear normal shoes and stay warm.

Mostly, I was looking forward to having an adorable Pikachu at my side. "I'm never going to look at Ash and Pikachu the same again."

She turned from side to side like she was at the end of a catwalk. "In a good way or a bad way?"

"All good." When she beamed, I just wanted to herd her to the bedroom and strip her yellow pajamas off.

"The Ash look fits you, honestly." Appreciation shone in her eyes. "You're a chameleon."

"How so?"

Pink dusted across her cheeks. "Well, there's computer-nerd Van, who's quiet and introspective but alluring." Her flush deepened. "And then there's boardroom Van, who acts like he makes everyone at a meeting beg for it." I ticked up a brow, loving how her blush stole over her whole face. "And this makes you kind of an avant-garde Van, with maybe a little tough-guy edge."

"With my red hat?"

"It's what cinches the deal," she said solemnly, but she failed at biting back a smile.

I chuckled. "I've been called worse. Come on, Pikachu, let's go catch 'em all."

Less than fifteen minutes later, I parked in front of the Perez house. Alder and Daisy were just pulling up.

Clover nearly skipped all the way to the door, waving at Alder's family. "Look at you, Laila!"

The young girl had petals around her head like she was some sort of flower. "I'm a monkey orchid."

Daisy smirked. "In case I thought I'd be able to just buy a simple costume."

Alder carried the car seat. "There was a run on monkey orchids as soon as we showed up."

Evander appeared at the door, lines bisecting his green

face. The monster of Frankenstein. Violet was next to him with her hair standing straight up, a white line sprayed into either side. The bride of Frankenstein. And little Willa wore a white lab coat. Dr. Frankenstein.

Evander pushed the door open, studying our costumes. "You're going to have to explain it to me."

"Ash and Pikachu from Pokémon," Clover said as she stepped in.

I tensed as I followed her. I hadn't met many adults outside the gaming realm who understood my hobby, and thanks to my family's behavior, I usually kept quiet. Why did I suggest this couple costume idea?

"Cool." His gaze danced back and forth, only approval in his gaze. "Perfect for a chilly night."

"No way." Auggie came from somewhere behind the crowd milling close to the door. "Dad! Aunt Clover is Pikachu." The kids moved over. He was dressed in a Liverpool soccer uniform, and his hair was slicked smartly to the side. "Whoa. You're Ash."

My night was already a success. If I could make a kid like him excited about what we were wearing, should I really hold on to what my family had thought?

Clover grinned and turned from side to side. "We thought of doing Pikachu and Eevee, but we couldn't find jammies in Van's size."

I snorted. "They had a pair for Eevee in your size, but you wanted to be Pikachu."

She snickered. "True."

Evander's eyes gleamed, and he met his wife's gaze. She smiled, and when she saw that I noticed, her grin grew larger.

Alder and Daisy came in behind us.

Lily poked her head out from the entrance that led to

the kitchen. "Pizza's ready. There's no schedule. Just eat and take off."

"You aren't dressed," Clover said.

Eliot appeared behind Lily. "Her costume would take out five people and a window."

Lily rubbed her hands together. "His isn't as bad."

Clover stuck her hand in mine and led me toward them. "Are you going to keep me waiting, or can you tell me?"

"I'm a banana," Eliot said drily. "And so are all the kids."

"A bunch of bananas?" Clover stopped next to the stack of pizza boxes on the counter. I rubbernecked around us while listening to their conversation. The kitchen had been recently refurbished with polished cabinets and gleaming woodwork. "Hmmm, what would Lily be?"

"A gorilla." Lily grinned. "You should see the costume. Its hands are the size of dinner plates."

Eliot draped his arm around his wife. "I was supposed to be the gorilla, but the costume was too short." He opened the top of a pizza box and spun it around to face us. "Help yourself. Jasper didn't make the trip. He wanted to finish working cattle, then it's time to sell off our herd."

Alder moved around Clover and grabbed a slice of pizza. "Then he's moving here. All the Dukes in one spot." He leaned against the counter before he took a bite. "Unless you're going to move to Williston."

A chill slipped and slid through my veins. Clover was moving out of town?

Wasn't I doing the same? I hadn't thought about my living situation beyond arranging all my meetings. I hadn't even looked at the rental information.

Clover shook her head. "I need to stay where you all are. After the baby's born, maybe it'll be easier to work remotely from there so I don't have to juggle the times I have to travel with finding childcare."

Fuck that. She shouldn't have to move away from her family. Not when I was around.

Only I wouldn't be. Would I? And why was I so bothered by where she chose to live? I could go anywhere.

My stomach cramped. I must need food in it. I took two paper plates and handed one to her.

Alder pushed off the island. "You don't need to move. Jasper will be here then. Who knows, maybe Uncle Jasper will open a day care just for all of our kids."

Clover laughed, and while I loved the sound and appreciated Alder putting her at ease, a part of me stayed disgruntled. What the hell for? Why wouldn't I want Clover's family to rally around her so she could continue living near them? Why wouldn't I want her family to help her out?

Because it would mean Uncle Jasper was a big part of Bean's life and Uncle Van wasn't.

Clover wandered next to me as we followed Auggie, Poppy, and Jensen around the block adjacent to the Perez house.

The wind gusted between the two houses as we walked by. She shivered and put her hood up. "I've been meaning to tell you thank you."

"For what?"

"For messaging Poppy."

"Oh. That. You missed her."

"But it was that simple for you. You could've been irritated at me for complaining about something I could very much do myself, but you reached out instead."

Auggie jogged up a walkway to a front door glowing under the porch light and hit the doorbell.

"Would you really think about moving to Williston?" The pizza had sat in my stomach so heavily I'd been tempted to ask Clover what type of mineral weighed more than a brick of lead.

"If I have to." She stretched her sleeves out to cover her fingertips. Poppy and Jensen were a few feet ahead of us. "It'd be harder in a way. I have so many people around here to help, but sometimes I might have to be gone Monday through Friday."

"You can call me."

She blinked up at me. Auggie had gotten his candy and was sprinting back down the sidewalk. "What?"

"Call me. About Bean. I can help."

"Oh." We walked a few more steps. "Do you have experience with kids?"

"Uh, none."

She giggled. "Okay. You get points for honesty though." She paused for a moment. "Does that mean you're going to move somewhere in the state?"

Would I move to Williston too? Good damn question. "I feel like I should stay close," I said honestly. "Bean's the only member of my family I can stand."

She laughed loud enough that Poppy turned around. She beamed at us and faced ahead, murmuring something to Jensen.

"Fair." Clover stopped again while Auggie darted up to another front door. "I would like you to stay a part of Bean's life, but not just because you're the only member of the other side of Bean's family."

I could've soared off the sidewalk. She wanted Uncle Van around her—around the baby. I really did want to be there for Bean. Jasper wouldn't be the only fun, single uncle. I also didn't like the thought of Clover scouring her siblings for help. She might be too afraid to ask for what she needs because they all have busy lives.

"I don't want you to put your career on the line," she continued, "and a fussy baby could interfere with that."

"Bean wouldn't do such a thing."

She smiled and tucked her arm through mine. "I'm going to tell you a secret." I tipped my head closer to her even though I heard her just fine. "I love my nieces and nephews, but sometimes I'm really glad I can leave them with their parents."

Grinning, I patted her hand, and we started our route again as Auggie excitedly showed his parents the toy car he got to pick out with his treat. "Your secret is safe with me, but if a kid can derail all the work I've done to start consulting, then I haven't done a very good job."

She looked up at me, her hood shadowing her eyes. "So does that mean you'll be close by?"

"Yes." I would move into an apartment right here in Coal Haven. I would be closer to Bean. And her. There was no reason to be anywhere else. The thought of staying in town didn't make my stomach acid go wild like it did when I pondered other places to live.

"Good." She kept her arm in mine as we walked.

Chapter Seventeen

Clover

I popped a Tootsie Roll into my mouth and sifted through the documents at my makeshift desk. It was officially November. I had one month to find another place to live. Van had scribbled some notes on a few of the sheets with info from when he had called the landlords—availability, deposit, monthly payment.

The front door opened. Van had been outside going through the shop. The lawn didn't need to be mowed, and the flower beds were ready for winter. He'd cleaned up the garden, and he'd even repaired a portion of the wooden fence along the drive. Today, he'd cleaned some of the junk out of the shop so he could make a trip to the dump in the morning.

"Look at this." He appeared at the doorway. A wave of fresh air, old dirt, and linen scent rolled over me. A memory surfaced of when I'd helped my mom in the kitchen, and my dad would come in from working outside. He'd wrap his arms around her waist, she'd laugh, they'd kiss, and then they'd break. It had been a normal day, and I hadn't realized at the time how much I wanted that.

I pushed the apartment information out of my way. I still wanted it, but I wasn't going to be dependent on someone for it again. I'd do my own research. "What do you have?"

He took the chair next to me and sat with the tub between us, removing the lid.

The container was half full of little plastic bricks of all shapes, sizes, and colors. "Are those Legos?"

The way he smiled when he nodded melted my heart. He was like a kid who'd found a giant bowl of candy, like what sat in the middle of the table, and it was just for him.

"Lookit." He dug his hand into the stash, and a loud, clattering whoosh filled the air. "They're not even dirty, but I'll still clean them. You gonna use the bathtub tonight?"

"I can wait. Need help?"

His gaze flicked to the apartment information. "You're not busy?"

"I'll call them tomorrow and set up some tours. Wanna go together? If I don't like a place, you might."

His expression stayed neutral. "Yeah, let's do it."

Now I was excited to look at apartments. I could be independent but not alone. He had gathered information, and I would set up the visits. Apartment hunting just got a little more bearable. But first, Legos. "Let's get to cleaning. I'll get the dish soap."

A few minutes later, we were on our knees, and the faucet was running full blast. He dumped the whole container inside, and we swished them around.

"Why is this so satisfying?" I asked above the sloshing noise we were making. I might not mind doing this on my own, but everything was more fun with Van. Hanging out with my family achieved a new level when I could come and go with him. When I had my own person to chat with at big gatherings, even if he wasn't *my* person.

His eyes brightened. "Because we work at a desk all day, every day, and we don't get to play."

We played most nights, but that was with clothes off, and it ended in orgasms. This was different. Lighthearted. It wasn't killing time watching movies—which was also fun. It meant that we enjoyed yet another thing together. We were cleaning toys, and it was a great time.

He dug out a few towels and laid them between us. We took handfuls of bricks out of the water, shook them, and spread them out. I was returning for another batch after dumping an especially satisfying load out when Van flicked his fingers lightly. Water droplets hit my face, and I jumped.

Laughter burst out of me. I did the same to him. He swished his hands through the water and tried to do it again. I dunked my fingers faster than him and sprayed him. His grin promised retribution, but when he lifted his arm, his hand dripping, I grabbed his wrist.

There was no way I could overpower him, but we wrestled over our pile of Legos. Him managing to wiggle his fingers. More water sprinkled onto me.

"You're fighting dirty," I accused him, gasping for breath.

"Prove it." He wasn't even out of breath.

"You have a longer reach." I didn't let go of him.

He leaned over the towel of drying bricks like he was showing me that he had a longer everything. "You seem to be doing just fine."

"You're toying with me."

"Yes, Clover." He tugged me closer, and I had to let go

of him to catch myself on his chest. There was no way I would fall, though. He wouldn't let me. "I absolutely like toying with you."

Our faces were inches apart, our mouths a breath away. It wouldn't take much to kiss him. We'd already kissed. Just once. Since then, we'd used our tongues on each other a lot. Used our hands. But we hadn't made out. We hadn't done anything more intimate than a sizzling-hot orgasm. It'd been the one unspoken line we hadn't crossed, or it'd make our late-night pillow-talk sessions more dangerous. It'd make what we were doing more alarming. More real.

"I like when you toy with me," I said playfully, but my mouth had gone dry. We were so close. How easy would it be to feel his soft lips on mine again?

His gaze tracked over my face, dipping repeatedly to my mouth. "When we move..."

"I suppose we'll have to quit." My gut wrung out like a rag. One month left.

"Yeah," he said quietly. "I guess you'll be even more pregnant and probably not interested."

"Actually, my sisters said they enjoyed sex almost to the end. Then it could get a little uncomfortable." Was I supposed to tell him that? Did he think I was begging for us to continue?

He'd want to get on with his own life, right? He'd want to meet someone who wasn't complicated from the beginning. Someone who could support him and his job beyond putting a roof over his head. Someone who didn't need help raising her kid.

He didn't move, but his muscles were taut underneath my hands. "That's interesting."

"Yes. But I suppose we should make a clean break." The Tootsie Roll I'd had was going to launch itself back out of my stomach. "Hormones are one thing, but friends with benefits could get..."

"Messy."

"Complicated."

"You might fall head over heels in love with a buff geologist who isn't a blatant nerd."

I took the branch he held out, the offering to make our agreement casual with an end date, and swung on it. "Ew, yes. Nerds? Who needs them? I need a guy who rappels into volcanoes."

"And I need a woman who can name at least a hundred Pokémon and rattle off Python in her sleep."

"I feel like you're not talking about a snake."

"See? It'll never work."

I chuckled, but I couldn't bring myself to agree. It couldn't work. I had to be a good role model for this kid. No falling out of one relationship into another. No depending on someone else. No having it bad for its uncle.

Slowly, he released me, helping me straighten so I didn't fall over on the Legos and get hurt.

His phone buzzed. Without taking his eyes off me, he dug it out of his pocket. Finally, he broke eye contact and read what was on his screen. Interest lit his face. "What are you doing at eleven tonight?"

Van

I brought several blankets with me in the pickup as we drove to the middle of the pasture closest to the house. The person leasing the land had moved their cattle out a few weeks ago, so I parked at the highest point on the four-wheeler trail running through the grass.

Shutting the engine off, I killed the lights. Silence fell. Clover had her face pressed to the window, and I peered through the windshield. My mind was not on our task for the evening.

One month. Then we were done.

"Oh!" Clover twisted toward me. "I think I see them. Should we go out?"

Yes. We were outside to see the northern lights. An alert went off to notify me that they might be visible in my area tonight, and the sky was clear.

I wiggled my phone. "I'm ready to be our professional photographer tonight."

I turned off the cab lights. Nothing lit up as we got out.

"It's so dark out," she said, meeting me in the back.

I dropped the tailgate and spread a blanket out for us to sit on. Instead of having her clamber on in the dark, I put my hands on her shoulders. "May I?"

"Sure?"

I dipped to lift her under her ass. She let out a whoop and clung to me. Once she was settled, I took a seat next to her. Yeah, I liked doing all that way too much.

The temperature wasn't down to freezing yet, but it was cold. I draped a blanket around the both of us.

She scooted closer to me. "You're a heater."

I couldn't let her be cold. I put an arm around her and stared at the faint green haze in the sky. "Is that it?"

"Have you ever seen them before?" She gasped when I shook my head. "Seriously?"

"Too far south, and we lived in town. After I moved, I read about things I shouldn't miss in North Dakota, and one site mentioned the northern lights. So, I set up an alert for whenever they were predicted to be visible."

"I'm glad you got to see them," she murmured. "The camera will pick up the other color wavelengths, but sometimes you can see them with the naked eye."

The green got brighter like a surge of power had been plugged in. "Is it moving?"

"Yes!" She wiggled. I might miss the show if she kept doing that. "They're dancing."

Waves of green light rippled across the sky, and for the briefest of seconds, a flash of pink appeared. "Damn, that's pretty."

I took some pictures, and she was right. In the images, the green was flanked by the pinks and purples that I had seen in snapshots growing up.

"It's really relaxing." She laid her head on my shoulder. "It's dark, and there's no rush. And they show you how big the world is, the universe, but it's just light, and it's so peaceful."

"I like the company."

She tilted her face up, and maybe it was the temptation of earlier when we were in the bathroom, and she was close enough for me to devour, yet I didn't get a taste. Maybe it was the nights we got each other off, and while it was amazing and the strongest orgasms of my life, there was something missing.

Intimacy.

Sex.

Losing myself all the way inside her.

I lifted her chin with the tips of my fingers and pressed my mouth to hers. She didn't pull away, and she didn't go stiff. I increased the pressure, and she opened for me. With that, I was a goner.

Sliding my hand around the back of her neck, I turned as much as possible, and she did the same. It wasn't enough. I slid back and lifted her to straddle me. She settled her weight on me, and *yes*. That was some of what I'd been waiting for.

She stuffed her hands through my hair and tilted my head back. I gave her all the access she wanted. She tasted as sweet as the Halloween candy we'd been munching on all day.

I tunneled my hands under her hoodie until I hit warm skin. More. I'd implode if I didn't get more. I broke the kiss to murmur, "I want to be inside you."

She touched her forehead to mine. "Is that a good idea?"

Valid question. "No, but we only have a month together."

"Yeah. Just a month. Less, really."

I spread my fingers out. The waistband of her leggings teased me with how easily I could get to her. I kissed her neck but kept my hands high. There'd be no coercion. If we were going to do this, we had to go in knowing exactly where we were. Sex. Nothing more.

We might be husband and wife, but we were friends with benefits. We couldn't be anything else. It wasn't what she wanted, but we both needed this.

"We wouldn't need protection." Her breath was a whisper across my lips.

I shook my head. Both of us had gotten clear bills of health after we'd been betrayed. I hadn't been with anyone since. "One month of messing around, then we divorce?"

"The countdown is on." She brushed her hands down my shoulders. "So I guess we should make use of the time we have."

Yes. "Want to move to the back seat of the truck?" I hadn't contorted myself for back-seat sex in a long time, but I'd do it in a heartbeat for Clover. It wouldn't matter if I drove a pickup or a Prius.

She tipped her face up to the sky. A long wave of aurora danced over our heads. "Let's do it under the lights."

I was hers wherever she wanted me. She wiggled out of her leggings, setting them on top of the shoes I helped her get off. I flung the blanket around her. There was no one but us, but she should be warm and feel like she had privacy. She straddled me again and helped me get my jeans open.

When her hot hand wrapped around my dick, I moaned. I returned the favor, sliding my fingers to her drenched pussy. She shuddered against me, and I swallowed the panting breaths coming from her.

"Van?" She gave me a hard pump that almost shoved me over the edge.

She was asking if I was ready. I'd been ready for longer than I cared to admit. "Sit on me, sweet Clover. Let me feel how soaked you are."

I held myself rigid, and she lowered herself onto me. Her mouth dropped open as I filled her. She fisted around me so tightly. When I was seated fully inside, she paused. We both had to catch our breath.

"Christ, Clover. You feel like heaven." My hands dug into the soft skin of her hips. I'd been sleeping next to her all this time without touching her?

"You're so..." She exhaled and rolled her hips. "Big."

If she had said it any other way, I wouldn't have believed her, but her breathy tone didn't lie, nor did she. She continued rocking, stroking up and down my length until she adjusted to my size. I held myself rigid, otherwise I'd come too fast. I'd waited too long for this, and I wanted to experience her climax while inside her.

She rose up and crashed down. A moan escaped me at the same time hers slipped out. We were in sync, taking from each other, giving as well.

I kept her in place to catch her mouth again. Burying a hand in her hair, I released her hips, and she rode me.

With no protection, I wouldn't last long, and I didn't want to. A green aura shimmered above us, and it was a gorgeous night, but I also needed to hold her. That wouldn't happen in a pickup bed.

The blanket fell from my shoulders. Her movements got longer, and her muscles were tense. She was close. I was veering toward my peak, but I'd make sure she tipped over with me.

One circle of her clit and she exploded. "Van!" My name rang across the pasture just as I detonated. I dropped my head back, squeezing my eyes shut as I came, my dick getting throttled by the walls of her pussy. Overwhelmed was an understatement. By the experience. By her. By how much she was the whole package—funny, smart, and mind-blowingly sexy.

"Fuck, Clover." I wrapped my arms around her to keep her from falling as she slumped against me, fitting perfectly.

The wall of lights faded and gained strength, shifting across the night sky. Stars dotted the darkness around it. How was I going to move on from a night like this?

❧

Clover

. . .

My back was pressed against the shower wall, and Van pumped in and out of me. This night had been the most amazing ever, and it wasn't over. First, it was sex under the stars and a painted night sky. Then we came home and went straight to bed, only to get fully naked and have sex again. I had only meant to clean up, but he'd knocked on the bathroom door.

A moan ripped out of me, and I dragged my mouth along his jaw. "I can't believe I'm going to come again."

Was it the hormones? Lackluster sex? I hadn't thought so, but Van was obliterating any previous description I had for good sex.

"You can do it." He grunted, plunging deeper than before.

Pleasure upon pleasure stacked inside me, growing and expanding. This shouldn't be able to happen again, but I wasn't going to stop it. My new favorite position was Van inside me.

My limbs were wrapped around him, and he was taking his time. His hands were at my ass, holding me in place. How long would we have warm water? I wouldn't. He was blocking me from the spray.

I tunneled my fingers through his wet hair. Droplets tracked down his face, and I caught a few with my tongue. The sly smile he rewarded me with only nudged me closer to my orgasm.

"You feel like heaven." He dropped his head and licked along my collarbone. My eyes rolled back. I was just ticklish enough that shivers broke out over my body. Mixed with the way he filled me and then withdrew, I was even closer to exploding.

A soft gasp left me, and I clung to him, tightening my

legs around him, giving my clit more stimulation. I was almost there.

How long would this last?

I tried to push the question away, but it came back. I backed away from the edge. No. I wanted to come. I wanted to soak up all this time with Van. Drown in him. This was how it was supposed to have been all along.

I squeezed my eyes shut. That was a lot to put on my husband. I had to be prepared for him to wake in the morning and tell me this was a mistake.

"Clover." He grunted and punched in with more force than before.

The way he said my name anchored me. I wouldn't worry about the morning. I wouldn't worry about us. That was decided. I would enjoy this while it lasted, and hope that maybe, someday in the future, I could have something like it again.

Could it ever be with Van?

My orgasm knocked into me, wiping out my thoughts and catapulting me into pure bliss. "Van!"

He fucked me hard, faster, his feet slipping as I shook in his arms. My climax kept going, and then he stiffened, releasing inside me. It was perfect. Just like the other times. And it was just one more thing I was counting down before I had to move on.

Chapter Eighteen

Clover

"I've really got to get to sleep, or I'm going to miss my alarm and be late for work." I was draped across Van's chest. It was late, and we'd spent all Sunday in bed.

It was like we'd never had sex before and were told the next month would be our last chance to.

For me, it might be. For at least a while, as I supported me and Bean. After being with Van, that was okay. Why settle for kibble when I'd tasted gourmet?

He kissed the top of my head. "I can think of many ways to wake you up."

"You mean like you did this morning?" My entire body heated as if I wasn't spent.

He traced circles over my hip as he held me. "I could wake up like that every day."

"Makes getting out of bed harder."

"We could get out of bed first and then have sex."

I laughed and brushed my hand down his side. I didn't get tired of touching him. Or talking to him. I probably wouldn't have gotten tired of living with him. "That sounds like a plan. Another shower escapade?"

"Or I can have you for breakfast."

My toes were already curling in anticipation. "Who's going to cook?"

"Ah, sweet Clover. If you're stopping to think of logistics, I've been doing it wrong."

"No, you aren't." I propped myself on an elbow. "You're just underestimating how much I think about food."

"And now you're eating for two."

I nodded even if he couldn't see me. This was the first time we'd acknowledged Bean since we'd started having sex. "I worried that would bother you?"

"That you're eating for two?"

"No. That you'd remember I was pregnant." He'd remember, and he wouldn't want me.

He rolled to his side. "You thought it'd turn me off?"

"Yes." The word came out a rasp. "I know it's only temporary, but I thought you'd come to your senses."

"Clover, you've knocked them all out, but aside from that, no. I've had my eyes wide open this whole time about who you are and my relation to that kid in your belly. I'm the guy helping you get back on your feet after my brother pushed you down, and you're the girl helping me reclaim the career my ex dismantled. Now roll over."

"You really mean it? We're having sex *again*?" I hadn't had a marathon day of doing it since, well, ever. I might be sore tomorrow.

"Roll to your back." He crowded me with his big body until I was sprawled on my side of the bed. Tingles spread from my belly to my sex, but then he put his face inches from my lower abdomen and stopped there.

"Hey, Bean," he crooned.

Shock rippled through me, but I didn't move. The view was too cute, too sweet, and it didn't matter there was no light.

"I'm your uncle Van. You can call me Sullivan, though I suppose that'll be harder for a kid to say."

I smiled, but I didn't want to interrupt him. These were the moments I thought I'd never get. The small things I was prepared to mourn. I had no husband, no fiancé, no boyfriend to share in all things baby. But Bean had an uncle Van.

He had come to the first doctor's appointment. He'd been there for the bulk of my morning sickness. Now he was here for the smallest of moments—talking to my belly.

My heart clenched, and my throat grew thick. I could do this alone, but geez, if I was getting this choked up over this? I had more work to be the independent, lady-boss role model for Bean.

Yet I wouldn't interrupt him. I was weak enough to need this too.

"Just don't call me Sully," he continued, a breath gusting over my skin, making this all the more intimate. "You're not going to have a choice. You're going to learn how to play Pokémon." He shared a grin with me. "You're also going to learn rockhounding. I bet you'll have a good eye, like your mom. I bet you're going to be smart, too, like her."

"I think Bean will get some of his uncle's intelligence. His fortitude." I swirled my fingers through his hair. "Bean might even start his own geological consulting company."

Van's shadowy smile was lopsided. "As long as Bean doesn't let some girl or guy wreck it all."

My heart dipped. No, I would not be that girl for Van. "Bean's going to have some good people to look up to."

"Yeah." His lips were a whisper away from my skin. He kissed my belly, a touch as light as a snowflake. "We'll set the example. Mama and Uncle Van. I'll be the example I almost never got."

"You're going to be around that long?" I was only asking to keep up the playful conversation. Not at all because I wondered if he would be around this time next year. Or in five years. Ten. Where would our lives be then? "You could be a tech millionaire and buy a house in Aspen, and I'll be a girl who plays with rocks."

A rumble came from him that sounded like a growl. "Don't diminish what you do."

"It is what I do."

"Tell me your job again."

"You know what it is. I've told you."

He flipped over, and cool air gusted over me before he nestled by my chest. I hadn't put my pajamas on yet. We hadn't made it any further after our last round of sex than this. He drew a nipple between his lips, and a shiver racked my body.

He let it go with a pop. "Tell me."

As if he wasn't making my brain a slurry, he blew across the damp tip. Goose bumps erupted over my skin, and a bolt of electricity shot through my bloodstream. "That's mean."

He sucked my nipple back into his mouth, licked across, then let it go and blew over it.

"Is this supposed to be torture?" I arched my back off

the mattress, like I was trying to stuff the peak back into his mouth.

He pushed up to reach the other side. "What do you do for a living?"

"I figure out where to store brine underground."

That breast got the same attention, and a quiver rippled under my skin. "There's more."

Was he going to keep going? I wanted him to. "I analyze data about dirt—"

A hot mouth closed around the same bud, only he let go right away. "Try again, just like you told me the first time," he muttered against my breast. "Or I'm not going to fuck you for breakfast."

I bit my lower lip. I liked this game way too much, but also, I could also be laid on the table or against the counter, or however he wanted to do me. "I determine the well type, location, and the rate for optimal pressure to manage the carbon dioxide plume. I also analyze data from the storage tests."

"Sounds like you do more than play with rocks." He moved on top of me, nudging my legs apart with his knee. "You make them your bitch."

"No, I can't do that." I swept my hands down his shoulders as he notched the head of his cock at my entrance. "The rocks will always show me who's boss. I just try to sweet-talk them into letting me work with them, and when they don't like it, they push back. Hard."

Just as I said that, he thrust inside, smoothly and slowly, as if he sensed I might be tender and didn't want to make it worse. While he was inside me, I didn't care. I was full, and all was okay.

He dipped his head to nibble along my jaw. "Every time

you want to diminish what you do, remember how good you get fucked if you don't."

I widened my legs to take him farther. Pleasure was building like a sensual mudslide in my veins, ready to crash over me any moment. "I won't forget."

Chapter Nineteen

Van

"This is no good." None of the places we had looked at all week were feasible. Clover and I were touring the third apartment. This one was up a flight of stairs behind an old house right off Main Street.

Clover squinted up at the entrance. "We haven't even gone inside."

"It's going to be winter soon, and those steps will become death."

She tucked her hands into her jacket. The rich blue brought out the dual colors in her eyes, and she had on a cream knit hat. "I'll keep them clear."

"No. Absolutely not." I envisioned her laboring up those stairs with a baby belly blocking her view. One small slip was all it would take. "We can call and tell the landlord we're canceling."

"She's up there waiting for us."

"I'll run up."

She tucked her arm through mine, a move that was starting to feel so natural it was like she'd been taking me by the arm for a decade. "It's not icy right now. Let's go look at it. You might like it."

If I moved in here, she wouldn't be able to visit me, but I'd humor her and do a tour. "Fine, but you're going up first." If she slipped, I'd catch her.

Her smile dipped a moment before returning in full force. "I kind of like this protective side. It's almost caveman-ish."

"Me, Van. You, be careful."

She laughed and took the stairs like they were nothing more than a few steps up a porch and not a full flight of wooden steps attached to the side of a house. The wind licked at the tendrils of her hair sticking out of her hat. I herded her inside as soon as we reached the top.

An older woman smiled at us. "Hello, I'm Zelda. Van and Clover?"

"Yes," I said, shaking her hand. "Nice to meet you."

"Ooh, this is nice." Clover clapped her hands together.

The place was cute, but it wasn't happening. I waited until she looked her fill, then I gave her a small shake of my head. She smirked and thanked Zelda, telling the landlord she'd think about it.

Not one ounce of guilt hounded me. I might be a caveman, but I needed her to be safe when she was visiting me. Or we could keep living together...

No, she wanted to do things on her own. Couldn't blame a girl who was left at the altar to be skittish about making long-term plans with a guy. Especially if that guy was her ex's brother. I've proven I'm nothing like him, but she wasn't the only one hurt by him. I had my own life to reclaim, and I was so close.

We had one more place to look at. It was a house rental, and it wasn't one that Alder owned. We'd looked at his open unit first, and she didn't mind it, but she wouldn't go for it. I didn't have to ask why. The rent was suspiciously low, and she didn't want to feel like she was taking charity from her brother.

The drive only took a couple of minutes. A little square house not far from the elementary school was wedged between two large ranch houses on a small lot with no garage and barely two dirt tracks for an off-street parking spot. The landlord's pickup was parked across the road, and the front door hung open. There was nothing visible of the place through the screen door.

"It's cute." Clover pushed a lock of hair behind her ear and adjusted her hat. "Not a big place to take care of."

It wasn't. The ad said it had two bedrooms, a separate bathroom, and was newly updated. "Let's see if it's the one."

I studied the houses around us as we walked to the door. I'd change locks as soon as she signed the papers. That was the advice I'd always heard, and I'd make sure it happened for her place. I stepped inside behind her. The landlord was my age, and he brandished flyers for houses for sale with his face on them. He was a real estate agent too.

She was going to pick this house. The floors had been restored to the original walnut, and all the trim was freshly stained. The walls were painted a clean off-white and all the holes in the plaster had been filled. I had expected a musty smell from an old house like this, but someone had baked an apple pie. Maybe it was a candle. Whatever. It worked.

Clover took a deep inhale. "Oh, this is charming."

I grew more dismayed as we walked through it, and her smile widened. The bathroom, while tiny, had a tub-and-shower combo, a new toilet, and a vanity with lots of storage. Clover gushed over the equally small linen closet in the hallway before breathing a sigh of relief in the bedroom.

"This is it, Van." She glanced past me to make sure the landlord wasn't around. "It's clean, and the rent is reasonable. There's not much of a yard for me to take care of."

"There's no garage."

"A shed's in the back." She crossed to the rectangular window and lifted the blinds. "All I'd need is a little push mower and a shovel."

That wasn't good enough. Her car would be out in the elements. If she didn't leave the house for days during a cold spell, would it even start? Then what?

She'd call me or one of her many family members.

Didn't change how much I couldn't get on board.

She closed the blinds. "I won't have to buy much to fill the space."

My stomach twisted on itself. She didn't have any furniture, not even a bed. Goddammit. "I'll help you with that."

"Thanks, but I've saved enough to get my own."

I bobbed my head and held her brilliant gaze. Her eyes lit with excitement, but she couldn't hide the trepidation in their depths. All my misgivings about this being the perfect place for her to begin a new adventure vanished.

"It'll be okay," I murmured.

A crease formed along her brow. "Will it?"

"I'll make sure of it."

Her smile started and then dropped. "*I've* got to make sure of it." She raised on her toes and kissed me. I gripped her elbows, but she pulled away. "Sorry. I forgot we're not at home." Her smile was tight. "At the house."

That house was the best home I'd ever had. This might be her chance at a real, secure home for her and Bean. Guess

I'd call Alder and ask him what the real price of rent for his property was.

She wandered into the next room, and I trailed behind her. I was following this woman anywhere, it seemed. Perhaps she was right to create distance between us. I'd worked too hard to get back to a semblance of my earlier self, the Van from before my brother tore through my life.

"This will work." She spun to one wall and spread her arms out. "The crib would fit here. A glider rocker. I don't need a changing table, but maybe I could find a cheap dresser–changing table combo."

Note to self: find a combo she'd like. Cost be damned.

"What about you?" she asked. "Which one of the places we looked at are you going to pick?"

"The first." The first house rental we checked out was the one Alder owned. If Clover and I grew apart, I'd have one link to her.

Was that too stalkerish?

She was about to walk out when her phone rang. Frowning, she checked it. "Oh, it's Dad." She didn't turn her back on me when she answered. "Hello?"

I paced the room as she talked. Would she find a suitable rental? One that didn't make me think of everything that could go wrong for a single mom? I was being unreasonable, but I didn't care. She deserved the best.

"Yeah? Oh." Her tone went flat. "Uh, yeah. He's right here. I'll ask him."

I stopped and leaned against the bare wall where the crib would go.

She lowered the phone like she was going to cover it, then brought it back to her ear, her gaze holding mine. "Dad said his lawyer friend can help us out right after

Thanksgiving. He's taking a long Christmas holiday and will be out the rest of December."

Divorce. Heat prickled the back of my neck. It'd be the middle of winter, and Clover would be growing bigger. Divorce. Living separately. Just what we both wanted. "Okay."

"He can meet us early that Monday."

I didn't fly out for my investor meetings until January. I was free all of December. This should be a boon. I would be on my own for a month to refine my pitch. I could even take on smaller consulting projects that would show I was already greasing the wheels.

"Yeah, that'll work." My voice was raspy.

"Eight o'clock?" She gnawed on her bottom lip. "Dad says it'll be a quick visit. Just some signatures."

That was all that would be needed to end us. The back of my throat burned.

"Eight would be fine. I'll let work know I'm coming in late that day."

"Yeah, same." I shrugged, but my shoulders were tight. "Perks of being my own boss, right?"

Our divorce was on the schedule.

❧

Clover

There was no snow on the ground yet, but it was Thanksgiving morning. The date of the divorce was approaching at lightning speed. On Monday, I would be a single woman.

Van had movers all ready to go. Aunt Linda hadn't

been able to line up another renter thanks to the holidays. I tried not to think about when she would, or who would get to make that house their home. Who would have a nice, big garage attached to the house. A huge shop that would hold a sizable tractor to push snow and mow the lawn.

What couple would watch TV in the cozy living room and make meals with their spouse in the kitchen? Would they laugh about the squeaky cabinet and how no one could get away with sneaking snacks for long? Would they find the bin of freshly washed and dried Legos in the garage?

After we spent time building various pieces, mostly related to our hobbies, we'd dismantled everything and packed all the pieces back into the tote. Since we didn't know which previous owners the Legos belonged to, we decided that what came with the place would stay with it for the next owners.

Would they know how lucky they were?

Van turned down Alder's driveway. My siblings' cars and pickups lined the drive.

"This is where you grew up?" he asked.

"Yep. Lily has Grandma Annie's old place, and we used to go there a lot. After we moved to Billings, that was the house we partied in if we returned to Coal Haven. When we moved to Billings, I never would've thought that this would stay in the family, or that one of us would be back in it, raising our own kids."

"Glad to be back?"

"Yeah. I am." I wanted to experience this with Van. Next year, would he be willing to go to whatever brother or sister of mine hosted? Would he get on his own and realize Coal Haven wasn't the place to be? That I was surrounded by family, and he was free to find somewhere else to live? "Thank you for coming."

"I'm getting used to Duke family gatherings."

I recalled each time—kickball, pumpkin harvest, and Halloween. "After only three?"

"Technically four if we count the wedding, but they made that much of an impression." He wasn't kidding. He tipped his head to the tote bag. "And I get to have cookie salad."

"I left a container of it at home."

"Breakfast tomorrow?"

"Naturally." I chuckled. I'd have to keep him supplied with cookie salad. It'd be an excuse to see him if he didn't join in on the fun.

He carried the food and hovered next to me as we picked our way across the drive until we reached the path to the house.

Auggie flung open the front door. "Aunt Clover!"

"Happy Thanksgiving," I called.

"You get to see Dad's cabinets." He darted away from the door.

"That kid needs to go into marketing," I said. "I've seen those cabinets countless times, yet he makes me excited to see them again."

"Jensen installed them?"

"How'd you know?" I asked lightly.

We shared a grin.

"Hey." Jasper held his arms up like he was cheering for us. "I'm gonna fight you for a place to sit."

"You get the kiddie table," I said, shrugging out of my coat.

"When'd you get so pregnant?" Jasper took the tote from Van.

I smoothed a hand over one of the maternity tops I'd bought with Violet and had combined with a pair of insulated leggings that I'd bought a few years ago that were too big and couldn't return. My maternity pants were waiting in the wings. They weren't packed yet. "It's the shirt. It poofs out and makes me look bigger."

"What if you're having twins?" Jasper asked.

I rolled my eyes. "I already showed you the image of Bean. There was just one. Besides, twins don't run in our family."

He jutted his chin toward Van. "What about him?"

Van thought for a moment. "Not that I know of."

The oddness of this moment sank in. I was abandoned by my baby's daddy, but Van was here to answer for him. Story of our relationship.

"Do you watch football?" Jasper asked him.

"At the risk of being stereotypical," I said to Van, "the guys watch football and us girls hang in the kitchen and start baking Christmas cookies."

Van's lips quirked. "Hmm, work or sit around?"

"Don't let her fool you. We have to clean up," Jasper explained. "After dinner, after second dinner, and after the baking."

Van pretended to wince. "Oof, I have a shortbread recipe I've been meaning to try, but I'll let Clover have girl time."

Laughing, Jasper led us to the kitchen. Alder had cleaned out the garage and set up tables. People were going back and forth through the dining room out to the garage with food and supplies.

"You made it," Lily said. She gasped when she saw me in the maternity clothes. "Look at you. So cute and pregnant."

"I'm barely four months."

She propped a hand on her hip. "When's the next ultrasound?"

"I made the appointment for right after New Year's."

"You did?" Van asked, his brows drawn together.

I swallowed, my throat thick. This had been put off too long. I squared my shoulders and faced Van. "Sorry, all the appointments were made last month, and I didn't think..." But I had. I'd thought a lot about telling him when all the appointments were. "You told me your travel schedule, and I didn't want you to feel torn."

Lily lifted her brows. Glancing between us, she forced a smile. "I need to grab the veggie tray. Jasper already brought the cookie salad out." She darted around us.

"I could've been here." A troubled line bisected his brow. "Is someone going with you?"

"No, other than an ultrasound, it's a normal appointment. I've already seen Bean, and I'm not finding out the gender, so I thought it wasn't a big deal." Each appointment was a big deal to me, but I couldn't have him changing his trip. What if he felt manipulated?

Disappointment clouded his expression. "You should have someone with you."

"If I feel like I need someone, I can call a sister or Alder. Maybe Jasper. He doesn't have kids, so he hasn't sat in on any yet."

A muscle in Van's jaw clenched. "As long as you're not alone."

I would get used to it. "I won't be."

Dad came through the door. "Van." He gave Van a hearty shoulder whack. "How's it going? Ready for the divorce?"

The corners of Dad's eyes crinkled like he was joking, but his gaze held more than humor.

"Divorce in the morning, then I'll take Clover to brunch and help her move."

Dad patted his shoulder again. "You're a good man. In case I don't have a chance to talk to you before then, thanks for taking care of her."

"I can't take the credit," Van said easily and aimed a smile my way. "She's taken care of me just as much as I've done with her."

Was he talking about cooking and cleaning and checking in with each other? Or sex? Because yes, to all of it. "I'll miss taking turns cooking."

There was so much more added to the list. I was going to miss a movie partner. I might've gotten a sour stomach from the popcorn and brownies, but I'd still love to experience it again. And there were the other things. Orgasms.

Would we be able to mess around after?

No. Bad idea. We'd both be doing each other a disservice if we continued having sex while we lived separately and planned our lives apart. Only he was staying in Coal Haven. That decision wasn't for me. It was for Bean.

That was our connection after the divorce. Bean. Nothing more.

Chapter Twenty

Van

The guys might say they watch football, but there wasn't much being viewed. Alder and Weston were talking about the oil business. Jasper dozed on the recliner, his legs stretched out and crossed at the ankles. Lily's oldest son was sprawled on the cushions next to him, in an almost identical position. Eliot and Evander were talking pumpkins and horses, and Jensen had his hands behind his head, slouched in a beanbag chair he brought from his house for extra seating.

"You're sticking around, then?" Jensen asked. "You're renting from Alder, right?"

Alder and Weston stopped talking, and it was like a spotlight hit me.

"Yeah. Bean's my only family, really."

Jensen cocked his head. "Bean? Is that what Clover's naming the baby?"

"No, it's what we call it." Defensiveness prickled along the back of my neck, and my muscles automatically tensed, ready for ridicule.

"Ours was Bud," Evander said, rubbing a hand over his shaved scalp. "I still call Willa that a lot. She loves it."

A light smile lifted my lips. If I kept calling the baby Bean after birth, would it like that? Something just for us when it came to a kid who was going to have loads more aunts and uncles than I had?

I wasn't competing with anyone, but...I was. Just another uncle in...I did a quick count. Fuck, five others? Why did I feel a need to elbow my way to the head of the line? Just because I'd been married to Clover?

Yes.

I'd give her all the space she wanted, but I didn't have to like it.

"Yes, Alder's leasing a place to me." Across town from Clover. Good thing Coal Haven was small.

Jasper's brows lifted, and he glanced at Alder. "Yeah? You got one for me, bro?"

"Tell me when," Alder said. "If it's not open, the same offer goes to you that went to Clover. You can stay with us."

Eliot and Evander murmured their agreement, offering a room.

Jasper raised his hand. "No offense, but it's bad enough seeing you all suck face and give each other dopey eyes at family gatherings. If I hear anything, I'm gonna hurl, and then I'd get kicked out."

"I've got a pair of noise-canceling headphones," Alder said.

Weston held up a hand. "Take pity on a poor father and save this kind of talk for when Magnolia and I hit the road."

Snickers filled the room just as a touchdown was made.

Jensen pumped a fist in the air and paused. "Wait, is this the team we're rooting for?"

"Is it the wrong football for you, soccer boy?" Jasper drawled.

Jensen grinned. "I'm a soccer boy because of your sister."

The guys groaned.

"So, Van." Jasper angled himself toward me. "Need a roommate?"

Shock filled me. "Roommate?"

Jasper touched his chest, a sly grin on his face. "You won't have to marry me." He thought for a moment. "Wait. You can, and then we could live in the lake cabin that's supposed to be mine."

Weston grunted. "If you can sell the story to Linda, be my guest."

"You won't mind having Van for a son-in-law? Again?" Jasper joked.

Weston dipped his head. "My kids can pick good partners. Why would I think you're any different?"

Humbled by his response, I didn't know what to say. Jasper was joking around, but Weston didn't sound bothered to keep me in the family. They'd welcomed me in, and while we were just shy of three months, they'd been good to me.

"What'd ya say?" Jasper asked, crossing his arms, his expression sincere. "We can have Bean over for uncle sleepovers."

If I had said we had a nickname for the baby to my parents, they'd have found a way to make fun of it or me—or both. The Dukes didn't do that. They all pitched in to cook and clean. They were good to each other, and the people they had surrounded themselves with did the same.

To be embraced by this fold? It was an experience I'd never forget. One that would make me more discerning when I dated again.

My turkey dinner would waddle right back out of my stomach with that thought. I didn't need to date for a while. I had a company lifting off and a baby to help with.

"I don't know if I want to get married again." I was only half joking. My appointment to sign the divorce papers hung heavy over my head. "But I could use a room-mate if you're okay with me working from home."

"I'll be unemployed, but don't worry. I'll go hang out in a coffee shop or something." He scrubbed his hands down his face. "I've gotta reorient myself to the civilized world after being a cowboy for years."

"You wanna plant pumpkins?" Evander asked.

Eliot chuckled. "I don't think he's joking."

"I can plant pumpkins," Jasper offered.

"Me too." Hell, did I really offer that?

All their gazes landed on me.

"Yeah?" Evander's gaze got distant like he was thinking it over. "If you want to get out from behind the desk, I hit the ground running as soon as planting season hits. I'm thinking of expanding."

"Pumpkins?" Alder asked.

"Orchard," he said. "My cousin Isla was complaining that she can't get as many local pears as she wants for her brewery. I can take an acre or two from one of the grazing pastures. Could use some extra hands."

"Clover's due date is in May, so I'll be around." I'd make sure of it. If I picked up a contract or two, I could plan around it.

What if it caused an issue? What if Clover delivered early and I was gone? A client wouldn't like me taking time off if I just signed on with them. I stuffed that concern away. I'd figure it out later.

Clover popped out of the kitchen, and I rose and crossed toward her.

"Need anything?" I asked. A dusting of flour streaked across her cheek. I wiped it off, cupping her face and rubbing my thumb over it. "How are you feeling?"

"I'm good." She quirked her lips and glanced over my shoulder.

Oh. I was caressing her in front of her family. I was supposed to be just her roommate. Dropping my hand, I forced myself not to look back and see how many eyes were on us. They wouldn't trust me with their sister, or in Weston's case, his daughter, if they knew what I planned to do to her each day until Monday morning.

She swiped at the spot on her cheek that was now clean. "I just wanted to know if you like pumpkin pie or apple pie, and if you like sugar cookies or snowballs."

"Do I have to pick just one?"

She smiled. "One of each. Then on the second plate, you can do the other kind."

"I hope you made a lot."

"Trust me, we do," she said sagely and brushed the back of her wrist against her cheek. Another smudge of flour appeared.

I chuckled and wiped it away, never tiring of touching her soft skin. "Are you one of the desserts?"

Her eyes flared. Dammit. I did not say that in front of her dad. All of her brothers.

Jasper groaned. "See? This is what I mean. Maybe I can't be your roommate."

She chortled, but embarrassment flooded her face. "You're going to move in with Jasper?"

"He's going to move in with me," I clarified, helping her change the subject as much as possible without looking like we got busted having sex.

"Bachelor uncles," Jasper added, like he couldn't help himself. "Whenever the sale happens, I'll be living with your ex-husband."

A knife twisted in my gut. Ex. I was going to need a lot of dessert to get that bad taste out of my mouth.

❀

Clover

Why did it feel like I was cooking a last meal?

I knew why, and my appetite stayed tucked into a dark corner despite how good the Parmesan meatballs smelled. I had pasta cooked and waiting to go with the sauce I was currently stirring.

My bag was packed by the front door. In the morning, I would grab my toiletries and...move out. The movers were coming tomorrow afternoon, but Van was dealing with them. I'd be furniture shopping for my new place.

"Smells good." Van entered the kitchen and leaned against the counter. One plate of cookies we'd brought home from Thanksgiving was nearly empty. The rest were frozen. He plucked a broken Santa hat up and popped it into his mouth.

"You're going to ruin your appetite."

"I can eat this whole plate and then that entire pan." He peeked into the sink and let out an appreciative groan. "Is that penne? I'm never going to cook for myself like this."

"We can still do it. Cooking for one does get a little

old." Did I sound as casual as I hoped? Would he brush me off? Let me down easy?

"Sure."

Pleasure infused warmth into my blood. Moving wasn't looking as dismal as before. "Poppy invited us for Christmas. Daisy and Alder will be there. Lily and Eliot are going to his sister's place, and Evander and Violet will be hanging with his parents. Jasper's going to stay at the ranch in Buffalo Gully so the staff that hasn't moved yet can have the holiday off."

"She invited me too?"

I was about to say he was a part of the family, but that was changing. Yet, he was one of us. He fit too well, and even if he didn't, I couldn't let him weather the holidays by himself, not after I knew how he grew up. "Of course. Consider yourself an honorary Duke."

His hesitant smile cut straight through my chest wall to my heart. Did he realize how much it meant to me that he liked being around my parents and siblings? He knew the names of my nieces and nephews, and he was going to live with my brother. I had intended to ensure that I didn't mess up his business. I wouldn't interfere. But if I could make him feel welcome and like he had his own people? That was more than I could ask for.

Yet it wasn't all I wanted to ask for.

If I could get one thing for Christmas, it would be Sullivan Wagner.

His smile faded, and he swallowed, his Adam's apple bobbing. "I, uh, actually have plans."

"Oh." A stabbing pain went through my chest. I couldn't blame it on the baby. The pain was too high. Too close to my heart. "Good. That's good."

His brow crinkled, but he selected another chunk of sugar cookie. "I hate to miss your cookie salad."

I chuckled and stirred the pasta into the sauce. My appetite was returning, thanks to this chat with Van. "I'll pay you in cookie salad to babysit."

His jaw clenched mid-chew. "Yes," he said after he swallowed. "That'll work. You don't owe me though."

"I know," I said quietly. And there went my hunger again. "I know."

Dinner was fairly quiet. Van chowed into his meal, and I ate more than I thought I would. Afterward, we both did the dishes and then retired to the couch to watch a movie. He sat in his spot, and I tucked myself against the armrest.

The cloud over my head grew darker with each passing hour. Soon it was time for bed. Van tapped his fingers on his leg. The remote was between us, but neither one was going for it.

"I suppose we should get to bed." Why did my voice have to sound so small?

"Yeah. Early day."

"We actually have to leave the house." My thready chuckle got lost in his weak one. I might as well address the elephant holding divorce papers in the room. "Is it weird that I'm not looking forward to it?" I waved my hand to gesture to the whole room. "Leaving this."

"And the sex."

"I will miss that too."

He tugged my feet out from where they were curled under me. "One more time for the road?"

"Only one?" Some of the anxiety retreated, and I stretched out under him. He shut the TV off and tossed the remote onto the end table.

"I could muster two." He rolled my leggings down.

Cool air wafted over my legs. "But I don't want you tired for tomorrow. It's going to be a busy day."

I'd rather be tired and distracted for tomorrow. I yanked his shirt off. We were in leisurewear, cozy and comfortable and easily accessible. It took both of us to get his pants down. Soon we were naked, and he went one step further and put a blanket under me. He was so sweet and thoughtful. I would miss— No, I would not think about that. I would not be sad on our last night in the house. He'd helped me get on my feet. This was a celebration.

My head would convince the ache in my chest later.

"You got big plans?" I cradled him between my legs.

"I've got wet plans—for you." He pushed to his knees and shoved mine wider apart. The stricken look that passed through his features happened so fast I nearly missed it. It echoed what I felt inside.

He looked at me like he would never see me again.

I lightly scored my nails down his chest and abdomen.

His pupils blew wider, but he didn't move. "I need to watch you come."

Lust hit hard, but it was tinged with sadness. Would this really be our last time?

He propped a foot on the floor and leaned forward enough to cup his hands against my breasts. "You know what I'm going to think about when I jack off in my new place?"

I moaned at the rasp of his palms over my nipples and wrapped my hands around his wrists.

"This," he said roughly. "These tits and how they fill my hands." He skimmed his fingers down my torso, outlining my stomach and stopping at my lower abdomen. "The little swell that Bean makes." A shadow passed over his face.

Was he thinking about how he wouldn't see how big I'd get? Would he miss it? Would he have moved on by then?

Instead of thinking about that, I covered his hands, framing my baby belly with mine. "You'll still be able to talk to Bean. Anytime you want."

"Just not when you're naked."

"Not naked." I chuckled, and his gaze hooked on how my boobs jiggled.

He continued his trek, snagging my hand on the way down. My fingers twined with his. "Show me how you're going to touch yourself."

This would be the second time he watched me. The first was in that hotel bathroom. Now it was because he wouldn't be able to touch me when we weren't living together.

The hungry look in his gaze prompted me to slick my finger farther down. He stayed with me the whole way. Wet heat surrounded my finger, and I found my clit. Pleasure pumped through me.

Rolling my hips into our touch, my eyelids fluttered.

"Fuck, sweet Clover. Show me how you're going to get off when you're not with me."

"I'm going to do this." I undulated my hips with the rhythm. "And I'll think about when you use your tongue and your finger at the same time." I was going to be thinking about him. The whole time.

He ran his hands up and down my thighs. "Push a finger inside you."

I shifted to ditch my clit and do just that. His intake of breath when my finger disappeared inside me heightened the sensation. "How tight are you?"

"I...don't know." I didn't have any experience outside of my own body.

As if he sensed my logical brain wiping out the passion, he threaded his index finger inside next to mine. I could feel myself inside and out, but I could only feel him in a weird mix that flooded me with more heat.

A hard groan left him. "So fucking tight. So damn wet. No shower is going to replicate this." He thrust in and out. "Rub your clit."

I did as he asked. Pleasure ping-ponged through my veins and built within my belly. As I circled faster and paired with his thrusts, I cranked closer to the top of a cliff I'd gladly fling myself off.

"Fuck, I can't wait." He removed his hand, but before I could whimper at the emptiness he left behind, he stroked up and down his hard erection. "Keep going."

I hadn't realized I'd stalled. I resumed my pace, and he drove inside.

"Van!"

His growl was his only response before he started pumping. Our grunts and moans filled the living room as we each pushed the other closer to climax. He bracketed my hips and devoured me with his eyes.

We'd had a lot of sex, but this was different. The lights were on, there was nothing between us, and we knew it'd be one of the last times together, if not the last time.

I backed away from my peak as a wave of melancholy crashed over me, but he put his thumb on my finger, adding pressure to my clit.

I was back on the edge and teetering. "Oh God."

"That's it, my sweet Clover. Let yourself go."

It was the way he'd added to my nickname that shoved me over the edge. "Van!"

Ecstasy rolled over me in wave after wave, like the most blissful electrocution imaginable. I clenched down on him, and at some point, I ended up holding his hand instead of working on myself. The tips of my fingers grazed the slick flesh of his cock, but we held still, our breaths sawing in and out of us.

His gaze traveled from where we were connected, up to my face, and back down. "Well," he said quietly, "that should get me through a few shower sessions."

Chapter Twenty-One

Van

It shouldn't be this easy to get divorced.

"I've seen a lot of divorces," Mr. Sewell said, his hands folded on his desk. His office wasn't what I'd expect for a lawyer. The old house he worked out of creaked more than his chair. The inside could be as nice as the Perez house, and at one time it probably was, but the wood varnish had long worn off, and the walls were a shade of yellow that time could only paint. "But this is one of the easiest, and you two don't hate each other."

"Thanks?" Clover said nervously.

I let out a small chuckle and caught her eyes. Last night had been amazing. This morning, we couldn't sleep, so I pulled her into the shower. One last time. Our last time.

"I'm glad you could stop in today." He grinned, flashing pristine white teeth. His hair had been freshly trimmed, and he was wearing a polo and khakis. "I've gotta get to Bismarck to catch a flight."

His December in Turks and Caicos would be more pleasurable than mine in my new rental.

Why did I turn down Christmas with the Dukes? It'd probably be warm and inviting and relaxing. Good food and better people.

I had to. The more I clung to Clover, the more she'd have to drag me around. She'd been held back long enough.

He rose and shook our hands before shuffling us out of the office. We stood on the front stoop as the door clicked shut behind us.

"Well," she said, tucking her face into the collar of her coat, "that was fast."

I should protect my face from the bite of the wind, but the pain was welcome right now. "And easy."

Her faint giggle carried across the yard. "Aunt Linda texted and said you could just leave your set of keys in the house. She'll get in through the garage."

"I'll put them by yours."

Her set of keys was on the island. The movers were coming, and then I would do a quick cleaning. Until then, I was helping Clover unload her things into her apartment. Her siblings had pitched together a spare bed, a dresser, and a scattering of furniture. Jasper has supplied the most, insisting he would have to store it if he moved in with me.

"Okay." Her smile was tight. "Thank you for closing out the house."

"Thank you for marrying me."

Her soft laugh echoed the sad sting in my chest.

This was it. We'd just drive away from each other and resume living separate lives. That had been so much easier before I knew what being married to her would be like.

Yet I wasn't ready to completely part ways. I hadn't

been married before, and the whole divorce-papers thing messed with my mind. "Ready for some breakfast?"

The bathroom quickie had pushed us closer to our appointment than I had meant it to, but she'd insisted that she wasn't that hungry.

She pressed her hands to her stomach over her blue-and-white jacket. The material crinkled. "I could definitely eat something heartier than a banana."

"I've got some time. Wanna go to the diner?"

Her smile came out like the sun peeking through the clouds overhead. "I haven't eaten there since I've been back. Let's go."

I hated driving different cars, but it only took a few minutes until we were both parked outside the small diner downtown. Several spots were open. The morning rush was gone, but a few older people having their morning coffee could be seen through the windows.

Clover got out, and I scrambled to meet her by the front. I held the door open for her.

"It smells delicious," Clover said as she passed.

"Morning," the server called. She was about my mom's age, wearing jeans and a gray sweatshirt and a name tag that said Joni. "Have a seat anywhere."

I led Clover to a booth by the window. We sat across from each other, and silence descended between us. Joni delivered two glasses of water, said she'd be right back, and scurried away.

I let my attention wander up and down the street of my new hometown. My rental house was several blocks away. Tonight would be the farthest I'd slept from her since she returned from her work trip.

Clover put her chin in her hand. "It's not Omaha."

"No." Coal Haven's main street didn't stretch much

more than five or six blocks. "To be fair, I wasn't getting out much in Omaha."

Joni appeared. "Hello." She tapped her pen against her notepad. "I'm gonna be that guy and ask if you're the new couple that moved into the old place where the Henkes leased the pastures."

Clover's eyes lit and then died. Did she recall the papers we'd signed this morning? "Yes. Actually, we aren't together like that."

Joni peeked at Clover's ring finger. "Oh, dang. I'm sorry. I presumed too much, and that's why I shouldn't open my mouth."

"No, it's fine. We were mar— We're just friends."

We *were* married.

Joni smiled. "That's sweet. One of you is a Duke, right?"

She chatted a little more, mining for information that would likely get passed along to regulars, like the ones sipping their coffee. Then she took our order and was gone again.

"We're going to be the talk of the town," she whispered.

"I think we already are."

"Now they'll just be confused." She scrubbed her face with a hand and checked her phone. "Jasper said he's on the way with a load of furniture. That'll give me time to pick up kitchen utensils, and I'll work all night to catch up."

"Same." I wouldn't concentrate well today. "When's your next appointment?"

"I have one next Monday."

"I can go with you."

"Oh, you don't have to."

I wanted to. "Clover," I said gently. "I'm in town now."

"I never know how long I'm going to be waiting, and

you're so close to getting everything shored up for all your pitch meetings."

"I'm ready for those." I had some polishing to do on my programs, but I wasn't worried. I should have been, but I wasn't. "What time?"

"I got one right at eight."

"I'll be there." A knot loosened in my chest. I had another date set to see her.

"And Christmas?" she asked. "You still have other plans? You're always welcome at Poppy's."

"I've got plans," I lied. I'd spent the day alone before. This year would be no different. Only it felt like the loneliness would crush me. But that was for me to deal with, not her or her family.

She narrowed her eyes. "Do you have plans for Christmas Eve?"

I gave my head a little shake. My parents usually went out, and Elijah had never included me in his life, not that I would've joined him. I should tell her I was tied up. She hadn't asked what, so I hadn't had to lie even more. But I could only be so strong. "No. Nothing for Christmas Eve."

"Then come over. We'll have pizza. I don't want to ruin a big dinner for you the next day."

A dinner for one. "Are you inviting me to your place for Christmas Eve out of pity?" Did I care? I'd give her all the space she wanted, but I'd take whatever scraps she left me. It was to stay in Bean's life.

And hers.

A divot formed between her brows. "Would you be joining me out of pity?"

"Not at all." The last thing I felt around Clover Duke was pity. "Christmas Eve is yours."

❧

Clover

I pulled up in front of the clinic. I didn't see Van's truck. He offered to pick me up, but I was on my journey of being on my own.

Mostly, I was missing him, and a strong sense of home-sickness would not let up. My first week living in my new place sucked as much as it was liberating. For one, I did it. I was doing it. I had a nursery. The baby had a roof over its head.

I had an old bed that used to be Laila's, but she'd upgraded to a bigger size. The living room was filled with a love seat and a recliner. Neither matched. Jasper even brought me a TV he claimed he didn't use anymore. Either he bought it for me, or Alder did. Perhaps my parents.

I should've turned them down so I could accomplish it myself, but it left me with more money to outfit the nurs-ery. Except Haven Furnishings delivered the perfect dresser–changing station combo. Thanks to Van.

Mom called every day to check on me. I assured her that I had lived on my own pre-Elijah days, and I could do it again. But working at my little round table I found in the thrift store and not seeing Van walk by was a constant shadow on each day. He'd texted to check in, and I'd had to refrain from sending him something every day.

I would get to see him today.

I gathered my things and was about to get out when he pulled in. His expression was thunderous. He had his phone to his ear, and his lips were moving with enough force I'd be able to read them as he drove by if I had the skill.

I dropped my hand off the door latch. Was he running into issues with his business? Was he missing something important because of this?

He parked a spot away from me and threw his pickup into park. Resting an elbow on the window, he kept the phone to his face. His other hand punctuated the air several times.

Fuck you. I could read that.

He punched the screen with a finger and then slammed his phone against the steering wheel.

Oh no. All that hard work he'd been doing. Was it all down the drain?

My phone buzzed. I'd tossed it into my purse when I loaded into my cold car.

I dug for it. Who could be calling? Was my doctor canceling for some reason? I'd miss out on an hour with Van, but at least I'd get to see him.

There was a knock on the window, and I jumped, barking out a cry.

"Don't answer it." His muffled voice carried through the glass.

I stopped with my phone in my hand. "What? Why?"

He opened the door, and cold air gusted in. "It's Elijah."

I dropped the damn thing back into the depths of my purse. "What? Why?" My vocabulary shrank to two words. Elijah? Calling?

"He's found out about us."

"How?"

Van shrugged. "Maybe some of the town gossip hit socials. He's pissed as hell." My phone continued vibrating in my bag. "Don't answer. He's being a bigger asshole than normal."

Before, I wouldn't have been able to imagine what Van could mean. How could he be worse than usual? But after hearing how Van grew up, and what happened as adults, I could fill in the blanks.

"That selfish prick has no right to harass us." I snatched my phone up without looking. Elijah's name streaked across the screen, and it brought back memories. Mostly of when I was in the hotel room in Vegas and couldn't get a hold of him. The hurt and fury lifted to the top of my brain.

"Clover, don't. The things he's saying—"

"Hello, Mrs. Wagner speaking."

"Mrs. *Wag*— Clover? Is that fucking you? How could you—"

"Excuse me?" I said politely. "I don't speak to little men who ditch women right before a wedding to run off with a stranger."

"I didn't—"

"And don't think you can call me and demand any answers. You lost that right when you got handcuffed and fucked around."

"I—"

"Do *not* for one second think I will let you back in my life."

"What about my kid?"

A giant palpitation jumped in my chest. So he had gotten that message. A pressure lifted off my shoulders. I wouldn't be the one to hide his kid from him. Elijah had to be an adult and think of more than himself. Or not.

"Do you want to see your kid?" There was a pause, and as much as it stung that I'd gotten pregnant by such a poor choice of a dad, I'd capitalize on it. "Do you want to *pay* for your kid? Are you going to put money away for college for this kid?"

More silence.

Figured. What a jackass. I had seen my siblings pairing off, and I'd wanted to join them so bad I picked a man like Elijah. "I know everything, by the way. Not just the cheating, but the lying. And now you're just mad because two people you've hurt to make yourself feel better teamed up and fixed some of the damage you did. So, unless you want to start paying child support, I would recommend not stepping one foot back into the country. As soon as the sole of your shoe hits US dirt, I'm going to find you, and I'm going to drain your wallet for the next eighteen years. And with Van's help, I will find you."

Van smirked, pride radiating across his face.

"What you can do," I continued, "is email me within forty-eight hours and let me know if you want a role in this kid's life. Otherwise, it'll just be mine, and you owe us nothing."

I didn't want to take the chance that he'd decide to turn a new leaf in five years or ten years. I wanted all the power if he ever dealt with Bean. I could no longer trust him, and I'd do everything I could to protect us.

"I assume you didn't lose my email address during your drunken honeymoon?"

"I can't believe you married my fucking brother." His seething snaked through the line.

"I can't believe you'd fuck his girlfriend. Oh wait—I can."

"He's lying." There was that petulant tone, the one Elijah used when he was busted for not being completely truthful. I'd heard it at enough cocktail gatherings.

"Between the guy who left me pregnant and broke at the altar and the one who's been there for me through everything, I think I know who to believe. Goodbye, Elijah. Tell your new wife she has my condolences." I hung up and then, for good measure, I blocked his number. We'd communicate in writing from now on and only about Bean.

"Holy shit, Clover." A cloud blew out of Van's mouth with his laugh. "You gave him no way to weasel out of his excuses." He held out his hand, and I gripped it to get out of the car. "I wish I could've done that."

"I had warning, thanks to you."

His gaze softened. "How've you been?"

Lonely. I missed waking up to him. Falling asleep next to him. I even missed the pillow wall since he'd been on the other side. But I'd just told my ex off and got some closure on a shitty situation. Small steps. I could do this.

But I didn't have to do it completely alone. "By the time this appointment is done, my toast will have burned off. I owe you breakfast this time."

The corner of his mouth tipped up. "I could always eat. Since I'm not accountable for meals, I haven't cooked much."

"Well then. Let's go give Joni and the coffee drinkers something to talk about."

Together, we walked toward the entrance, our shoulders nearly touching.

Chapter Twenty-Two

Van

It might be the end of my workday, but I checked my schedule for the tenth time today. After Clover's appointment last week, the admin reviewed her upcoming appointments. There was no way I could join Clover for even a small part of the next ultrasound visit and make it to my first investor meeting.

There had to be a way.

I scrubbed a hand down my face and spun around in my chair. My office was upstairs in the house I was renting. It was all one open space, and Jasper promised he'd only need a bedroom. I didn't believe him, but I was flexible. I was actually looking forward to his arrival, which wouldn't be until the new year.

I folded my hands and gazed out the small port window. The place was old, but it had charm, and Alder had restored it nicely inside. Jensen said he'd done the cabinets for him and also helped lay new flooring in the kitchen after they discovered water damage.

This place was a dream to work in. Yet each morning, I woke up and stared at the popcorn ceiling, willing myself to get out of bed.

This was the first time since my breakup with my ex that I was truly alone. I hadn't liked living with my parents, and as aggravating and interfering as they'd been, they were still human interaction. Since I had no clients yet and was only peddling my business to potential investors, I had myself for company.

My parents had tried contacting me for the first time. Elijah had likely gotten to them.

Now I had them all blocked. As far as I was concerned, my only family would be Bean.

The whole situation was an adjustment, and I missed Clover. I missed seeing her stuff in the bathroom. I missed having her in bed next to me. I missed those breathy moans when she came.

That fast, I was hard and aching. I pushed at my dick like that'd help. Only one thing would, and jacking off in the shower wasn't it. I spun back around to face my monitors. They had gone blank.

Another evening with nothing to do.

I could go to Bismarck for a Pokémon tournament, but a few snowflakes drifted past the glass. The roads might be slick.

The doorbell rang.

Was it Clover? I raced downstairs. It didn't matter that there was no reason for her to call me. I sprinted across the house to the front door, but when I opened it, there was no one there. A box sat on the welcome mat.

Clover's Christmas gift that I'd ordered. She hadn't said

not to exchange any, and we were friends. She was damn near my only friend.

Just then my phone buzzed.

I grabbed the package and looked at the phone. Jasper's name appeared, and my heart sank. I had more friends than just Clover, but they were all her relatives. Thanks to her, I had them in my life. But I'd rather she was on the other side of this line.

"Hey, Jasper."

"Do you have my bed warm, or do we have to share like you did with my sister?"

"She required a pillow wall."

"No kidding?"

He didn't have to know how long it lasted. "And she cooked every other night."

"I can handle that, but you might get sick of steak."

"Challenge accepted. Do you like popcorn and brownies like your sister?"

He chuckled. "You're going to have to specify which one."

I liked all of his sisters, but there was only one I dreamed about.

"I was calling to let you know that I paid Alder for half of December's rent, but I'll be there a little later in January than I thought."

He didn't have to pay for half of December, but I'd been around him enough to know arguing wouldn't change his mind. "Thanks for the warning. I can walk around naked until then."

He snorted on the other end. "I've lived around a bunch of cowboys for years. Nudity is part of the territory. No need to let me stop you. I'm sure it's freeing after living with my sister."

"Yeah, right." Did my laugh sound as nervous to him as it did to me? My last night on the couch with Clover claimed the forefront of my mind.

"See you at Christmas, Van."

We disconnected, but I kept my phone, staring at it. Talking to Jasper had been a nice reprieve from the quiet house, but he hadn't given me any new info on Clover.

Fuck it. It was snowing, and she was on the other side of town. I called her.

"Hey," she answered, and all sorts of knots loosened inside of me at the sound of her voice. She sounded happy, and that was all I wanted.

Not quite all. Happy under the same roof as me would be better. Like she'd told my brother, I'm there for her. She just didn't want me there *with* her.

"Hi. It's snowing." I winced at the way I blurted it out. "The forecast said four to six inches."

"Yeah, I bought a couple of shovels. Different-sized ones."

"I'll dig you out."

"You don't have—" She sighed. "I'd appreciate it. I was maybe regretting getting the option with no garage."

"If you have to get anywhere, I'll pick you up." Since I had the better vehicle.

"No. Nowhere."

"Me either." I draped my hand across the back of my neck and paced the hallway. I wasn't ready to get off the phone. I had a long, Clover-less night ahead of me. "Your brother called. Jasper. He's moving in the middle of January."

"And then all the Dukes will be reunited."

"Yeah. Elijah hasn't bothered you since last week?"

"Not a peep, and no email. I'm going to be the sole

parent. I mean, he can always try to prove his parental status, and if he does, well, there'd be no money in it for him."

"So he'd have to be actually interested in his kid to go through that effort."

"Exactly." Another long exhale. "I might be a single mom, but I'm going to be a mama bear."

"Good."

"Yeah." Dishes clinked on the other end.

"What are you making?"

"Spaghetti. I'm having a major carb craving. What about you?"

"No plans yet. Are you making meatballs?"

"I thought I'd work it into my busy social life," she said wryly.

I didn't mean to let my groan slip out. "Homemade sauce?"

"Actually, yes. I've had it simmering for a while, and now I have a portion set aside to cool and freeze."

Hunger rumbled in my stomach, but it wasn't the food I was craving. "Sounds good."

"Do you... Would you like to come over?"

Yes. Goddammit, yes. But how much did I crowd her? She was being nice. Thoughtful as always.

Christmas Eve was soon enough. I should wait until then. Prove I could get through tonight without seeing her.

She hadn't been going to invite me until I had called. I would continue to be there for her in the way she needed me to be. "Thanks, but I'll stay in. You can feed me after I dig you out."

I could only be strong so long.

"Deal. I'll keep some in the fridge so I can cook while you're working."

Once the last flake fell, I'd be there.

❧

Clover

It ended up snowing closer to ten inches, but the temperature climbed high enough once the storm passed that much of it was already melting. Which also meant the snow was heavier.

I peered out the living room window. Van was outside, carving a path from my parking spot to the road. He'd already cleared the sidewalk and the steps.

I had meatballs and sauce warming on the stove. I'd cook the pasta as soon as he was done, and I had brownies in the oven. Honestly, I was so damn glad not to have to shovel, I'd make him anything. I'd give him a blow job.

Who was I kidding? I'd do that anyway. My hormones were going wilder than when I was in my first trimester. It was Bean's fault I was this bothered watching a man with every inch of skin covered do manual labor in my front yard. He was in black snow pants and a black winter coat. His gloves were black with red panels, and he'd pulled his black hat down low. Van looked like the most sinister snow removal service ever, and it was a bigger turn-on than I could've anticipated.

He paused and propped a hand on the shovel handle, surveying his work. From my post in the living room, I could see his chest heaving. Those muscles I used to be able to have my hands on were getting a workout, and it wasn't from me.

He carefully leaned the shovel against my car and took

his gloves off. Then he shrugged out of his winter coat. I stayed riveted to the cool glass as if he was stripping all his layers off.

Need ripped through me until I half gasped, half cried. He wasn't mine anymore.

He never was. We'd had an arrangement, and I had to be able to leave that behind. I could do this.

He tossed his coat onto the hood of my car, hitched up his snow pants, put his gloves back on, and continued shoveling. And I continued staring out the window, my breasts heavy and desire pooling between my legs.

Ugh, I had it bad.

What would be the harm?

A Van who was free to go anywhere and do anything once his business took off. The company I wasn't going to stand in the way of.

Van's job would take off. I'd have a broken heart.

The oven beeped, and I left my post. He had to have seen me gawking at him like the worst stalker in the world.

Was he going to Bismarck for Pokémon tournaments? He hadn't said, but then why would he? Wanting to keep him wasn't the same as being his keeper.

Was he meeting new people? New women?

None of my business.

I took the brownies out and forced myself to stay away from the window. I could do this. I could be friends with Van. He was Bean's uncle. We were family.

The sour taste in my mouth wouldn't go away, so I dug out a glass of milk.

The front door opened. "You are now free to leave your property," Van called from the entry.

I rushed out like I couldn't miss one second of him in my place. His hat and gloves were off, and his jacket was already hung up next to mine. I took a mental snapshot for my wishful-thinking folder. He stomped snow off his boots, toed out of them, and shucked his snow pants.

When he saw me, he grinned. "I'll try not to get your floor wet."

"For all the work you did, I'll forgive you if you do."

He straightened and ran the back of his hand across his forehead. "Now I need a shower."

His hair was a little longer than when I moved out, but he'd gotten it trimmed recently. I clenched my hands together so I wouldn't walk right over and run my fingers through his damp strands.

"I'll put the pasta on. Relax and warm up." I had to retreat to the kitchen. Seeing him in my living room flipped my heart all the way around. Couldn't I even make it through a month? I was no longer dependent on his help to keep a roof over my head, and I should be euphoric about that. But all that resonated inside me was loss.

After I got the pasta going, he wandered to the kitchen table. "Did everything come from Jasper?"

"Most of it. I thrifted the table, and I have my eye on a nice living room set at Haven Furnishings, but I'm going to wait until after the holidays."

He tapped the surface of the table. "It's nice."

The kitchen was so much smaller when he was in it, and I didn't mind.

"Where's your office?" he asked.

"Right where you're standing, but I put it away."

"You didn't have to."

"Then it's a real day off." One full of winter eye candy. "Sit. You've been working. How's your back? Your knee?"

"As long as I don't slip and fall, they'll be okay. I

messaged Linda and asked if she wanted me to clear out the driveway at the house."

At *our* house. A weight plopped right on my chest. Tears pricked the backs of my eyes. How nice would it have been to ride out a snowstorm with Van?

I flashed back to the Vegas hotel room, getting told my fiancé ran off with another woman he'd just met. The hurt. The embarrassment.

How easy it was to forget that Van witnessed it.

I might've told Elijah off, but it was in a *your brother took care of me when you wouldn't* way. Wasn't exactly empowering—unless I was Van.

I had given up everything when Elijah asked me to. I couldn't do it again.

"Something wrong?" His deep voice cleared the cloud of my thoughts, and I blinked.

I was watching water boil. "Oh, no. Just thinking about the weather and if I should park on the street next time."

"It's a toss-up."

"How's work going?"

"I just keep writing and rewriting my pitch." He scratched the back of his neck. "I've fucked it up once, and they already know the deal. I know meeting them in person is more about proving I'm serious and making sure I'm not a mess."

"You're the least messy person I've ever met."

"Only because you met me when you did."

He'd changed himself. So hot. "I still think you're hard on yourself."

"Nope. The breakup was messy." He took the lid off the meatballs and groaned. "You're only getting better at making these."

I straightened my shoulders, and my boobs pushed out. "Thank you."

When I glanced over, his gaze was on my chest. He jerked away to inspect the rest of the kitchen.

Did we really have to stop messing around?

Yes. I'd fall for him, he'd launch his business, then he'd meet someone else. Someone who was having his baby, not his brother's.

The water finally boiled. I dumped the pasta in and set the table. Van jumped in without asking, probably because I would've told him to sit. We talked about superficial stuff, mostly our work and my family, as we ate. When he finished, he refused to sit while I cleaned up.

"You don't make a very good guest," I finally said when he blocked me from washing dishes.

He grinned and kept scrubbing. His sleeves were rolled up. As if I didn't need more reminders of all the parts of him I liked. All the bits of him I'd had my mouth on.

I boosted myself on the counter next to the drying rack. "Have you gone to Bismarck again?"

"Why?"

I stroked my gaze along the width of his shoulders, glad he was paying attention to the dishes. "Pokémon."

"Oh. No. Maybe when I get back."

"When you're rolling in all that investor cash?"

"Those fanboys are going to have to watch out for me."

"Or all the pretty Pokémon players." Where had that come from? No, I knew from where, but why did the question leave my mouth?

He made circles with the dishrag on a plate. "You think I'm there to pick up women?"

Well, there weren't a lot, but if he met someone there,

they would start with something healthier in common than he and I had. "You might meet your soulmate."

He frowned and drew back. I got one blink from him, then he focused back on the dishes. "My soulmate?"

"It's a given I'm not going to date for a while, but nothing's stopping you." It was hard to talk around the lump in my throat and sound casual.

He stopped again to look at me. His gaze was carefully neutral. "No, I guess not." He rinsed the plate, a furrow in his brow. "Except for all the men at the tournaments."

"I'm just saying."

"Noted."

Erase that note, dammit.

He dipped his hand in the soapy water and came up with forks. "I thought I was supposed to be staying away from women who might tank my company."

"Right." I smiled from the small surge of triumph. Was he on a hiatus too? "But after you attract all those new investors, it'll be smooth sailing."

"Then I'll need clients."

"That'll be easy. You're the best."

He blew out a soft breath. "You don't really know what I do."

"You're still the best."

He ran water over the forks and shook them out. Once they were in the drying rack, he didn't go for another dirty dish. He wiped his hands and stopped in front of me. "You have that much faith in me?"

I nodded, loving how close he was. If we were at the other house, I could twine my arms around his neck. We'd be naked and fucking in less than five minutes, and only because the man liked his foreplay.

I liked his foreplay.

Gripping the edge of the counter, I swallowed. "I do."

He worked his jaw back and forth, his gaze narrowing on me. "My soulmate will have the same faith in me."

Acid washed into my throat. "Even more, probably." The tears threatened to gather in my eyes again. To cover for my reaction, I gave him a playful shove in the shoulder. "Buddy."

Shock passed over his face a second before he choked on a laugh. "Sweet Clover, did you just call me 'buddy'?"

"Maybe," I said with a giggle. "Just trying to talk you up."

"I don't need a wingman," he said quietly. "I just need a friend like you."

"You have me." As a friend, and nothing more.

Chapter Twenty-Three

Clover

Poppy stepped inside my house. "Wow, it's small."

I shot her a scowl. "You say that every time."

"I've only been here once."

She'd stopped by another time to give me some presents to hide from her family. According to her, Jensen had accidentally found her stash twice. "I know it's small, but it's all I need."

She didn't follow up on her dubious look and held up a paper bag that smelled delicious. The Rattler's logo—a rattlesnake around a beer mug—was on the outside. "Girls' night."

Grinning, I led her to the kitchen. "Girls' night is going to end much earlier than it used to."

"Us soon-to-be mamas gotta get our beauty sleep."

My gasp rattled the walls. "Is that your way of telling me you're pregnant?"

She nodded furiously. "Yes!"

I clutched her arms and we jumped around, screeching and cheering. This was how it was supposed to be. Good news. Joy. Celebrating. I didn't get this reveal, but I'd give it to her.

"I'm so happy for you," I cried. "I have so many questions, but let's eat first."

When we were seated at the table, and I had a container with steak bites and mashed potatoes opened in front of me, I inhaled a contented breath. "Smells delicious."

"Haven't you been eating well?" She dropped her gaze to my belly like it was going to shrink right in front of her as a testament to how much I didn't cook for myself.

"Yes. Not quite like when I was living with Van, but I cook." I stuck a fork into a steak bite. "If Van hadn't come over the other night, I would be so sick of spaghetti leftovers. I miss going out once in a while. I should see if he's free one night. Maybe New Year's Eve." I stuffed the food into my mouth and groaned over the flavor.

Poppy stared at me.

"What?" I asked around my savory mouthful.

"That's a lot of Van you're talking about."

"He's a friend."

A brown brow ticked up. "He's your ex-husband."

Don't remind me. "You know what that was about."

She took a bite of her mashed potatoes, but her gaze didn't stray from me.

I didn't know what to say without inciting more questions about him. If I talked too much, Poppy would keep digging until she found the rare gem that was how I felt about him and had kept buried nice and deep.

I continued to gobble my dinner. "How are you feeling?" I asked around a bite.

Her expression turned stubborn. "Avoiding the subject won't help."

"I'm not avoiding anything."

She pushed her food away and crossed her arms. "How close did you get?"

"I told you. We're friends."

"I didn't believe you then. So you were messing around and caught feelings."

She read me too easily—or thought she did. But she was happily married and settled in life. I was embarking on a new adventure. She didn't understand. She took care of herself before she got with Jensen. I was the one with something to prove.

"We lived together." Why was I insisting on downplaying everything? Talking about it might make me process everything, help me move on from reliving so much of the months we lived together. "Okay, yes. I really like him. He's who I should've been with from the beginning, but it's too late. Now I have a life to build, and so does he. I'm not holding him back."

"Is that what you think you'd be doing?"

"You don't know his history, but he's lost everything before. Because of a woman. Because of his brother."

She dropped her fork and leaned toward me. "So now you're both just going to be lonely because of that douche?"

"Yes! Wait—no? That's not what it is." How wasn't it? The reason seemed important. "I'm trying not to be dependent on a guy, yet the guy I wouldn't mind leaning on can leave at any moment, and he probably will. He should. He deserves it."

Her back thumped against the chair. "I can't believe I didn't know you were going through all this."

"You have your own life."

"But you didn't talk to me."

"Van had to message you last time." I didn't mean to say it so bitterly, but there it was. I pressed my fingertips to my temples. "Sorry. We're both adults with our own lives. I clamped myself to Elijah, and it was the worst decision of my life." But it was also the best. I was in the town I grew up in with the rest of my family. I had a good job. I was going to be a mom. So many changes. "At the very least, it was life changing."

"Are you afraid he's going to be like Elijah?" Sympathy shimmered in her eyes.

There was no way Van would ever be like his brother. "I'm telling you that he'll be so successful that he'll run his work online, move to the Bahamas, and never look back."

"Is that what he said?"

No. He was staying in Coal Haven. But for how long? "You're missing the point. He can do anything now. He was stuck living at home with his awful parents after his ex slept with Elijah and blew up the first company."

"Elijah fucked his brother's girlfriend?"

I nodded. My righteous rage was satisfied at how scandalized my sister sounded. "Van's a catch. Any girl he lands would be so damn lucky."

"But you caught him."

"No, I didn't," I mumbled, miserable. We talked about him finding his soulmate. "I'm not going to manipulate him like everyone else has in his life. He's important to me, and that's why I'm not going to tie him down."

She crossed her arms, her food forgotten. "What if he's lying down and holding the ropes?"

I scoffed and pushed mashed potatoes around. "He's not."

"He's living in Coal Haven, and Jasper's moving in with him," she said pointedly.

"It's his launchpad."

She shook her head. "You're just afraid."

Terrified, but that wasn't the real issue. "Poppy, if he fell head over heels in love, don't you think he would've said so? He hasn't. He's been a good friend. He's a red-blooded male who wanted sex. Then he moved into his own place. I'm not throwing myself at a guy just to bounce off him. I'm not putting myself in that position again. I'm making my own home, saving my own money, and raising this kid with only my name on the birth certificate."

"Oh, Clover. I would hate for you to miss out on something really special because of what Elijah did."

"Bean is special. I'll have that."

She drew her brows together. "I don't like it."

Neither did I, but Van seemed satisfied with how everything was going, and that was without me as his girlfriend. "I'm happy, and we're still friends. He was over the other night for dinner, and we kept our hands off each other." It seemed easy for him. "He's coming over for Christmas Eve."

"What's he doing on Christmas Day?"

"I don't know." It was like I was breathing through a damp washcloth. I wasn't his wife, and I didn't get to know his plans. "Maybe he's found someone already."

"Pssht. He has not."

"He turned down your invite, and he hasn't said what he's doing. It's not my business." Either it was another woman, or he didn't want to be with me. Didn't matter which one, the outcome was the same.

She let out a small sigh. "And you're ringing in New Year's Day alone?"

"It'll be better than last year." I'd been recovering from bronchitis, and Elijah had insisted he couldn't go out with friends alone. For some reason, staying home alone with me hadn't been an option, so I'd let him drag me out.

She exhaled a gusty sigh. "I guess if it works."

"Yes, it does. We're friends."

She picked up her fork and stabbed into a piece of beef. "You're so stubborn."

For the security of me and Bean, yes, I would be.

Van

My third attempt at wrapping the present for Clover was the best. The seams were still crooked, but it was covered. I held it and knocked on her door.

She opened it, dressed in an oversized cream knit sweater and red plaid leggings. Her hair was gathered behind her in a loose bun.

My mouth went dry. "Damn."

She looked behind her. "The tree? It's sad, isn't it?"

What tree? Behind her was a small tree that didn't reach two feet tall. The fake green needles were barely visible under the garland and silver and red ornaments.

"The tree isn't sad at all. It matches you." Only I didn't want to strip the tree down. I didn't want to lift its garland and see how big the baby belly had gotten. I didn't want to frame my hands around the tree and imagine a life with it.

But she was thriving on her own. Her cheeks glowed, and she looked as sweet as a Christmas cookie.

"Come in."

When I stepped inside, a familiar smell reached my nose. "Oh good, the pizza arrived."

"Thank you for doing that."

"No problem." I passed her the gift, wincing at the crooked wrapping.

"I knew it. I got you something too." She smiled and put the gift under the tree next to another box of a similar size.

"You thought I'd come over on Christmas Eve without a gift?"

"No, and that's why I made sure to get you something. I would've anyway though."

I knew that too. I followed her into the kitchen. She'd put up a few drawings on the fridge. One was from Auggie of Santa with a soccer ball, and another from Cali of a Christmas tree with a bright star above it. A third was hard to make out, much less have a signature of any kind.

"I like your decorations."

"Thank you. I kept it low-key this year. Next year, they'll have to be babyproof."

A radiant Clover with a seven-month-old crawling around wasn't the gut punch I expected, but I had to put a hand to my stomach. I'd better fucking be here for that.

By this time next year, would she be ready to let a guy into her life? Into Bean's? In more than an uncle capacity?

You might meet your soulmate.

Those words had killed a lot of lingering hope inside me, but clearly not all of it had been shut down.

Buddy.

Fuck me.

My nerves were ramping up. Would she like her gift?

Would she think it was kiddish? She'd been cool about Pokémon, but dammit, I didn't know anymore. The anticipation about my investor meetings was killing me. Realizing how empty my life was now that I was out of Omaha and didn't have to weather my family bugged the crap out of me. And being friends with Clover? Well, that was stressful.

I ate pizza, and we chatted about our week. I didn't have more to add. Anything I wanted to say would make it all worse.

Do you know how much I miss you?

Do you think you could make room in your life for me?

What if I ran my company from an office that isn't far from yours and we raised Bean together and maybe had more?

It was the holidays, warping my conviction. Tomorrow, I'd be on the couch, watching movies, only I wouldn't have Clover with me. I wouldn't be carrying her to bed. The thought was messing me up, threatening to make me cave. I had to hold strong. She needed Uncle Van, not needy Van.

She wiped her mouth with a napkin. "Poppy called a couple of days ago. They're having trouble with their septic system, so my parents are hosting instead. So I'm going to Billings for a night. I'm riding with Poppy."

The heaviness inside me crowded my lungs. "Good. That'll be fun."

"Are you sure you don't want to come with us? I could drive."

I wanted very much to hop in and drive to Billings. But then I'd have to reveal that I had lied, and I was over looking pathetic, especially around Clover. "Thanks, but I've got a full day planned."

I had nothing to do. Good thing she hadn't asked what the hell I was doing. What would I say? *Trying to make sure you don't have to entertain me.* I could've said a Christmas Day Pokémon tournament, if those existed. A tournament for those of us who were trying not to gauge whether or not a day was good or bad by how much he saw his girl smile.

She searched my face like she sensed I was lying. How could I have barely known this woman until four months ago, but she could read me better than anyone?

"Are you taking a trailer to haul all the gifts?" I asked lightly.

She laughed and rested her hand on the top of her baby belly. There was enough of a ledge now. She was getting bigger, and I was missing it.

I'd seen her once a week since we'd moved out.

"No, everyone said they'd exchange at home and pitch in to do something fun for the kids in Billings, like rent a room for a few days so we can play at a pool. With a big family, it gets to be too much stuff if we exchange gifts."

"Fair."

Sitting at the table and eating with her felt off. This wasn't the right table, the right room, or the right house. It was the same sense I got each time I walked into my rental. It was off. The silence was off. Not having any clacking away at a keyboard that wasn't me was off. My mood would turn dour if I continued on this line of thinking.

"I thawed some Christmas cookies." She retrieved a plate from the counter and took the plastic wrap off.

"I forgot how much you all made." But I remembered how nice that day had been. The best Thanksgiving I'd ever had.

Good thing I wasn't going with her tomorrow. I'd probably beg to become a Duke, and that wasn't fair to her.

"Which is your favorite?" She picked through the selection, settling on a sugar cookie.

"You know I'm a sucker for the kisses."

"Hershey's are the best."

"Sure." One kiss ranked higher, and that was everyone with her. I plucked a cookie off the plate and popped it into my mouth. Then I dusted my fingers off. I might be unsure about my gift, but I needed to see her open it. Maybe she'd sneer or roll her eyes, and that would be definitive proof that she wasn't damn near perfect. Something to dull my misery. "Ready to open gifts?"

She popped up. "Yes! The whole no-gift-giving thing is great when you have a big nuclear family, but I don't think Bean is going to be getting me presents for a few years."

"Not until at least kindergarten, when Bean makes you a paper something in class."

"I can't wait, but that's a long time with no presents." She went to the living room, then spun around and ran into my chest.

I caught her by her shoulders, and her heat seeped right into my skin. A groan nearly slipped out. I rubbed my thumbs along her fluffy sweater. "Can't open presents if you knock yourself out."

She blinked up at me with those big eyes. "Right." She sounded almost breathless. "I was going to grab the cookies."

"I'll get them." I hadn't taken my hands off her, but she hadn't moved either.

"I also bought sparkling juice."

"You didn't tell me this was a party."

"You should know by now I'm a wild child."

I chuckled and continued running my thumbs along that soft, damn sweater. "I do know you."

She looked down, and the faintest pink dusted her cheeks. Was I making her uncomfortable?

Peeling my hands off her, I stepped back. "I'll get the cookies. Only because I don't know where you keep your glasses."

The cupboard to the left of the fridge.

A few minutes later, we were sitting by each other on the love seat. I held her present to me, and mine was on her lap. Two glasses of sparkling red grape juice were on the end table, and only two cookies were left on the plate.

"I'm nervous," she admitted, tipping my box. A telltale, but muffled, clattering sound filled the air between us. "That's familiar."

"Open it."

I held my breath like I was five and giving my mom a handmade gift, which was probably why I was so nervous. I didn't have a litany of good experiences with this type of thing.

She didn't hold back, tearing at the wreath-covered paper, her smile growing as more of the box was revealed. "Legos?" She gasped. "Lego rocks?"

"You can't rockhound in the winter. Thought this was the next best thing." Plus, I couldn't forget the day we cleaned old Legos together and created fun little scenes.

She laughed and lifted the box. "It's perfect." Giving it a light shake, she giggled harder. "I knew this sound was familiar. I can't believe I didn't guess it. Ohmigoodness, I'm going to have this all together before I go to bed if I don't pace myself." She squealed. "An amethyst geode. I love it."

Everything inside me melted at her excitement. I'd never had a response to a gift like that. "Good," I said gruffly. "I'm glad you do."

"Ugh, now I feel like I went off track with mine."

"Doubt it." I ripped off the paper with more enthusiasm than intended. That disappointed five-year-old in me made a resurgence. The plain cardboard box inside didn't tell me anything.

When I opened the top, I started to chuckle. What other reaction was there for the best gift?

"Pokémon cards?" I took out several packs. The perfect gift.

"Are they the wrong ones?" She wrung her hands together, the box of Legos on her lap forgotten. "There are so many types."

It wouldn't matter. "They're just right." My throat grew thick. "A lot of places let you only buy one pack at a time."

"Yeah, but I have my ways. And there are a lot of different retailers that sell them. As long as I could catch them stocking their shelves."

Now my chest was tight. She'd had to plan this gift. She would've had to stalk stores, ask questions, and then do it all over again at another place. She had, and the proof was on my lap. "Thank you. This means a lot."

"You like it?"

"It's the best present I've ever gotten."

She did a double-take at my expression. "Seriously?"

I nodded and sifted through the plastic packs. "Yes, sweet Clover. I'm not exaggerating."

Her lips parted, and shock filled her gaze.

It was Christmas. I had to lighten the mood. "My grandparents got me socks and underwear, but you knocked their gifts off the top of the podium. Right to first place."

The sympathy didn't disappear from her expression, but she laughed. "It was a toss-up between the cards and the Santa boxers I saw."

"No Pikachu underwear?"

"Sold out."

I grinned, and we held each other's gaze.

"Merry Christmas, Van," she said softly.

"Merry Christmas, Clover." *And thank you for making it the best one yet.*

Chapter Twenty-Four

Clover

"Oh my God, we lost her again," Poppy said and waved her hand in front of my face.

Blinking, I shook my head. My sisters were staring at me from across my parents' large table. Mugs of hot chocolate rested in front of each of us. The kids were getting entertained by their dads and grandparents, and we got some girl time. "What? I'm right here. I'm listening."

Poppy pursed her lips. "Then you should've reacted when I told you I'm having triplets."

"Oh my God, Poppy. Really?" How was she going to handle that and run her own business? Would she need help? Would my hands be too full to help?

"No," Poppy cried.

Lily smirked but did a poor job of covering it. "I think her brain's back on yesterday."

Violet nodded. "It's been on whatever day is Sullivan day."

"He's just a friend," I reiterated for the millionth time. I hated that phrase. It should be banned from the English language.

"Even I can tell that's not true." Daisy shot me an apologetic look. "Sorry. I don't mean to get involved, but it's hard to see you missing him the whole holiday weekend."

"I've only been here for a few hours." Not counting the drive down and Dad's excellent prime rib dinner. How could they evaluate me in that much time?

"Were you thinking about him?" Poppy asked.

Was I recalling the heartbreaking wonder on his face when I got him something completely simple like Pokémon cards? The whole process took some planning, but not that much. The box hadn't been that big.

Was I thinking about how nervous he'd been when I'd opened his gift? He'd been tense like he was afraid I'd laugh at how stupid it was—it wasn't—or that I'd fling it back at him like it was a thoughtless gift. He'd shown me how well he knew me with one gift.

"He got me rock Legos," I said.

"You mentioned that," Violet said softly. "A few times."

I had? "It was a perfect gift."

"You said that too," Lily pointed out.

I clamped my mouth shut. Heat seared the backs of my eyes. "It was really sweet." Horror filled me as a hot tear washed down my cheek. I batted at my face. "Hormones."

"You love him." Poppy wasn't asking a question, but I shook my head.

"Of course I care about him. We're frie—"

"Literally don't ever say that again." Lily didn't usually interrupt like that, but she'd gotten more outspoken with all of us since the divorce from her deadbeat first husband.

"You care about Van way more than just a friend, and I'd be willing to bet he feels the same way."

I chewed on my lower lip. "No." They all stared at me. "It's not going to work. Van's a *great* guy." Nice. Thoughtful. Good in bed. But he's off somewhere private, being a great guy with someone he hasn't told me about. If he was alone, then he chose that over me. "But he has his own life."

Violet rolled her eyes. "At Thanksgiving, he looked like he wanted to be stuck all over you."

"He didn't come here today, did he?" I snapped. Crap. I was strung tight, and I couldn't blame hormones. "He's only had good things to say about all of you, but he still made other plans." Without me.

"You don't know what he's doing?"

A vise gripped my heart. "Nope. Like I said, he's moved on with his own life. The man is single, and he can mingle all he wants."

"I'm sorry," Violet murmured. "But I don't buy it. It's been less than a month. He's not mingling, and he's not doing it on Christmas."

"We should've made him come," Poppy said.

I should've made him come with me. Just the two of us road-tripping. "I put the invite out more than once. Trust me, if he wanted to be with me on Christmas, he would be." My sisters seemed to want there to be some star-crossed love between us. Maybe I did too, and that was why I had to move on. "He's got a lot of business travel coming up. I'm sure he's preparing for his pitches."

"What if he thinks you're the one who wants space?" Violet asked.

My ribs closed around my lungs. "I can't."

Triumph filled Poppy's face. "So you do want more?"

She threw her hands in the air. "Finally, we're getting somewhere."

"We're getting nowhere." I folded my hands across my stomach. "I've told you all how it is. Can we drop it?" My volume ratcheted up. "He's the best person I've met—my family aside." The sting was back in my eyes. I blinked back tears. "He's focused, and while he takes care of me, he does it because he's got a big, good heart."

Poppy snorted. "Is that all that's big?"

I tried to glare at her. "Big organs aside."

Lily snickered and closed her hands around her mug of hot chocolate. "What if he doesn't know that you want him as much as he wants you?" I opened my mouth, but she shook her head, warning me not to interrupt. "What if you both are pining away and wanting what you think is best for the other person when what's best is actually the two of you taking a chance."

I tried to answer, but no sound came out. The problem was Van was the best guy I'd ever met. He was everything I would want for the father of my baby and for a life partner. The stakes of rejection were higher than they'd ever been. I cleared my throat. "I can't be rejected. Not by him."

Van didn't break the news that way, but it was how I felt.

"Oh, Clover." Violet leaned over and grabbed my shoulder. "Sometimes you have to put yourself out there. Same with Van."

Poppy studied me, her lower lip stuck out. I tensed, automatically knowing that I wouldn't like what she had to say. "Maybe you're right."

She might as well have dropped a brick on my heart.

"If neither of you is willing to take a chance on the

other," she continued, "then I guess that means neither of you is the one."

Van

Being alone on Christmas sucked as much as it always had. In fact, I had the pleasure of finding out it was even worse. I had skipped a boisterous family gathering and a day with Clover to do what? Make a point?

To keep my unspoken promise to be better than my brother.

Yes, and no. To give Clover what she wanted.

Now it was New Year's Eve, and I was alone again. I could go to the bar, see if I could find that soulmate, but a large part of me didn't want to look. All of me didn't want to look.

I was so close to launching my company. New year, new me.

So why was I sitting at my desk staring at my phone? The screen was black, like it had been all day.

Fuck, I needed friends.

I had them, and I had ditched them all on Christmas.

Shoving a hand through my hair, I blew out a breath. Maybe Clover was onto something. Learning to be alone might be critical to how well I'd do at all this. Enjoy my own company when I didn't have to handle my parents and their narcissistic neediness.

Yeah.

I picked up my phone.

Me: Happy New Year! Partying hard?

I carefully set it down. Why'd I go open that door? New year, new her. New Bean. New niece or nephew.

Several minutes ticked by.

Fuck me. I really did need to be comfortable being alone.

I needed friends—ones I haven't fucked and obsessed over.

Happy New Year to me.

There was a knock at the door. After dinner?

Frowning, I checked the time. Oh. It was much later. A few more hours and I'd be ringing in the new year.

I brought my phone with me. Was Clover having a blast with her nieces and nephews? Sipping on sparkling juice, having pizza and junk food? Envy tugged at my chest walls. Not for Clover, but for everyone else.

I needed to get a life.

Opening the door without looking, my pulse spiked. "Clover?" I peered out behind her. "Everything okay?"

A smile burst through her pensive expression. I stepped back, gently tugging her inside.

"Yes, it's fine." She clutched her mittened hands together. "I should've called first. Are you in the middle of something?"

I closed the door behind her. "No, not at all." Did that sound light enough to play it off like I was a computer nerd who had no friends?

"Okay. It was a last-minute thing. I was talking to my sisters over Christmas..." Her gaze froze on me for a second before she shook her head. "Anyway, I didn't want to ring in New Year's Day by sleeping through it."

Delight filled me like a helium balloon. My night turned around. "I could've come to your place."

"I know. It's good for me to get out, and it's been such a

slow week." She took her gloves off and shrugged out of her coat. "A lot of people are out until after the holidays, so it's quiet even for working at home."

Her belly under a plain black sweater was even bigger than last time. A weird sense of loss filled me. It'd only been a week. She looked down and winced. "I didn't change out of the sweats I wore all day. It was kind of an impromptu decision to come here."

"No problem." My gray sweatpants almost matched hers. I scratched the back of my neck. "I, uh, don't have anything planned."

She lifted the tote she brought. "Sparkling apple juice and Oreos."

"I can't think of a better way to celebrate a new start." I took the tote from her. "Make yourself comfortable."

In the kitchen, I retrieved a couple of glasses and napkins. I didn't have champagne flutes, but this would work for sparkling juice.

She was sitting on her normal side of the couch, and a beat of nostalgia went through me. Like usual, I kept all my feelings to myself. That was a lot to put on Clover when she was getting back on her feet.

I handed her a glass, and she held it up until I sat.

"To new beginnings," she said, lifting it higher.

"Hear, hear." I clinked my cup to hers.

She folded her legs under her as she drank.

"Good stuff," I said as I swallowed. I barely noticed the sweet liquid. Her cheeks were still pink from coming in from the cold, and it made her radiant. Her halo of hair would be soft if I ran my hands through it.

"I don't know if I can go back to champagne. I really like this stuff."

"I never drank much of it either."

She wiggled to face me, and my attention stuck on her chest. Her tits were bigger too. I skated my gaze away. "Are you ready for your trip?"

"Yes." I hadn't packed a damn thing. "The weather forecast looks good."

"I'm sure Denver is pretty nice. You gonna go anywhere fun while you're there?"

"Just a work trip for me. What would you do if you could go?"

"Oh, that's easy." She grabbed an Oreo and held it up with a flourish. "Hello? Look for rocks." She punctuated the air with her cookie. "I heard jasper is hard to find, but it only makes me want to look more. And that area is known for fossils."

"Now you're into archaeology?"

"When fossils are in rocks, I am." She chomped into her cookie. I grabbed one to keep from staring at her. What would it be like to go to Denver with her? To have her next to me on the plane? To watch her wonder as she got a glimpse of the city?

I turned the TV on. "Do you want to watch the ball drop an hour early?"

"Let's celebrate twice."

Taking our normal spots on either side of the couch, we watched New Year's celebrations all over the world, eating cookies and polishing off the juice. She'd yawn and blink when she thought I wasn't looking, and I'd smirk at her. I was tired too, and it was nice to be sleepy with someone next to me. With Clover.

A minute before midnight, she stood up and gestured for me to do the same.

She grabbed my hand, and dammit, I held on tight. I hadn't touched her in too damn long.

She squeezed and let out a little squeal. "We're getting close."

I gripped her fingers in mine. "Ten."

"Nine."

"Eight!"

"Seven." I stroked my thumb along her soft skin.

"Six," she said a little quieter, aiming that big gaze right toward me.

"Five." I moved a little closer to her.

"Four." She turned toward me.

"Three." I clasped her other hand.

"Two," she whispered, tipping her head back.

"One," I murmured, my gaze glued to her sweet, pink lips. "Happy New Year, sweet Clover." I pressed my lips to hers. Finally. She released her hands and twined her arms around my neck. I delved into the warm depths of her mouth, and she met each swipe of my tongue with her own.

I could gobble her up. Drink her down. Consume her. Her body was pressed to mine, every inch of that belly I hadn't been able to see. The couch was right here. It'd be so easy. She could be on top. I wouldn't let her up for air. I could be inside her in minutes.

Her whimper traveled right through me, and instead of sinking further down, I came up for air. And logic.

I ripped my mouth away. "Shit. Sorry." I wasn't. How not sorry I felt was definitely an issue.

"No. It's fine." She still clung to me.

I wrapped my hands around her wrists. "It's not. I don't want to wreck things between us."

That wide gaze was on me, so intent, so innocent. "What if it doesn't?"

I hadn't heard her right. "What?"

She licked her bottom lip, and my brain flipped the

switch to shut off again. "I was talking... Something my sisters said..."

I flicked my mind back on. She was nervous to tell me something, but my thoughts whirled in a lust-filled haze.

She steeled herself and lifted her chin. "If neither of us is willing to take a chance on the other, then I guess that means neither of us is the one."

Making sense of the sentence shouldn't be so hard, but my blood was on the way to my dick. Every nerve remembered how she felt in my arms.

Her gaze dipped down before lifting to mine. "I'm taking a chance. I think there's more between us than friendship."

Fuck yeah, there was. I wanted her, but she didn't want me. She only thought she did. "It's been a month."

She sucked in a breath and released me. "Right."

"You wanted to prove to yourself you could do it."

Swallowing, her eyes darted from side to side. "Sure. I mean, yes. That's what I want. And you have your work."

Hell with my work. Yet I had to hold on to it. This wasn't what she wanted. I wasn't what she wanted, not really. "I'm entering a busy time. An unknown time. I don't want to leave you behind." I grimaced. Did I really say that? "I mean—"

"Of course." Her chuckle came out weak. "Being left behind definitely isn't my thing. Fool me once, right?" She curved around me and went for the door. "Well, happy New Year. Thank you for indulging me. Next year, wow. It's going to be a new experience."

"Clover." I messed this all up. I was trying to make sure she got what she wanted, and to do it, I was giving up what I wanted. "I just want you to—"

"No need to worry about me." She stuffed her feet into

her boots and yanked her coat out of the closet. She wasn't looking at me. "Thanks again."

"Clover—"

"Night." She was out the door. If I ran after her, would she sprint and hurt herself? Slip and fall?

I stood in the doorway, getting bitch-slapped by the cold as she drove away, her tires crunching in the snow and ice. I deserved so much worse. Clover put herself out there, and I batted her away, claiming it was for her own good.

It was. She'd realize she was just scared.

Only the Clover who kissed me didn't act terrified. The Clover who came here tonight had been nervous but excited. That Clover had planned to tell a guy how she felt about him. I'd swung the door closed in her face, and I was getting hit in the ass by it on her way out.

Chapter Twenty-Five

Clover

I had one leg crossed over the other in the clinic waiting room. Three other patients waited for their appointments. I squirmed. I needed to pee thanks to my upcoming ultrasound, but I had to wait.

My phone buzzed.

Poppy: When's your appointment?
Me: Tomorrow

Her sister's radar was too strong. I tucked my phone away. She wasn't the only sister who'd been hitting me up this week. Alder and his damn memory probably told them all he thought my big appointment was today. I had told them when it was at Christmas. And then after my New Year's Eve humiliation, I had hoped they'd forget about it.

My embarrassment knew no bounds around Sullivan Wagner. The two worst times of my life had been witnessed by him.

First, getting ditched by Elijah. And getting dropped by Van.

The poor guy. He would be on his way to Denver at this very moment. Probably grateful to be taking off.

I'd put him in such a tight spot. We'd been wrapped up in the New Year's Eve thrill, and I'd crawled all over him. I'd read into it all and put myself out there. He'd set me gently back down.

I bobbed my foot and stopped. That wasn't helping the bladder situation.

Was my face hot over the memories, or was it hormones?

My phone buzzed again. I wasn't going to look. I would let my family know how everything went after my appointment. It wasn't like I was finding out the gender.

I'd just get to see Bean again. See how much Bean had grown. Hear the heartbeat. Get more pictures to hang on the fridge. It'd be exciting. Then I'd use that high to tell my sister what happened between me and Van.

The door to the exam rooms opened, and Emery popped out in lilac scrubs. "Clover. Come on back." Her smile was just the right amount of friendly and excited. I needed that.

I smiled for the first time in a week and pushed out of my chair. This would be a good appointment. I'd have a pleasant time, get some blood drawn, and then I'd stare at the images tonight and think about my future. My very single future.

Emery stepped back to let me pass through and hit the handicapped button. The doors clicked all the way open. "How are you doing today?"

"Good."

The hum of the door stopped, and another click sounded before they started to swing shut.

"Clover!"

I spun around just as the last guy I expected to see pushed through the door, ramming it with his shoulder. "Van?"

He was breathing heavy. "I'm sorry. I meant to come earlier."

"What are you..." Emery and the other nurses were looking our way. I'd moved to town, married to a different man than I'd planned to be. Only Emery knew that, but the others might also know Van and I were no longer married. And here we were on the verge of making a scene. Yet I didn't care. "What are you doing here?"

"Denver can wait."

Everyone around us vanished. "No, it can't." A horrible thought bashed into my brain. "Did you cancel? For this?"

He formed a lopsided grin. "Yeah."

"Why?" I screeched. Glancing around, I gave everyone an apologetic look. "Sorry."

"Why don't I bring you to an exam room?" Emery said. Her tone was the perfect amount of supportive and hopeful. "I'll get your vitals in a few minutes and then take you to radiology."

"Okay," I said numbly, but I couldn't take my eyes off Van. He was dressed in jeans and a sweater. Had he left the house without a coat? It was below zero outside.

He came closer, and I couldn't move until he gently cupped my elbow. We followed Emery into an exam room.

When we were shut inside, I spun on him. "What are you—"

His mouth landed on mine. A high-pitched sound

escaped me, only to be swallowed by him. He didn't take the kiss further but slowly drew away. "I'm sorry."

"For what?" For ending the kiss? Me too.

"For running you off on New Year's Eve. I thought I was doing the best by you."

"You were. You were right. I need more time."

"You're a smart girl, Clover."

Okay? Was this the beginning of a brush-off? I was so confused.

"You don't make rash decisions. You came to my place that night to talk about us. Right?"

I nodded.

"And I got scared. I got scared you'd realize that you deserved more than me. But here's the thing—I'm willing to work every day to be worthy of you. Because I fell in love with you."

A small gasp escaped me.

"I'm so damn in love with you," he continued. "I never wanted to divorce you. I never wanted to move out. I only did it because that was what you wanted."

It wasn't. "But your company?"

"I talked to them all. Explained everything." He shrugged. "A couple pulled out."

He didn't have much more than a couple interested. "Van."

"I'll do it without them." He pushed a lock of my hair behind my ear. "I've made it this far; I can keep going and continue building. As long as I have you."

"But..." This wasn't right, yet all of it was what I wanted. There had to be a way he didn't lose out by being with me. "What about what you want?"

"I want you. I know you don't want to depend on

another guy, and I understand. We can do everything separately, as long as I'm right next to you."

The last words chimed through my head. A pretty melody. "I want you right there with me, too."

His grin spread wide. "Yeah?"

My vision grew blurry as happiness swelled so big I could burst, and it wasn't just my bladder. "Yeah."

He wrapped me in his arms, hugging me tight.

My face smashed into his shoulder, and there was nowhere else I'd rather be, except for the house we made into a home.

"I love you, sweet Clover. So damn much. I tried to be strong, but when it comes to you, I'm too weak to stay away."

"That's a confession I like to hear."

His chuckle rumbled against my shoulder.

I hooked my arms around him. "I love you too, Van, but I can't believe you did that."

"Believe it. My Denver investor still wants to meet with me, and he said that if I can bring you, he'd like to meet you too."

Smiling, I snuggled into him harder. "If it seals the deal for you, I'll go anywhere."

"That's what I love about you. We're a team. We're a team in life, and we'll be a team with Bean. I'm going to be the best uncle-dad a kid's ever had."

I pulled back. "It really doesn't bother you?"

His gaze was solemn. "It's an honor. Truly." He released me and stepped back. "I was late because of this." He dug a little black box out of his pocket and started to drop to a knee.

There was a knock on the door, and it opened. He paused in a half lunge.

"Oh, hey." Emery's eyes went wide. "I wouldn't do that. Not that." She gestured to the ring. "Definitely do that. But the kneeling part. Don't do it. We clean and disinfect, but you know, it's a general rule. Never touch the floor in a clinic if at all possible." She backed out of the room. "Why don't you two come out when you're ready. I'll let the tech know it might be a few minutes."

"It won't be that long," I said. "I'm going to say yes." He opened the box to a simple but gorgeous band of browns with a subtle blue. "Oh my God. Is that made from petrified wood?"

He took the ring from the box. "I drove as fast as legally possible so I could get to the gift shop, grab this baby, and get back before your appointment."

I practically shoved my left hand at him.

He gently gripped my hand and slid the ring on. A perfect fit. "Once my company takes off, I can get you one with a gemstone." He smiled. "But not a diamond for my geologist."

Van kissed the back of my hand and pulled me into his side. "Ready to go see our baby, sweet Clover?"

"I'm ready for anything as long as you're with me."

Epilogue

Clover

I rocked on the chair Van bought for the front porch. The grass had been neatly mowed earlier this weekend. I leaned back and enjoyed the sunshine on my face.

The front door opened. The sexiest uncle-dad in the world exited with a small wrapped bundle in his arms.

I smiled. I could get pregnant again just looking at that, and actually, we weren't doing anything to stop the possibility. "I thought you were going to lay him down."

"I can't bring myself to actually do it." He lightly dropped into the matching rocking chair next to me. "I'm going to spoil him."

"My mom is a fan of saying that you can't spoil babies."

"Your mom's a smart woman." He steadily rocked, and little Nolan scrunched his face and passed out again. Adoration crossed my husband's face. He was smitten—with Nolan and with me.

Looking back, that month living alone seemed like years. The months back with Van? A blink.

"I want to take you out next week for our anniversary," Van said.

"I didn't know we decided which one to celebrate." We remarried on Valentine's Day in a small courthouse ceremony. Aunt Linda let us move back into the house. She had canceled a prospective renter right before the lease was signed when she'd heard Van and me were getting married for real because we couldn't stay apart.

"Easy—we're celebrating both, and to be fair, Valentine's Day is already a holiday. Can't be cheated out of a real anniversary."

"I approve of that plan. What are we doing?"

"I heard it through the grapevine that you wanted a wedding by the lake."

Poppy must've started that rumor, and it was a true one. I told her when she was planning her wedding what I envisioned. "You want to celebrate our anniversary with a wedding?"

"What better way than to gather on a beach? You in that dress with the clovers on it. I'll get a fresh trim so my hair doesn't blow in my face. It'll be our turn to host the Duke crew."

"Mmm, sounds divine." So much happened in the last year. We'd be the same people, but doing it our way. "What about our anniversary night?"

"I've got a sitter."

"Jasper?"

He chuckled. "That man could start a career as an uncle day care, but he won't take money."

My brother accepted food as payment. "I'll make him

some cookie salad." I caught Van glancing at me and grinned. "I'll make extra."

"Good."

I admired my husband and son. The baby wasn't the only one spoiled. Van catered to me, and since his company took off faster than he thought possible, he was planning a remodel. The room that used to be his office was now a nursery, and he'd had the shop remodeled to make offices for each of us. He'd added a small bathroom and a little nook for Nolan to nap in while we worked.

Plans were already made to add onto the house if we had another baby, and I was more and more certain that was happening sooner rather than later.

Van slid his gaze to me, and an appreciative look crossed his face. "I might have to lay him down, so I can lay you down."

"Sullivan Wagner, are you hitting on me?"

"Clover Duke Wagner, I'm never going to quit."

"Good."

———

Thank you for reading Clover and Van's story!

Jasper is the last single Duke, and he has no plans to change his status. But he wouldn't mind changing his employment situation. Then Sheridan Bishop slams into his world outside of a coffee shop, and offers him a job. There's something about the damsel in distress that he can't ignore.

Besides, it's only temporary... right? Find out in Dandelion Sighs.

You're invited to the birth of Van and Clover's baby and to their vow renewal in a special bonus epilogue on mariejohnstonwriter.com/newsletter.

About the Author

Marie Johnston writes paranormal and contemporary romance and has collected several awards in both genres. Before she was a writer, she was a microbiologist. Depending on the situation, she can be oddly unconcerned about germs or weirdly phobic. She's also a licensed medical technician and has worked as a public health microbiologist and as a lab tech in hospital and clinic labs. Marie's been a volunteer EMT, a college instructor, a security guard, a phlebotomist, a hotel clerk, and a coffee pourer in a bingo hall. All fodder for a writer!! She has four kids, cats, lots of cats, and a corgi.

mariejohnstonwriter.com

Follow me:

King's Treasure

King's Country

King's Queen

www.ingramcontent.com/pod-product-compliance
Lightning Source LLC
Chambersburg PA
CBHW032250070726
47590CB00016B/1826